SERIOUSLY, NORMAN!

SERIOUSLY, NORMAN!

Chris Raschka

MICHAEL DI CAPUA BOOKS
SCHOLASTIC

Text and pictures copyright © 2011 by Chris Raschka

All rights reserved

Library of Congress control number: 2011927653

Printed in the USA 23

Designed by Steve Scott

First edition, 2011

for
ingo
puzzle & solution

SERIOUSLY, NORMAN!

stop

"Pencils down, please."

Norman Normann put his pencil down and listened with half an ear to the final instructions.

Of all the miserable ways to spend a miserable Saturday morning in the miserable month of January, this had to be the miserablest. In fact, the most miserablest.

So thought Norman.

Norman shrugged, heaved his body out of his chair, and then dutifully placed the completed test booklet facedown in the upper-left-hand corner of his desk. Scooping up what remained of his number-two pencils, he arranged himself in the line forming at the door, to be marched back to the cafeteria, where his mother, he guessed, awaited him.

"Norman!" said his mother, rising like a small hot-air balloon. "Norman—sweetie-monkey-muffin-puffin-honey-bumpy-lumpy—my Norman. How was the test?"

Norman considered the question. As a whole, the test just taken is best described as being like:

A. A four-hour dental appointment, only without the comfortable chair, the painkiller, or the raspberry rinse

B. A grilling, barbecue-style, to the point of charring, leaving not an ounce of juice

3

C. Having each of one's twenty fingernails and toenails removed slowly by a little old lady with dirty tweezers

D. Death

E. All of the above

Norman said, "It was fine, Mom."

"Oh, I'm so glad, my darling," said his mother, folding her short arms around him. She pressed her warm cheek against his and rocked him gently back and forth. "And because you did fine, next year you'll be able to go to a super-duper-super school to make you more and more smarter than ever!"

She gave him a squeeze. "Oooooo, I'm so proud of you!"

"Yup," answered Norman thoughtfully.

Norman executed an expert duck-and-twist to escape his mother's grip and reached a distracted arm into his winter coat. Normally, he didn't think much about the future, but now he wondered what a super-duper-super school might actually be like. If he really had done fine on the test, maybe he would find out. And if he had done only medium fine, he guessed life would go on much as it had before.

He slipped his other arm into his coat and looked at his mother, who had begun to knead moisturizing cream into his face.

"Mom, I'm twelve years old," said Norman.

"Exactly," said his mother. "And it is extremely cold out and I'd like to avoid chafing."

Having finished with the moisturizer, Norman's mother wrapped Norman's head in three turns of a red scarf, then, unwrapping him, rewrapped him in four turns, as it was, she believed, very, very cold out indeed. She patted his hair and, leaving just a slit for his eyes, pulled a thick woolen hat onto his head.

It was within these four turns of scarf and beneath this woolen hat that Norman wondered: But what if I did less than fine—say, really, really badly? What then?

Norman had no answers.

He couldn't even make an educated guess.

abyss

Exactly three weeks and three days later, Norman's mother looked up from her plate of slightly burned pancakes and then, taking a nervous sip from a glass of orange juice, said, "Norman, we got a letter from that nice testing agency. It arrived yesterday afternoon."

She put down her glass and folded her hands. "It was such an impressive-looking envelope, too, really good-quality paper. Lovely paper. Inside, the paper was nice, too. I thought it might be some horrible machiney paper with machiney writing on it, but no, this was typed out very nicely, with your name beautifully printed, two Ns in Normann, all exactly correct."

"Three Ns in Normann, Mom," said Norman.

"Really, I was very impressed and tickled," she said, her eyes growing wide. "Of course, there was *some* machiney writing, numbers mainly, but I guess that's to be expected."

Norman stopped eating his pancakes and looked at his mother. He loved his mother. He had to admit, to his innermost self anyway, that he loved his mother. How could he not help but love her, knowing as he did how she had met his father in college, when she was Norma Peasley-Knapp and his father was a young man who knew where he was going, with a captain-of-industry name—Orman Normann. How cute everyone had thought it was that someday she might be Mrs. Norma Normann. It was fate, written in the stars, they said. And it *was* written in the stars, for they did marry, and when a baby had come along and it was a boy, well then, it could only be named Norman. Fate again. And now she was his mother. For all of this, he loved her.

However, there were moments, like this one, when Norman wished that his mother would just get to the point.

"Mother, what do the numbers say?"

"Well, dear, that is just what I was getting to. The numbers indicate—that is, your father and I feel that, seeing these numbers in relation to—well, the numbers would seem to be a little . . ."

"Mom, I bombed on the test, right?"

"Well, dear, 'bombed' is such a harsh, such a violent word. And you know I don't like anything to do with explosives, you know that. No, no, you mustn't think you bombed."

Norman skewered a portion of pancake.

"Okay. I stunk. I stinked. I stank. I blew it. I choked. I crapped out."

"Norman!"

Norman could not help it. Tears came into his eyes.

His mother reached her arms across the kitchen table and grasped Norman's syrupy hands.

"Norman. This is what I wanted to tell you. Your father and I have decided that because your numbers are, well . . ."

"Abysmal? In an abyss? As low as you can go?"

"Not super-duper-super high—well, your father and I have decided to . . . well, what I mean is, your father is home now and would like to discuss everything with you in his study. He's waiting for you."

Norman's brow furrowed darkly. He pulled his sticky hands from his mother's wet grasp and stood up from his chair.

"Listen to what your father says, darlingest, and then you'll feel better." Her eyes widened a smidgeon more, entreating.

"Oodles better."

* * *

"Oodles better?" said Norman to himself as he walked along the hall to his father's study. "Oodles better? Oodles better, oodles better, oodles bedoodles better, oodles better, oodles better oo."

He approached his father's study door quietly and knocked.

"Come in, Norman!" sounded his father's booming voice.

Norman pushed open the heavy door to the study, a room he was very rarely allowed in. He stepped in and looked around.

It was not a pretty room, nor was it a cozy room. A large black metal desk stood in its center, facing away from the French doors leading to the backyard. No bookshelves lined the walls, only mismatched metal filing cabinets, a heavy green safe, and, opposite the desk, a couple of vinyl armchairs. A large fluorescent ceiling fixture cast a minty shimmer over the metal furnishings. The scent of drugstore aftershave hung in the air. The thick, whitish shag carpet, which went wall to wall, hushed the faint whistle of the fluorescent light but did little to dampen the whining of a toy bomber that buzzed around at the end of a stick, creating a kind of mechanical halo two feet above Norman's father's benevolently beaming face.

"Come in, come in, come in," said Orman Normann, putting aside some papers. "Come in, this isn't going to hurt."

Norman stepped farther into the room and then jumped, startled by the discovery that his father was not alone.

Seated in a chair along the wall

to his right was an elderly gentleman dressed in careful business attire, who was unremarkable but for two things: an enormous silky gray mustache and a cone-shaped fur hat that rose a foot and a half above the old gentleman's skull.

"Son, meet the foreign minister of Alfur. Minister, my son."

Norman bowed his head sheepishly to the old gentleman, whose dark eyes flashed as he tipped his own briefly in response, causing the great hat to nod like some deaf-and-dumb beast.

"The minister here wants to buy some of my airplanes," said Orman Normann, and on the word "airplanes" he made the two-handed, two-finger waggle that means "quotation marks." "But that can wait a minute. Minister, you'll excuse us?"

The old gentleman nodded and closed his eyes, and the great fur hat appeared to sleep.

Orman Normann put the tips of his fingers together. "Norman, your mother tells me you crapped out on your test. Well, she didn't say 'crapped out,' of course, but that's what she meant. You know that and I know that. And we're not afraid to say it. Ha! Heck, we could even spell it: C-R-A-P-T O-U-T."

Norman's eyes began to brim again.

"Now, then, there's no need for tears, son," said Orman Normann, standing up. "Norman, I've crapped out on plenty of tests myself. Plenty! NO, this just goes to show you what I've always said all along: That school of yours is just no darn good. NO darn good. I mean, you learn the same thing every year. Every year it's the Colonial Era Eastern Woodlands Indians! Now, how's knowing about the Colonial Era Eastern Woodlands Indians going to help you in your life? It heap big no darn good! How!"

Norman wiped his nose. "That's not very funny, Dad."

"You're darn right, it's not funny!" Orman Normann struck his hands in the air. "And you know what else it isn't? It's not good business. What you need is a good business plan for your education." He pronounced it "edgercation." He hooked a thumb under his lapel and rocked on his heels. "I want to see quarterly statements for your edgercation with net and gross gains and losses on a percentage of the capital!"

"Huh?"

"Huh! I want to see a turnaround in the fortunes of that hot little property I like to call my son."

"Huh?"

"Son"—he stopped rocking and, stepping around the desk, placed both hands on Norman's shoulders—"what does the CEO of a parent organization do when one of its subsidiaries is about to go belly up?"

"Huh?"

"I'll tell you. He brings in an expert. A turnaround man. A rainmaker. A shamus. Or, in your case, the best darn tutor we could get on short notice."

"Huh?"

"Stop saying 'Huh,' huh? First thing I'm going to have that tutor do is learn you some new words, a little better vocaberlary."

"What?"

"That's better. Now, that's our new business plan. Quarterly progress reports. Up, up, up! And a personal tutor to make sure you move up and stay up. Okay, get going. Your new tutor will be here in a couple of ticks. Can't remember his name. Your mother knows, she'll tell you."

"What?"

"Stop saying 'What?' Now get going already. Beat it. Scram. Vamoose. Hoof it. I've got business of my own to conduct with my elderly friend here, har, har!"

What else could Norman do? He beat it.

* * *

Oodles better! Oodles better! thought Norman as he beat it, and beat it furiously. A tutor! Norman beat it through the entrance hall. His own personal tutor to point out all of his own personal mistakes. Norman stamped his slippered feet up the carpeted stairs. A tutor—to fill his head with what?—more useless stuff! Norman stormed down the hallway, shaking his fist at the flowered wallpaper. What about his free time? What about seeing his friends?

In his room, he paced and muttered. He stopped at his bookshelves and considered his collection of action figures. He hated action figures! He hoped that his father would never bring him another single robo-vulture or technomasher! This was an insult! This was an insult to him and to his school! He liked his school. He did not care about those other fancy schools. His father said they studied the Colonial Era Eastern Woodlands Indians too much. It was true that they had studied the Colonial Era Eastern Woodlands Indians the last three falls running, but so what? Norman liked the Colonial Era Eastern Woodlands Indians. Norman wished he were studying the Colonial Era Eastern Woodlands Indians right now. Darn it, Norman wished he were *in* the Colonial Era *with* the Eastern Woodlands Indians—in a longhouse, rolling around on the deerskins on a platform bed with all his cousins in the smoky air, eating whatever it was the Colonial Era Eastern Woodlands Indians ate, which he could not remember exactly at this moment but would be sure to learn about again next fall.

Norman looked out into the backyard, imagining where he could build a longhouse, which would have to be a short longhouse, because his backyard was not that big.

It was a beautiful day. He was annoyed by the dazzling snow;

11

he hated the brilliant sunshine and the fluffy clouds. What good was dazzling snow? Who cared about brilliant sunshine? It was dazzling and brilliant just to be annoying.

Norman turned from the annoying sky and clenched his fists to his temples. Why were there tests? Why should he go to a new school? Why couldn't he just stay home, here in his yard—in the short longhouse? And why did he need some strange and horrible tutor?

balthazar birdsong

The shriek of a blue jay startled Norman, and he looked back out the window. Other blue jays joined in, and Norman peered through the pine trees to find them.

As he searched the branches, the gate to the alley swung open and through it strode a thin man wearing a long overcoat and a gray scarf and hat. At the same time, one of the French doors to his father's study opened and out stepped the foreign minister, his tall fur hat now bent forward and leading the way down the path as if, like a dog kept too long indoors, it sought the fresh open spaces and maybe a bush. The thin man hesitated, but then strode forward and bowed to the foreign minister, who took no notice of him. Turning to watch the elderly gentleman pass, the thin man shrugged and continued toward the house. The foreign minister passed through the gate, adjusted his hat, and was gone.

Norman waited. Then he heard the soft sound of the back doorbell, which was just beneath his room in the small hall off the kitchen, and then the first notes of his mother's piccolo voice skittering up and down, apparently greeting his new tutor—for who else could the man be?—and then a voice like a bassoon, smooth, low, and a little gooselike. There was also a smattering of percussion, supplied, presumably, by his mother's tripping over various outdoor implements, such as sleds, shovels, scooters, etc., which always littered the floor by the door.

"Norman!" his mother called. "Norman! Please come downstairs, dear."

Norman remembered the foreign minister. Perhaps he could make his escape with him to a foreign country. He calculated the force needed to launch himself from his bedroom window into one of the pine trees. Then he estimated the force of his impact on the lower branches. Would the branches withstand the impact and catch him? Would his ribs withstand the impact of his being caught? The little pine tree had not been looking too healthy the last couple of seasons. His ribs had been feeling a little crackery just the other day. What about over the roof? No, it all required planning! For the first time, Norman acknowledged to himself that perhaps he had spent too much time reading comics when he should have been perfecting escape plans A, B, and C. Why wasn't he prepared for this?

"Norman! Come down here, now! Please, dear, if you're ready, do, please, come, now, immediately, please, do come."

Norman took a breath and a long look around his room, as if it were his last, and walked to the top of the stairs.

At the base of the stairs, in the front hall, stood his mother and the man.

"Norman dear, come meet your new tutor," said his mother.

Between the stair posts, Norman could make out the man's sharp eyes and beaky nose.

"Norman, come down now. This is Mr. Balthazar Birdsong. Shall Norman call you Mr. Birdsong?" Norma asked.

"If I may call you Norman, you may call me Balthazar," said

Balthazar Birdsong, unpocketing his right hand for Norman to take as he reached the bottom step.

Norman shook the man's hand and nodded, hesitantly.

Balthazar Birdsong said, "Norman Normann is a fine name. The name of a conqueror, I should think. A discoverer. A seafarer. Even a devastator and pillager, I would not be surprised."

"Oh!" said Norma.

Norman goggled.

Balthazar Birdsong turned on his heel and stepped toward the dining room.

Both Normanns hurried after him.

"I expect you have vision, Norman. You see the possibilities," Balthazar expounded as he walked, glancing about the rooms.

"You see many possibilities, good ones, reasonable ones," he continued, pausing to pick up and examine a porcelain model of a Conestoga wagon with *Greetin's from Moose Gut* painted on it. "You weigh the consequences. You have great imagination and the perception of your surroundings attendant upon this. But what you lack, Norman"—he replaced the Conestoga wagon on the mantel and turned to him—"is preparation."

A quiver ran through Norman. This new tutor apparently could read his mind. Whether Norman should have gotten out of bed this morning was no longer a question; the answer was "Obviously not." The question now was "Should I pretend to have a heart attack and hope to be taken to the emergency room?" Norman tried to remember what exactly the symptoms of a heart attack looked like.

Balthazar Birdsong continued: "If you want to avoid the unpleasantnesses of life, you must be prepared." He crossed his arms and looked down his long nose. "This is where I can help you, Norman."

"My heart feels funny," ventured Norman.

"Yes, quite possibly," said Balthazar Birdsong, and he strode away again, in the direction of the kitchen. "Now, before we begin, where can I find your espresso pot, please?"

Norman hurried after him, wondering if he should try one more time. "My heart—"

But his tutor interrupted him. "Norman, you are not prepared to tell me where the espresso pot is?"

Norman gave up on the heart-attack scheme and only wondered whether an espresso pot was some kind of torture device. Since he did not know *what* it was, he certainly did not know *where* it was. He said, "I don't know."

"I see," said Balthazar Birdsong. "Mrs. Normann, could you please tell me where your espresso pot is kept? And the coffee?"

As his mother shot past him, twittering like an apologetic emu, Norman blew out his breath, thankful that his tutor's interest appeared to be no worse than coffee. "Please, Mrs. Normann, calm yourself, calm yourself. It is not necessary. Let us leave it at this. Next week at this time I shall return, prepared to make the coffee."

He turned to Norman again.

"Norman, we have approximately one year to ready ourselves for the next Amalgamated Academic Independent City Schools Test. As you probably already know, there are fifty-two weeks in a year. We have missed three of these since the examination just concluded, and I am sure your family will insist on having some vacation this summer. Still, let us remember, fifty-two weeks. Now, how many letters are there in the alphabet? Twenty-six, of course. Therefore, we merely need to master, on average, one letter of the alphabet every two weeks. In the coming week, Norman, I would like you to master the letter *A*."

"Master the letter *A*?"

"Precisely," he said, pleased that Norman, at last, could speak coherently.

"Master?"

"The letter *A*." Balthazar Birdsong paused, now doubtful. "Do you require further explication? Very well. I wish you to get to know the letter *A*. Explore it. Walk around in it. See what's there. I have brought for you a copy of the Ingmeister's Third New International Dictionary, Unabridged." He stooped to his briefcase and slowly pulled out a very large book, which he placed with a thump on the kitchen table.

Norman cleared his throat, preparing to say his heart felt funny again, but Balthazar Birdsong, retrieving his coat and slipping in an arm, said, "Now, I am not asking you to memorize the entire section *A* of the dictionary, though I would not think ill of you if you did so. No, all I am asking is that you read the section *A* of the dictionary and know it. Norman, Mrs. Normann, I will see you again in one week."

"*Au revoir*" came his voice from the backyard as the door closed and the blue jays shrieked once more.

Maybe Norman *was* going to have a heart attack.

* * *

That evening, after an afternoon full of tears and tantrums— and that was just his mother—Norman sat at his desk and opened the Ingmeister's Third New International Dictionary with a heavy hand. He read:

airplane *n* : a self-propelled flying craft with wings

"Everybody knows what an airplane is," said Norman.

air potato *n* : an Asian vine with heavy tubers

"I knew there were air guitars, but an air potato?"

airsickness *n* : a feeling of nausea and dizziness

"I'm feeling it." Norman paged forward.

alfiona *n* : rubberlip perch
Alfredian *adj* : having to do with
    Alfred the Great
alfresco *adj* : outside
Alfur *n* : any one of a group of ancient peoples of
    many backgrounds from Celebes and the islands
    of the Moluccas
algo *n* : pain
algogenic *adj* : causing pain
algophobia *n* : the fear of pain
algophobic *adj* : afraid of pain

alfiona

"Reading the dictionary is algogenic. Wait a second." Norman scanned back up the page.

"Alfur," he said. "Alfur, why does that name seem familiar? Oh well." He closed the dictionary and collapsed onto his bed, resigning himself to the end of what had been a fairly happy childhood. He closed his eyes.

Twenty minutes later his eyes snapped open. "The foreign minister of Alfur!"

leonard

"Read the dictionary?" asked Leonard in disbelief. "Hoooeeee-yaaah!"

Norman walked with his best friend, Leonard Piquant, through the slushy snow of the neighborhood sidewalks. Snow piles, minding their own business, were being abruptly obliterated by Leonard's wet sneakers and Norman's slick boots.

Buddingdale Heights, the place in which both boys had lived all their lives—Norman with his two parents and Leonard with his mom (Leonard's parents having divorced when he was two)—was nestled among the hills along the river, above Manhattan, which kept it safe from some of the excitements and terrors of that great place. It was neither exciting nor terrible, made of medium-large and medium-small houses with front yards and backyards, usually enclosed in diverse fences with pretty gates to the alleys and garages where the cars were kept, thus making it safe to walk to the nearby couple of streets with shops, like shoe-repair shops, locksmiths, grocery stores, and so forth.

It was to these shops that Norma Normann occasionally sent Norman on his own to fetch something, such as a couple of slabs of fish for dinner, as on this day. However, this time, Norman was not on his own; his dearest friend, Leonard, was beside him, or in front of him, or behind him, or jumping on top of him with a yell.

"Hiiiiyoah!" yelled Leonard.

"Eeeeeyouuuuff! Youff! Yuf!" said Norman.

"Aaawwwww Waaahhh Cheeeeee!" said Leonard, as another snow pile was pulverized. "Whoever heard of reading the dictionary?"

"Not me, but that's what he said." Norman scuffed his boots.

"I think your dad is being mean. Look, he's a nice person, I like him a lot, but this is mean. What made him do it?"

"He's the greatest dad in the world, hiyaaa! But I don't know what made him do it, I always thought he liked me so much. I know for a fact that he said I was perfect a bunch of times."

"Did you write it down—I mean, when he said you were perfect, with the date? Because then you could use it as evidence and make him take back his stupid old tutor."

"Hihaaah, hiyaaah! Nah." Norman looked at the sky. "Maybe all the air travel he does is starting to shrivel his brains. There's less air up there, you know."

"Not to mention all those security-gate thingies. Beep, beep, ultry-violet microwavers frying human brain material-o-rooni."

"Maybe my stupid old tutor made my dad do it!"

"Watch this, watch this, watch this! Uloo uloo uloo oop!" said Leonard, showing an unsuspecting snowdrift no mercy at all.

"No, look, look!" said Norman, and he quickly created a little snow manikin. A moment later it, too, was vaporized.

"Wow gooomaaaah!" said Leonard appreciatively.

Norman took a little more time over the next snow manikin, making it long and thin, with a pointed head.

"Leonard, Leonard, look, my new tutor. Wahoo googoomagoo! Ftang!" And the tutor manikin burst into a hundred bits.

The boys walked on.

"Let's eat the granola bars your mom gave us," said Leonard.

"Ahhhh," said Norman, unwrapping a bar, "dining alfresco."

"What?"

"Dining alfresco. It means eating outside."

"Ah ha, dining alfresco. I was eating outside once," Leonard continued, through a mouthful of granola, "and a bird pooped on my uncle's head. It was really funny. He was just about to bite into a chicken-salad sandwich when the pigeon, I think it was a pigeon . . ."

Leonard rolled his eyes and flew like a pigeon. Then he gave an impression of the gagging sounds made by his uncle—gagging sounds being one of Leonard's specialties, and one very good reason why he was Norman's best friend.

"It was hilarious. I wish a bird would poop on my uncle again."

They were quiet for a moment, conjuring pleasant thoughts of birds pooping on their relatives.

"What's the name of your new tutor again? Didn't you say it was something like bird poop?"

"Almost. Birdsong. Balthazar Birdsong."

Leonard clapped his hands. "Bald Beezer Bird Poop! And now, ladies and gentlemen, I give you the next president of the United States: Bald Beezer Bird Poop!" He leaped up onto a snowbank. "Vanessa Beautiful Person, do you take this man, Bald Beezer Bird Poop, to be your lawfully wedded husband?"

"I do," said Norman, batting his eyes.

"You may kiss the Bald Beezer Bird Poop."

"Bald Beezer Bird Poop, this is your life! EEEEE-YOOOWWWF!" said Norman, and he kicked into an enormous slab of snow, sending showers of slush and himself into a snowbank.

Climbing to his feet, he said, "Come on, I've got to buy some fish for our supper."

* * *

The door closing with a jingle behind them, the boys pressed their noses against the glass to consider the slabs of fresh dead fish arrayed on the fields of ice.

"Boys, don't press your noses against the glass," said the fish man through his beard.

"Aw, look at the squids, they're so cute," said Norman, trying not to become dejected by the sight.

"Eeyaa," said Leonard in agreement.

"Boys!" said the fish man.

"Oh my gosh, look!" said Norman, pointing.

"Eeeeyaaa! What?"

"Don't you see what that sign says? It's rubberlip perch!"

"Eeeeeyuck! Sounds like some kind of a gangster."

"Rubberlip perch. That's alfiona."

"What?" said Leonard.

"What?" said the fish man. "Say that again."

"Say what—'alfiona'?"

"Alfiona," said the fish man, now smiling. "Alfiona! That's right! You are the first person to come into this store who knew the proper name of that fish. Alfiona. Just for that, if you buy a couple of fillets, I'll knock a dollar off the price."

"All right," said Norman. "I'll take three."

"That'll be fourteen dollars, and here's a dollar back for being so smart. I'll give you four quarters so you can split it."

"Eeeeeyes!" said Leonard, karate-chopping a basket of garlic.

"Boys!"

Norman and Leonard ran along the sidewalk, Norman clutching the bag of alfiona.

"I wonder what rubberlip perch tastes like?" said Leonard.

"Don't worry, I think the lips have already been cut off."

"Eeeeyuck."

"What'll we do with our dollar?"

"Easy question," said Leonard, in his guru voice. "We spend it in magic toy dispenser. Ah, magic toy dispenser is great purveyor of ancient wisdoms, sometimes blessing young child with treasure like super ninja gnome, sometimes smiting young child with terrible girlie pinky ring, or silly paper puzzle. Yes, yes. Only magic toy dispenser knows what you will receive. Sometimes young child receive empty plastic container. Terrible blow to child's feelings, of course, but worth the risk."

"Yes, master. You are wise and all-seeing. Let us proceed to magic toy dispensing machine outside of noble and revered Corner Super Market."

They hurried along, leaping over the long shadows cast by the bare trees.

Arrived at the trinket machine, they again pressed their noses against the glass to take a look at what they might receive.

"I want that magic eight ball."

"I want that blue ninja."

"I want the skateboarding homie."

"I want that bloody eyeball key chain."

Leonard placed his quarters in the slot and twisted the handle. The machine grumbled, the pile of toy containers shifted slightly, and a clank indicated that a toy had fallen and was ready to be taken.

"Eeeeegebummer! A pinky ring!"

"Ufff!"

Norman deposited his coins. The machine proceeded to clank and churn again. Norman flipped open the metal flap and pulled out an egg-shaped container and peered inside it, disappointed by the small plastic figurine of some kind of gray-bearded medieval royal personage, then looked at the name stamped along the bottom.

"Alfred the Great? Leonard, this is getting ridiculous. We've got to get back to my house!"

"Why?"

"I've got to read the dictionary!"

bombastic bombshell

The following Saturday morning, Norman smiled as he remembered Leonard's jokes and hijinks the day of the alfiona and Alfred the Great. Leonard had nibbled at the rubberlip perch and wiggled his own lips in a wobbly way. His mother had asked both of them to please chew with their mouths shut. Leonard had pulled the old "Do you like seafood, see food" joke. Norman had seen Leonard do this a thousand times, yet somehow Leonard always managed to bring something new and fresh to the way he rolled his eyes up, opened his mouth wide, and pointed to the half-masticated, partly dissolved gobs of foodstuffs within.

That was the last of the real fun Norman had had.

Norman lay across his bed and contemplated the events of the past days. First, he considered Balthazar Birdsong, who was weird, apparently could read his mind, and was, therefore, a great new pain in the neck; second, Norman held up his Alfred the Great toy, which was also weird but fun; and finally, Norman remembered the old gentleman in his dad's study, the foreign minister of Alfur, who was just weird. Why, Norman asked himself, would the foreign minister of a place Norman had never heard of (until he read the dictionary) come to his father's study, all by himself, to buy "airplanes"—Norman made the quotation-marks-finger-waggle sign—entering and leaving the house by the back door? And what was it with the finger waggle, anyway, whenever his father said the word "airplanes"?

Norman balanced the mini–action figure on his nose.

Alfred the Great had stood guard over Norman all that week from a perch on a small stack of books on his bedside table. Norman turned the toy in his hands, allowing the bedside light to cast shadows on its face, watching as the yellow and pink and green molded plastic seemed to become quite alive.

Norman had indeed returned to the dictionary to look up who Alfred the Great was, discovering that he was a king of England, son of Aethelwulf and defeater of the Danes.

"Hoooyaaaeeeeh!" Norman whispered as he made Alfred the Great chop a few heads off some Danish attackers.

Norman gazed at his action figure, holding it close enough to his eyes to make him seem fully human-sized. He said, "Alfred, I mean, Alfred the Great, I have to tell you something that is very hush-hush. I think my father is hiding something from me and maybe even from Mom. Alfred the Great, it is your mission not only to defeat the Danes but to find out what that thing is. What is my father's secret? Find that out and you will no longer be Alfred the Great, you will be Alfred the Super Great! Hiiiyaaaaa!"

* * *

"Norman!" his mother shouted.

Eeeyooof! thought Norman.

"Mr. Birdsong is here!"

Norman shook himself, sat up, and stuffed Alfred the Great into his pants pocket. If it was Alfred the Great's mission to find out his father's secrets, it was his mission to keep his tutor from finding out his own. Today, Norman would keep his mind carefully screwed shut, unopenable, like an old jar of strawberry jam.

He wormed his toes into his slippers, then shuffled out of his room to meet Bald Beezer Bird Poop for the second time, finding him in the kitchen with his hands moving swiftly but carefully around a little silver pot.

Norman sat down at the table. With his inner eye, he imagined sealed jars of jam that no amount of banging on with a knife would open.

"Good morning, Norman. This week, the letter *B*," said Balthazar Birdsong, now filling the small metal pot with water from a glass bottle, which he had removed from his satchel.

"'Bald,' of course, you know already," he said, now spooning in a brown powder from a small silver can that also appeared from inside his satchel.

A shiver passed from Norman's heels to his ears.

"You realize, I hope, that 'bald' means not only 'hairless' but also 'white,' as in our nation's bird, the bald eagle."

Norman shifted in his chair, picturing ancient jam jars, rusted shut and covered in glue.

Balthazar Birdsong continued. "Beezer!" he said, and Norman jumped about five feet into the air.

"'Beezer' is a fine word, combining the words 'beak' and 'sneezer' to create a composite, meaning 'nose.'" Balthazar Birdsong screwed the spouted top onto the silver pot, placed it on the stove top, and turned on the gas.

"'Bald' and 'beezer' are just two of the delights to be found in the *B* section," continued Norman's tutor. "Now, my own name, Balthazar, means an oversize wine bottle with a holding capacity of thirteen quarts, which I find rather fitting. You may remember Belshazzar the Babylonian king, who had such a bad name in the Bible, or more recently Balthasar Hubmaier, the Anabaptist executed in Vienna in 1528."

The small silver pot began to fizzle and hiss, and Mr. Birdsong removed it from the stove. He rummaged once more in his satchel, pulling out the smallest cup and saucer Norman had ever seen, into which he poured the steaming coffee.

Norman, realizing, at last, that his imaginary defenses were beaten and, hoping perhaps to create a diversion, said, "What does 'birdsong' mean?"

"'Birdsong' means 'birdsong,' my good Norman, but do not feel that I think it wrong of you to ask. Oh no. Many words mean quite otherwise from what they appear. But 'birdsong' means 'birdsong.' You see before you a man who sings like a bird with the capacity for thirteen quarts of wine." Balthazar Birdsong twirled the coffee slowly around and around in his cup, smiling oddly at Norman, then, bringing the cup to his mouth, he swallowed the entire cupful in a couple of gulps.

Rinsing the cup now, Balthazar said over his shoulder, "For the next two weeks, just read the *B*s. We've already discussed three of them, so the rest should be a snap."

* * *

That afternoon, as the day grew colder and darker, Alfred the Great stood staunchly on the kitchen table, nodding sagely, wiping a bit of Danish assassin's blood from his hands, as Norman read from the *B*s.

bombastic *adj* : given to bombast, using overelaborate words or manner

Bombastic Bald Beezer Bird Poop, thought Norman.

Bombax *n* : a South American tree with snow-white or scarlet flowers

Bombay *adj* : done the way it's done in Bombay (Mumbai), India

bombazine *n* : a silk fabric

bombe *n* : a frozen dessert of ice cream in a melon
shape

bomber *n* : an airplane built for bombing

bombilation *n* : a buzzing, humming sound

Bombini *n* : the bumblebee tribe; robust,
hairy, big, black-and-yellow bees

bombshell *n* : a huge surprise

Bombini

Slowly, Norman lifted his gaze toward Alfred the Great. An idea, like a silent little bomb, had exploded in Norman's mind. What if his father's airplanes were not just airplanes? What if they were bombers? What if his father sold bombers, to strange foreign ministers, in his study?

"Wait till I tell Leonard," said Norman aloud. "What a bombshell!"

the twins

Some days later, Orman Normann got in from San Francisco.

"Darn it, Norman, the Alfurnian foreign minister won't buy my airplanes!"

"I'm sorry to hear that, Dad," said Norman.

Norman fingered his fork. He looked at his father, who sat drumming the table and chewing his lips, looking like a neurotic alfiona.

"Dad, can I ask you something?"

"Sure, son, anything you like. Bombs away!"

"Are those airplanes you sell all over the place, by any chance, bombers?"

"Ha-ha!" Orman Normann slapped the table. "Boyo, you're getting smarter already! How did you figure that out?"

"I don't know, Dad, just a lucky guess, I guess."

"Son, I'm impressed," said Orman Normann, leaning forward and smacking his lips. "Thing is, I always call them airplanes to spare your mother's feelings. You know, she's awful sensitive about loud noises, death and destruction—stuff like that."

"I know, Dad."

"No need to mention this to her, right, son?"

"Right, Dad."

"But, darn it, that mustachioed geezer in the vertical headgear will not buy my bombers!"

"So sorry, Dad."

"Doggone it!"

"Maybe they don't need any bombers, Dad."

"Everybody needs bombers, Norman. Remember that."

Orman scratched his forehead.

"How's school, son?"

"Super-duper, Dad."

"How's the new tutor working out?"

"Well, he's kinda weird."

"You know, son, brainy people can be kinda weird," said Orman, pushing himself slightly back in his seat, "but that doesn't mean you can't learn from them."

"I know, Dad."

"It takes brainy people to build bombers, for sure." Orman slapped the table again. "Why won't they buy my bombers? I mean, of course, airplanes."

"Who won't buy your airplanes, dear?" asked Norma, entering the kitchen with the just-arrived pizza.

"The pesky Alfurnians."

"Eat your pizza, dear."

From the front of the house came a buzzing.

"The doorbell's bombilating," said Norman.

"What, dear?" said Norma.

"Someone's at the door, bombilating the bell," said Norman.

"Dear, what?"

"The door. Bombilation!"

"Dear?"

"Never mind, I'll get it, it's probably the twins," said Norman, pushing himself from the table.

It was the twins.

"Hi," said Norman. "Want some pizza?"

Anna and Emma were a year older than Norman and lived in the small house next door. Their mother was a dancer and their father was an opera singer, so both of them worked mostly in the evenings. Since the twins lived next door, and had always lived next door, they were considered part of the family. They referred to Norman as "our brother from another mother."

"How come your dad's home?" whispered Anna.

"The Alfurnian foreign minister wouldn't buy his bombers," whispered Norman, leading the twins into the living room so they could talk.

"Bummer," said Emma.

"That is a bomber bummer," said Anna.

"Four months from now it will be a summer bomber bummer," said Emma.

"And if you've just come from the dentist, and your dentist gave you one shot too many, it'll be a number summer bomber bummer."

"Can we stop now?" said Norman.

"I think not," said the twins together.

"I didn't know your dad sold bombers," said Emma.

"Shh, I'll tell you about it later."

Mrs. Normann came from the kitchen carrying a tray with small silver bowls. "Bombe, anyone?"

"Bombay?" said Anna.

"Bombe," said Norman, "it's a dessert."

* * *

The three friends sprawled across various sofas and chairs.

"So your dad sells bombers," said Anna. "That's kinda crazy."

Norman shuddered inwardly, suddenly worried about what his friends might think of his father. He felt his ears getting hot, but in answer to Anna's comment, Norman simply shrugged.

Emma, seeing his distress—his cheeks had turned a pretty shade of pink—came to his rescue. "I'll tell you what's really crazy, our science teacher, Mr. Kreidewand—that's what's crazy."

"Yeah, like, he'll stand on his desk to get our attention if no one is listening," said Anna.

"One time, he gave his whole lecture in a Donald Duck voice."

"We were studying birds. He is so weird."

"He sounds like fun," said Norman. "I think I like him."

"Me, too," said Anna.

"Me, too," said Emma.

The twins attended the oldest, most revered, perhaps not most fashionable, but still most elite private girls' school in Manhattan. A small bus picked them up each morning and took them into the city.

"We're studying insects now."

"We have to look up all the major family names, and let me tell you, there are a lot of bug families out there."

"Bugging us."

"Families of buggers."

"I think that's a bad word in England," said Norman.

"Excellent," said Anna.

"Wait a second," said Emma. "What do you call an insect collector who changes his plastic containers from pint size to quart size?"

"I don't know," said Norman. "What do you call an insect collector who changes his plastic containers from pint size to quart size?"

"A bigger bugger bagger."

"That's disgusting," said Anna.

"Say," said Norman, "I know the tribe name for bumble-bees!"

"Really?"

"Bombini."

"Really?"

"Bombini."

"How do you know this?" said Anna, raising herself onto an elbow.

"My new tutor is making me read the dictionary."

"Making—" said Anna.

"You—" said Emma.

"Read—"

"The—"

"Dictionary?" they said together.

"Really," said Norman.

"That's ultraweird," said Anna, lying back down.

"Yeah. I just read sections, actually. That's how I know about Bombini. It's kind of a cool name, really."

"Really!" said Emma.

"I wonder if your tutor knows our science teacher," said Anna.

"Maybe they're brothers."

"In the weird family," added Anna. "What's your tutor's name?"

"Balthazar Birdsong," answered Norman, examining a freckle on his left wrist.

"That's weird, all right, but it must be a different family," said Emma.

"Maybe they're just weird cousins," ventured Anna.

"Why are grown-ups generally so weird, I wonder."

"It is one of the great questions of the day."

"It's probably the eternal question," said Norman. "Selling bombers is kinda weird," he added, his cheeks pinking again. But this time he continued: "What's bugging me like a member of the Bombini is what if my tutor and your teacher and even my dad asked this same question when they were kids?"

"You mean?"

"Yes. Probably when they were kids they thought grown-ups were weird, too. Then they grew up, and look what happened. They started doing weird things themselves!"

"Ooooooo," said Anna.

The three were silent for a while.

"All right," said Anna, "let's get back to the bugs."

"Onward, onward," said Norman. "To the ants!"

"*You're* getting weird," said Emma.

* * *

When the twins had gone, Norman sat alone in his room, walking Alfred the Great back and forth across his desktop. Norman was proud of Alfred the Great.

"Alfred the G., I'm proud of you. And our hunch was correct—my father does sell bombers. Now, why does he sell bombers?"

Norman paused to allow Alfred the Great to chop off a few Danish heads.

"Hiyaaa! Let's put it this way. Question: What do the Danes want? Answer: England. Question: What does my father want? Answer:"

Norman paused.

"I don't know."

a little cloudy

Norman sat opposite Balthazar Bird-song at the green kitchen table, on which stood a mug of hot chocolate and his tutor's same small saucer from the week before, its matching cup held aloft by the tutor himself, who was twirling its contents slowly around and around. Outside, the last of the winter winds poked about the bushes

Norman had given up on trying to keep his mind closed and instead watched his tutor carefully to see if he could pick up any mind-reading tricks himself to use on his father.

"Did you enjoy the *B*s?" asked Balthazar.

"Yes," said Norman.

"Did you find your study of the *B*s worthwhile?"

"Yes, most," said Norman.

"How so?"

"Well, I was able to help the twins with their science homework."

"The twins?"

"Anna and Emma."

"Oh yes. I believe I know of these girls. A cousin of mine mentioned something about an Anna and Emma. I believe he mentioned them to me after a particularly long and tiring day. How old might these twins be?"

"Thirteen."

"Ah, they must be the same. Do you like them? Don't answer that. A silly question. Of course you like them, else why would they be your friends. No. I take this back. You have not yet told me that they are your friends. I assumed this, which is not so good, although I suppose I inferred it from your demeanor, which is not so bad. Are they your friends?"

Norman smiled. Here was what he was after. Apparently, his tutor was not a mind reader after all, just a very good guesser. Norman was not sure if he was pleased or disappointed to discover this; still, he was getting somewhere. He said, "They are two of my three best friends."

"Three best friends. As many as that?"

"Yes."

"I see."

Balthazar Birdsong swirled his coffee, then bent forward to bring his nose in close to the cup, looking to Norman, unavoidably, like a strange bird. But Balthazar Birdsong did not drink his coffee; instead, he straightened up again to resume his swirling.

"There is only one thing I regret about Anna and Emma," said the tutor.

Norman attended.

Balthazar Birdsong continued: "I regret that Emma's name is Emma and not Emmé," and at this he gave his cup a final twirl, then raised it to his lips and drank the coffee in a couple of gulps.

Placing his cup down, he said, "You see what I mean?"

"Oh yes," said Norman, not seeing at all.

"Now," said Balthazar, sliding his cup to the side, "before we move on to the Cs, I have another assignment for you for this week."

Norman did not groan aloud, but his eyes betrayed the fear that he was about to be assigned to read the phone book, possibly even the national online phone book.

"Do not worry yourself, Norman. This is an easy and pleasurable task. Here's what I want you to do. Each day during this coming week, at any time that you find yourself out of doors, perhaps when you leave your house first thing in the morning, or at recess, or at the end of the day, it doesn't matter, all that matters is that you have a good view of the sky, I want you to look up at the sky and take note of it. Just take note of it. That's all. Draw no conclusions. Conjure no hypotheses. Just take note of the sky each day. Is it sunny? If so, how sunny? Is it cloudy? If so, how cloudy? What do the clouds look like? Are they moving? Is there more than a single kind of cloud and are they perhaps at different heights in the sky?"

"Do I have to write all this down?"

"No."

"Do I have to remember everything and then tell it to you in order next week?"

"No."

"Will you somehow be checking up on me to see if I've done this?"

"No."

"How will you know if I've done my assignment?"

"I won't."

"Weird."

"Yes."

Norman sipped his hot chocolate, giving up any hope that this new assignment might be of any use in solving the problem of why his father sold bombers. Clouds and his father were

like chrysanthemums and a load of broken rocks—they had nothing in common.

From above they heard what sounded like a moose stuck in a bog, asking a friend for help. Norman knew this simply as the sound of his father getting out of bed.

"My dad's up," said Norman.

"Indeed?" said Balthazar.

Moments later Orman Normann arrived in the kitchen wearing a red-and-white checked shirt.

"You must be my son's new teacher," said Orman broadly.

"Yes," said Balthazar, rising from his chair and extending his hand. "I'm Balthazar Birdsong."

"Don't let that stop you, ha-ha!" said Orman, taking the tutor's hand in his robust grip. "Pleasure to meet you."

"Thank you," said Balthazar.

Orman Normann eyed his son's tutor for a quiet moment and then said, "Make my son smart!"

"That, he already is," said Balthazar Birdsong, sitting down.

"But not too smart! I don't want him figuring out all my secrets. Ha-ha!"

"Ha, ha," said Balthazar.

Orman proceeded to the refrigerator and peered into it. "Say, Mr. Birdsong, do you know anything about the Alfurnians? Where do these people live, anyway?"

He opened the crisper and pushed his head down toward it.

"I believe they live in Celebes and the Moluccas."

"In where and the wheres?" came the voice from the crisper.

"Celebes and the Moluccas, islands of the Pacific Ocean."

"Umph," said Orman, now emerged, clutching bagels, cream cheese, and a number of jellies and jams. "Hmm, maybe if I speak with some other foreign ministers? Some

Moluscans or Celebians. Hmm." He drifted from the kitchen.

After he had gone, Norman said, "He's still upset that the Alfurnian foreign minister won't buy his bombers."

"Is he?"

"He is."

"Well, no time for bombing now," said Balthazar Birdsong, getting up to rinse his coffee accoutrements. "I must leave you. I have much to do today. Remember what I said about your assignment. Give my best to your mother. Until next week, enjoy the *C*s."

So saying, he grabbed his bag and coat and proceeded out the door.

* * *

Norman sat at his desk, looking out at the clouds, which scudded by in several broken layers of gunmetal, slate, and sepia grays. Far above them, the scuffed blue sky was scratched by the long vapor trail of a high-flying jet. Norman opened the dictionary.

canned *adj* : **sealed in a can**

"I knew that," said Norman.

cannelloni *n* : **meat-filled pasta tubes**
cannibal *n* : **a person who eats human flesh**

But do they eat cannelloni? wondered Norman. Ah, here's something Dad might like.

cannon *n* : **a tube, usually metal, used**
 for shooting cannonballs

cannon

Suddenly Norman imagined little black specks falling out of a high jet, specks becoming larger and blacker, and louder, whistling in a high pitch that grew steadily deeper. And then, thought Norman, BOOM, there goes the neighborhood.

Norman looked at Alfred the Great and brooded. Wasn't his father always telling him not to break things? Norman, that lamp cost fifty dollars! And here he was selling bombers— if there was anything in this world that broke things, it was bombers. Norman shrugged and guessed that some things would just never make sense.

On the other hand, he had to admit, the dictionary was starting to make sense of his father.

"Norman!" It was the man himself, poking in his pumpkin-shaped head at the door. "Norman, are you doing your lessons?"

Norman, sliding Alfred the Great into his pocket, said, "Yup."

"Good, son. Do your lessons like Mr. Ding Dong says."

"Mr. Birdsong, Dad."

"Right. Do like he says and you could be the next Alfred Einstone."

"Albert Einstein, Dad."

"Him, too."

"Dad, you're talking a little bombastically."

"Shucks, I don't just talk bombastically, I sell bombastically! But remember"—Orman Normann lowered his voice—"that's our little secret." And he gave a final finger waggle and mouthed the word "airplanes," winked, and vanished like a weasel down a hole.

Norman turned again to the dictionary and mouthed, "Let's see what other secrets my dad won't tell me." And he read.

canoodle *vb* : to persuade someone with caressing words

cantal *n* : a hard cheese of France, like cheddar

cantaloupe *or* **cantaloup** *n* : a muskmelon with a warty rind and yellowish flesh

cantando *adj* : singing

cantankerous *adj* : ill-humored, contrary, and determined to disagree

a bit cantankerous

"I hope this isn't going to be algogenic," said Norman, "because, really, I'm a bit algophobic."

"Pardon me?" said Dr. Zahn, Norman's dentist, looking up from his instruments. "You hope it won't be what because you're who?"

Spring had arrived, bringing with it that special day that came twice each year like the harsh alarm of some celestial clock: the dental checkup.

"I said," said Norman, "I hope this won't be algogenic as I happen to have a bad case of algophobia."

"I still don't get you."

"I hope this won't *create* pain because I'm *afraid of* pain."

"Oh," said Dr. Zahn. "No, no, no, no, no. Just going to have a little look-see. Open, please."

Norman opened his mouth, closed his eyes, and listened as the plastic tube, hooked under his tongue, began sucking at his spit. The brittle, crinkly sound and slight pressure of a metal probe announced the commencement of Dr. Zahn's work. Dr. Zahn hummed tunelessly to himself, a tune which Norman thought might be, but hoped was not, a garbled version of George Harrison's "Here Comes the Sun."

Norman allowed his mind to drift, which was his restless mind's natural tendency at all times, even and especially at times of stress like this. He clutched Alfred the Great in his hand.

Alfred the Great shut his eyes. He was being held captive by a unit of Danish assassins. His tiny plastic imagination tried desperately to think of a way out. A small but intense fire crackled at his feet. One of the assassins held a red-hot iron close enough to Alfred's great nose for him to smell the heated metal.

"You have a couple of cavities in your lower-left second molar," said Dr. Zahn, "which, luckily for you, is still a baby tooth. After I give you a nip of novocaine, I think we'll pull it out."

Beads of sweat sprang to Alfred's clear brow, but he gave away nothing of his storming emotions, now looking his captors unflinchingly in the eyes, disdainful of their threats.

Dr. Zahn produced a pair of pliers from a drawer and began working them around the offending molar. He transferred the pliers from his right to his left hand as he placed his right knee onto the chair next to Norman's leg. Wrapping his right hand over and around his left, Dr. Zahn pulled.

Searing pain lanced through Alfred's cheek, flooding Alfred's inner eye with a burst of what looked like television static, if only Alfred the Great had ever seen a television. For a moment, Alfred felt he must either pass out or vomit. A low, satisfied chuckle proceeded from one of his tormentors.

"That's done it," said Dr. Zahn. "The tooth may have been bad, but that is some healthy-looking root." He chuckled again.

Norman opened his eyes to see his tooth, its dangly root looking pink and long, almost obscene, like something best left hidden.

Norman felt like vomiting.

"By chig pills lik a gandalup," he said.

"Your chig feels like a what?" said Dr. Zahn.

"A candalupp."

"One more time."

"A candalope."

"I still don't get you."

"Fuhgeddih."

"Eh?"

* * *

"Heeeeeyaaah!"

About half an hour later, Norman, standing outside the dentist's office, staring up at the sky, was assaulted by Leonard, whirling his air-karate chops. Norman's mother had asked Leonard to meet her son at the dentist's and then walk home with him, in case Norman was feeling a little woozy. Norman, who had been feeling a little woozy, now felt woozier.

"Ah!" said Norman, immediately wincing from having opened his mouth. "Ow, ow, ow," he continued.

"You really shouldn't do that," said Leonard.

"Ow."

"No, you really shouldn't do that. Standing on a street corner staring into the sky is an invitation to be attacked. All I can say is thank goodness I attacked you first. Who knows what might've happened otherwise. Someone from school might have found you. You'd be in the hospital by now if it weren't for me."

"Ow."

"You owe me a lot. What were you looking at, anyway?" said Leonard.

"De sky."

"What about de sky?"

"Juss de sky. It's one ob by assignments from Mr. B., by dudor. I'm supposed to notice the sky."

"Notice the sky?"

"Just notice de clouds and deir colors and whedder it's windy or not. Stuff like dat."

46

"That's gonna get you a good grade on your next test?" said Leonard, taking Norman by the arm.

"I don't know. It's just what I'm supposed to do."

"How much are your parents paying Mr. Bald Beezer? And wouldn't they like to hire me instead?" said Leonard, as they began to walk.

"I dunno, and no, they wouldn't."

Norman and Leonard crossed the street.

"At least I would give you some genuine test-prep value for your dollar," said Leonard. "In the following text fragment, what best describes the relationship of middle-school girls to cucumbers? *A*, middle-school girls are exactly like cucumbers. *B*, middle-school girls are somewhat like cucumbers. *C*, middle-school girls are not at all like cucumbers. *D*, all of the above."

"*A*."

"Incorrect. The correct answer is '*D*, all of the above.' And I'll tell you why. Because this question comes after a question about thermodynamics. Invariably, a question immediately following a question about thermodynamics has *D* as its answer."

"But I didn't know what the previous question was!"

"Exactly! Precisely. Right. This is why you need to convince your parents to hire me to be your tutor. When we get to your house, I suggest that we go to your father and lay out this plan. Wait. I thought of something. Just so there will be no hard feelings, I'll give you twenty percent of my wages. For instance, if, say, I get, let's see, twenty-five dollars for each session, I will give you, um, twenty percent of twenty-five, that's two, take away . . . Let's just say I'll give you three dollars each session."

"I don't think that's right," said Norman.

"You mean immoral, like some kind of gangster scheme?"

"No, it's not right."

"First of all, your father has probably done this to all kinds of people. It's probably the first thing he suggests when he's trying to get some foreign minister to buy his airplanes."

"Or bombers?"

"Or bombers, why not?"

"Or bombilating bombers?"

"Or bombilating bombers."

"Or bombastic bombers?"

"Or bombastic . . . or whatever! You buy three hundred bombilating bombers and I'll give you three dollars or three rubles or three pesetas back. See, everybody wins. What's wrong with that?"

"Nothing, I guess. It's your math. Your math is wrong."

"It is?"

"Definitely wrong. Would you be my math tutor, too?"

"No. I'd be your test-taking tutor. That's the beauty of it. You don't learn things, you learn how to take tests. Get it?"

"I guess so."

They crossed another street.

"Look. You don't need to learn about the world, life, the universe, history, butterflies, rocks, and math. You need to learn about text fragments, multiple choice, all of the above, true or false, process of elimination, and educated guessing, my best subject. You know I'm a great test taker. I'm a great test taker. True or false?"

"True."

Leonard, now running, shouted over his shoulder, "We will now present our plan to your father. True or false?"

"False. My dad isn't even home. He left yesterday for Celebes and the Moluccas," said Norman, hurrying after him.

Leonard stopped and turned. "He left for who and what?"

"Celebes and the Moluccas. They're somewhere in the Pacific Ocean. He wants to talk to the foreign ministers there."

"He probably wants to sell them three hundred bombers."

"Yup. Eeee yaaah!" Norman hooted, but then immediately put his hand to his cheek. "Ow, ow, ow."

"You really shouldn't do that."

*　*　*

"Hi, Mom. What's for dinner?"

"Macaroni and cheese," said Norma Normann, turning from the stove to greet the boys.

"Yum," said Leonard.

"How was the dentist, dear?"

"Horrible. In fact, I'm a little cantankerous."

"A little cantankerous! Is it serious?"

"No, Mom. I mean, I'm grumpy. I'm in an ill humor. I am disagreeable, because Dr. Zahn pulled another tooth out."

"My!" said Norma Normann, placing two large plates loaded with gooey noodles on the table for Norman and Leonard. "Well, at least it's not cantankerous."

"Hiiiii yaaaah!" said Leonard, plunging his knife into the macaroni.

"Dear!"

*　*　*

After dinner, the twins arrived.

"Mom's dancing *Cinderella* and Dad's singing *Carmen*," said Anna.

"No, Mom's dancing *Carmen* and Dad's singing *Les Pêcheurs de Perles*," said Emma.

"No, wait. Mom's dancing *Petrushka* and Dad's singing *Turandot*."

"Do you have any idea what they're talking about?" said Leonard behind his hand.

"I just know it has something to do with their parents," Norman answered.

"Maybe some kind of disease symptoms."

"Do you think they're cantankerous?"

"You mean contagious?"

"Yes."

"No."

"Good."

"Bad."

"Is today Wednesday?" asked Anna. "Because if it's Wednesday, then Mom is definitely dancing in *Swan Lake*."

"Today is Thursday," said Emma, "which means Dad is singing in *Oklahoma*."

"Now they seem to be making travel arrangements," said Leonard. "By the way, I've changed my mind about what I said before."

"About what?" said Norman.

"The answer to the question. It's definitely *A*, after all. Middle-school girls are exactly like cucumbers."

"*Anyway,*" said both girls, together shooting the boys a silencing look.

"We're only here for a few minutes," said Anna. "We're just waiting to be picked up for volleyball practice."

"Everything all right, dears?" said Norman's mother.

"Coach Munster is serious about volleyball, Mrs. Normann," said Emma.

"But on a weeknight? Good heavens!"

A car honked twice in the street.

"Someone's bombilating!" said Norman. "Well, not bombilating, exactly, but tootling, anyway."

"Bye," the twins trilled, running out the front door with their packs, full of gym shoes and water bottles, flapping on their shoulders.

how to eat a chip

"Cucumber city!" said Leonard, putting his feet up on a chair.

Norman watched his mother bustle about, moving dishes and cups from one counter to the next. The kitchen was her battlefield, always covered by an army of dishes, books, car keys, glasses, napkins, and notepapers ever circling around Norma Normann, who whirled and flitted as their commanding general.

"I'm going to check to see if your father has e-lettered," said his mother.

"Okay. By the way, it's 'e-*mailed*,' Mom."

As she retreated, Leonard eased a large bag of Doritos closer to himself with his foot.

"Ahem," said Leonard, drawing a chip out of the red-and-yellow bag. "Now, as your new tutor, I must instruct you as to the proper way to eat Doritos. It is done in the correct manner, as follows. First, you must consume the entire bag. Second, never allow your lips or teeth to touch your fingers. Only the chip. You must also—this is very important, please pay especially close attention here—never wipe your fingers on a napkin, your pants, or the tablecloth. Okay, now, when you have completely finished the bag, and your fingers are completely covered in Dorito dust, then, and only then, do you slowly lick each of your fingers clean. You may start with

your pinky or with your thumb. That is, of course, up to you."

Leonard crunched his first chip and continued.

"No, but seriously. I could be your tutor. I won't even charge your parents any money. Your mom could pick me up every Saturday. I could tutor you all day!"

Norman said, "Uh-huh."

"No, seriously. Seriously! Listen to me!" Leonard implored. "What is the point of tests? To get you into a good school. What is the point of a good school? To get you to pass the next test. What is the point of the next test? To get you into college. What is the point of college? To get you to pass the next test. What is the point of the next test? To get you a job. What is the point of a job? To make money so you can retire. What is the point of retiring? So you can die!"

Leonard dropped a chip from his upstretched arm—like a bomber, with appropriate bomber noises—into his mouth.

"All this tutor business is just bringing you one step closer to the grave," Leonard continued, crunching hollowly.

"My dad thinks it's important," said Norman.

"Oh, what your tutor is teaching you is important all right. Look at the sky and notice the clouds! I ask you!" Leonard circled his right index finger, which was covered with fine red dust, in the air. "You shouldn't be looking at the sky and noticing the clouds, you should be spending what's left of your precious childhood wisely, playing computer games, skateboarding, eating entire bags of Doritos, or at least getting up to some rewarding mischief, before it's too late. Which reminds me, did I hear you right? Did you say your dad actually sells bombers?"

"Yup, but don't tell my mom."

"Bombers! This presents a rich field of potential mischief!"

"Oh no!"

"Oh yes! We've got to make plans. First thing, you have got to sneak into your dad's study and have a look around." And as he said this, Leonard opened his eyes wide and let them roll from side to side, which, in a face now covered in red paprika chip dust, made him look like a very large fire ant, or a very small devil.

* * *

This time it was his mother who leaned her head in at Norman's door.

"Norman dear, I haven't yet heard from your father, but there was an e-letter thingie from Mr. Birdsong. He says he is unable to come see you this Saturday but will make it up sometime, and he says to go ahead and start on the *D*s and to continue to do your sky assignment, whatever that means. Do you know what that means, Norman?"

"Yes, Mother."

"All right, then. Well, if you're all ready for bed, I'll kiss you good night. Good night, sugar-taffy-honey-licking-smacking sweetikins!"

"Good night, Mom."

Alone, Norman was surprised to find that he was actually disappointed that Balthazar Birdsong would not be coming. Norman peered out between the curtains. The moon was a new sickle moon, soon to set, following the sun, which was quite possibly beginning to shine on his father somewhere halfway around the world. Did they see the same stars there? It was the same sun, Norman knew that much. But was the moon the same? Did it actually look different on the other side of the earth? He would have to ask Mr. B. on Saturday. Then Norman remembered that he was not coming.

Norman mulled over the idea of having a look-see into his

father's study. Maybe Leonard was right. Maybe Leonard was wrong. His father would get pretty mad, Norman was fairly sure, if he ever found out. But how could he find out? He was on the other side of the world.

A few low clouds coasted along outside Norman's window, weakly lit by the bit of moonlight. The rest of the sky was a deep blue-black, inky-looking but clear. Norman would definitely ask his father what the moon had looked like, but would he have noticed?

Was his father up to no good? No. Yes! No . . . yes.

Should he sneak into his father's study to find out for sure? No. Yes! No . . . yes.

Norman sighed. He had never thought of sneaking into his father's study before, because he had known it was wrong. Now he was unsure even of that. Norman was a hopeless mess of indecision.

He sighed another long sigh and opened the dictionary.

diffident *adj* : **without self-confidence, doubting one's own abilities**

"Boy, oh boy, oh boy, this dictionary seems to know everything," muttered Norman. "First it tells me about my dad, now it tells me about me. *Diffident*, I'm diffident. I always knew I was different. But now I'm diffident."

difflugia *n* : **a protozoan relative of the amoeba but having a shell made of sand grains**
difform *adj* : **oddly shaped**
diffract *vb* : **to break into pieces**
diffuse *vb* : **to pour out and let spread**

diffusionist *n* : one who stresses the
idea that bits of culture scatter and
mix throughout history
dig *vb* : to turn up, loosen up, or lift
out dirt

Norman picked up Alfred the Great. "Alfred the G., get out your boots and shovel. We're going to do a little digging in my dad's dirt."

dig

In the small, muddy front yard of a ranch-style house, Leonard crouched on a patch of last year's grass, wet and matted, where a circle of sun shone through the still-bare  branches of the trees. He pulled a piece of glass from his coat pocket, held it before him, and studied its frosty rectangularness. It was a prism. Leonard rolled it in his hands. He held it to his eye and looked up at the sky and then down at the grass. He scratched his cheek. He held it at arm's length again, then back up to his eye, peering this way and that along the grass and sticks. Then Leonard placed the prism on the grass and examined the small rainbow of color thrown onto one of last year's large, pale maple leaves.

"Cool!" said Leonard. "How does it do that?"

"The light is diffracted," said a voice from somewhere above him.

From his crouch, Leonard leaped—oh, at a guess—between three and four feet into the air, and said, "Eeeyaaah?"

The voice went on: "The light of the sun contains all the colors of the rainbow, each being carried by its own wavelength, shorter on the red end, longer on the violet, which differences, when passing from one medium to another, such as from air to glass and then back to air again, cause a separation of the color bands, which are regrouped and become visible when they

57

strike an object, such as this leaf. It is not unlike a marching band stepping from asphalt to cobblestones, where, let us say, the trombones reach and leave the cobblestones first, becoming separated from the glockenspiels, or conversely. Do you follow me?"

"Who," said Leonard, now faced around, having twisted himself about as he leapt—not unlike a cat, very much like a cat, in fact—"are you?"

"Balthazar Birdsong, Norman's tutor," said the owner of the voice, extending his hand to Leonard. "You may call me Mr. B., if you like."

"But how did you find me? How do you even know where I live?"

"It might be that I have supersensory, extramaterial powers, or it might be that I am familiar with the Internet."

"Okay, *why* did you find me?"

"As you may or may not know, I am behind in my obligations to Norman. I owe, I am in debt to the tune of one tutorial session. But more than this I owe Norman an apology because, though he would not admit this even, I think, to you, his dearest friend, he was disappointed by my absence yesterday, the knowledge of which I acquired through purely human channels, neither supersensory nor Internet—from his mother."

Balthazar Birdsong paused to let this sink in.

He continued: "So, I thought, what better way to make this up to Norman than to ease myself round to your attractive mid-twentieth-century home, gather you like the wild bloom you are, whisk you by public conveyance to Norman's abode, press you unto Norman's bosom, then transport you both, after many tearful yelps of joy and forgiveness toward myself, again by public conveyance, to my domicile, perched on a high floor in an apartment dwelling of our fair city, for a cup of tea."

Leonard stared a bit.

"How's about it?" said Balthazar. "Go ask your mother."

Leonard wasted little time worrying about the oddness of his visitor or the strangeness of the circumstance. A day with his best buddy was a day with his best buddy and should not be missed. He ran into the house, returning to the door with his mother, who extended a firm, fact-finding hand to Balthazar, who offered his with a smile.

She said, "Norma has told me about you. You're sure it's no trouble?" still sizing up Balthazar B.

"No trouble at all, Mrs. Piquant," he said. "May I compliment you on your beautiful home?"

"Thank you."

"Nineteen fifty-three, perchance?"

"Fifty-seven."

"Ah, of course. Natural redwood siding?"

"Naturally. I could never have fake siding."

"Certainly not."

Mrs. Piquant paused before saying, "Okay. Mind that you have Leonard back by dinnertime."

"Of course, Mrs. Piquant."

Quickly hugging his mother around the middle, Leonard dashed back into the yard, grabbed his prism, then, shouting "Bye, Mom!" over his shoulder, ran in pursuit of Balthazar Birdsong, already in full stride toward the sidewalk.

* * *

Norman, meanwhile, sat at his desk staring at the *E*s.

entropy *n* : the perpetual tendency of things to become disorganized

epoch *n* : a new beginning, a memorable time

epoche *n* : a way of studying observable things in
    which one does not care whether a thing exists or
    can exist as the first step in observing the thing

epollicate *adj* : thumbless

epomophorus *n* : a kind of fruit bat

eponge *n* : a soft woven fabric
    with an uneven look

eponychium *n* : the quick of a nail

epollicate

eponym *n* : the thing or person for which some other
    thing is named

epopt *n* : someone who has learned a secret system

"Epopt," said Norman to himself. "Hmm, sounds like
something I'd like to pop up as. I think I'll go dig for some
secrets." A twinkle, not unlike his father's own best feature,
began to form in his eyes.

The hall was quiet outside the study door; the only sounds
came from the kitchen, where Norman's mother chattered on
the phone.

Would the door be locked? It was not. Norman eased the
door open and slipped himself inside. Quickly he glanced to
his right to see if by chance the Alfurnian foreign minister had
returned with his terrible hat. No, the room was unoccupied.
Since that last visit, he could see that it had acquired a condition
of mild to extreme—what was the word? "Entropy," that was
the word.

It looked like the place had been hit by a proper bomb,
possibly dropped by the toy B-29, which still buzzed eerily
overhead. Norman set Alfred the Great down on the loose
papers flooding his father's desk.

"Alfred," he said, "show some greatness. Dig for clues."

Norman wandered around the room. He opened the bottom drawer of the right-most filing cabinet. It was full of files, files filled with incomprehensible papers.

He tried the safe. This was locked.

Norman returned to the desk.

"Anything?" he asked Alfred the G.

Alfred the Great stood on a pile of fast-food wrappers, junk mail, newspapers, and magazines.

Norman pulled out one of the magazines, *Bombing People*. He glanced inside. "The one hundred most beautiful bombers."

"Hoo boy," said Norman. "Oh wow, a B-29."

Under a stack of Chinese food containers, Norman spotted something extra glossy. Gingerly, he pulled it out.

"Hmm, L. L. Bomb. Let's see what they've got on sale. Light bombers. Heavy bombers. Bombers for special occasions. Limited Edition bombers. Bombers De Luxe."

Norman paged ahead idly and was preparing to toss the catalogue back on the desk when an envelope slipped from between its pages onto the floor. He picked it up. It was a letter to his father from someone named N. T. McSweeney. The envelope had been roughly torn open on one end. Norman eased out the yellow paper folded within and was preparing to study it when he sharply jerked his head up.

"Alfred, did you hear something?" Norman thought Alfred had heard something. There it was again: a faint clatter against the house.

*   *   *

In the Normann backyard, Leonard said, "I can't understand it. He's usually so on the ball when I throw things at his window."

"Perhaps he is lost in thought," said Balthazar. "Try shouting."

"Norman!"

* * *

Norman hastily stuffed the paper back into its envelope and then into his own back pants pocket, and grabbing Alfred the Great, he glided to the French doors and listened.

Norman leaned slowly forward and, peering out, saw the most welcome sight he could imagine: Leonard, up to something, and in the background, Balthazar Birdsong. Unlocking the doors quietly, he eased himself out and then crouched behind a bush.

"Hey!" he shouted, jumping into the yard.

"EEEEyaah!" yelled Leonard, leaping back. "Where did you come from?"

"Oh, around," said Norman, giving Leonard the raised and fluttered eyebrow-signal to indicate *Tell you later*. "What are you doing here?"

"I've been kidnapped by Mr. B., and now he says we're going to kidnap you!"

"Hey!"

"Are you prepared to come with us?" called Balthazar Birdsong.

"Hey! I mean yes!"

"I've already spoken with your mother and she said, 'Well, it means he'll miss our favorite program, *Health Tips for the Home*, but so long as he wears his mittens,' et cetera, which I take as her permission."

a firm foundation

"The trip to my beautiful abode requires that we take not only a public omnibus but subterranean locomotion as well, which I am sure you will both enjoy," said Balthazar Birdsong.

"I've ridden the subway tons of times," said Leonard.

"I've never ridden the subway," said Norman. "My mother thinks it's unsafe. In fact, if she knew we were traveling by subway, she probably wouldn't have said yes, but I guess she trusts you."

"Please desist from looking quite so skeptical when you say that, Norman. Of course she trusts me. I am trustworthy. I practically define the term."

"Then why didn't you show up yesterday?" said Leonard.

"Ah, your quick mind has caught me out, young Leonard. Well then, your going with me will simply have to be a leap of faith on both your parts," he said as he himself leapt nimbly up the two steps of the just-arrived B22 bus. "Come along, boys."

Seated at the back of the bus, Balthazar Birdsong continued: "But to return to the question of trustworthiness, you, Norman, and you, Leonard, may always trust me to act in your best interests and to be honest and fair. Perhaps I will be found to be missing now and again, if you will pardon my rather baroque turn of phrase. Perhaps my methods will seem to you mysterious from time to time, if not, indeed, pointless." Balthazar Birdsong lifted a needling eyebrow in Leonard's direction. "Nevertheless, your best interests will always be to me as a rock, like the foundation of a mighty edifice, in this case the edifice of your proper education."

The bus took a great right-hand turn, over or through a number of deep potholes, throwing all three to the left and then up.

"Mind you," he said, righting himself, "to establish a firm foundation, sometimes one has to blast through several surface layers of soil in order to get an anchor into the bedrock," and all three bounced in their seats again.

Balthazar Birdsong looked out at the passing scene for a moment, homes and storefronts, tall gloomy metal lampposts, telephone poles with tattered bits of paper and rusty staples, while Leonard glanced quickly over at Norman, asking two quick questions with his eyes: "Is he crazy?" and "Are we in terrible danger?" Norman answered with an "I-think-it'll-be-all-right" smile.

"For instance," said Mr. B., "let's do some blasting. Rather, let me drill an exploratory core into your crusts to see what I can build upon. Leonard, can you tell me exactly what your mother was wearing this morning when we parted?"

"Umm, she was . . ." said Leonard.

"Norman, what about your mother, what was she wearing?"

"Well, I mean. She was . . ." said Norman.

"That's easy, my mom was wearing . . ." said Leonard.

Norman said, "My mother was wearing . . ."

"She was wearing clothes," said Leonard.

"Yes," said Balthazar. "What kind, what colors, what were they made of, how did they smell, these clothes?"

"Uh, ah."

"Fine. Norman?"

Norman looked up and looked down and bit his lip, and then said nothing.

"Very interesting. Yes. Here I have next to me two boys,

each, presumably, loving his mother, holding her in the highest esteem, and yet neither of whom can tell me what his mother is wearing today, even though each boy saw his mother not longer than one hour ago."

"No, no, no," said Norman, "my mother was wearing . . ."

"My mother was definitely wearing something red," said Leonard. "Blue? I think it was green?"

"Yes. Yes, your surface strata would appear to be very porous indeed. Swamplike, even. A quagmire, no solid ground anywhere. Perhaps a few muddy tussocks of dry grass poking up from the slimy ooze, but more than that I don't see."

Turning away from the boys, he looked out the window once more. "Not enough solid ground on which to build even a pixie house . . ."

Leonard and Norman sat, giving each other silent looks, as the bus rattled on.

"Do not despair. You are no worse off than ninety-nine percent of your peers and neighbors. We will begin the blasting and digging process almost immediately. But first, and for the record, I shall enlighten you as to what your mothers are wearing right now, unless for some reason they have altered their attire, but then, why would they alter their attire? Leonard, your mother is wearing a blue-and-white mock turtleneck sweater, of wool, not so smooth as Italian, I don't think, more scratchy, Icelandic, perhaps. Did you not find it scratchy when you hugged her around the middle?"

"It was scratchy," said Leonard with a half frown on his face, rubbing his cheek.

"To complete the ensemble, Leonard, your mother wore clean blue jeans and gray canvas sneakers without laces. She wears a Mickey Mouse watch."

"That's my mom!" said Leonard.

"Norman, have you come any closer to memories of your mother?" Mr. B. went on.

"She was wearing her red, shiny-smooth bathrobe, wasn't she?"

"Very good, Norman. Yes, she was wearing her dressing gown. However, it was yellow, not red."

"What?"

"Yellow, not red."

"Really? Does she have a red one?"

"Quite possibly. But today, I assure you, her dressing gown was yellow."

"Gosh."

"So you see—ah, excuse me, the next stop is ours—so you see, your next assignment, and, Leonard, you may join in this as well, is simply to take note of what the person with whom you are speaking is wearing. And perhaps it will be best if you begin with your mothers."

The bus came to a halt.

"Here we are, everybody out."

Balthazar, Norman, and Leonard stepped out of the back door of the bus; then, the boys following their tutor, they passed a few shops to the corner, turned left, then climbed a long flight of iron stairs and passed through a set of turnstiles onto the station platform.

"As you will have noticed, at this station our subterranean train is actually supraterranean. Perhaps we should call it the *sup*way instead of the *sub*way. It is curious to consider that the stem of the *p* of 'sup' descends, and the stem of the *b* of 'sub' ascends, yet each prefix means the opposite. This is reminiscent of . . ." But Balthazar Birdsong's words were lost in the roar of the arriving subway or, if you prefer, *sup*way train.

Having seated themselves comfortably in a row, Mr. Birdsong continued. "While we are traveling, you might as well get started on the *F*s."

"But I've just started the *E*s."

"Good heavens, but it's already April. Here, I've brought along a dictionary."

Leonard and Norman slumped forward a bit on the train bench and opened the book.

* * *

The train rumbled along and, having crossed a bridge, entered a tunnel into the first of Manhattan's many hills, becoming a proper subway after all. Balthazar Birdsong appeared to doze. Norman slid the piece of yellow paper, which he had pulled from his pants pocket, onto the open dictionary, smoothing and then quietly unfolding it. The two would-be epopts inclined their heads to it and read the following message:

```
ADO ZENE GGS
ALO AFO FBR EAD
ABO TT LEO FSE LTZ ERWA TER
THR EEO RANG ES
ACA NOFMU SHRO OMSO UP
```

Norman looked at Leonard and Leonard looked at Norman.

the maestro

"Huh?" said Leonard. "What does it mean?"

"What does what mean?" asked Balthazar Birdsong, turning to him as the train rattled along.

Norman hastily crumpled the piece of paper into his palm.

"Come, let us take a look," said Balthazar, lifting the dictionary from Norman's lap. He read:

> **firing squad** *n* : **a group carrying out a death sentence by shooting**

"That seems rather straightforward. Let us hope that you and your loved ones shall be spared one."

> **firk** *vb dial. Brit* : **to jerk, twitch, fidget, fuss**

firkin

"As in 'Norman, don't firk so.'"

> **firkin** *n* : **a variably sized wooden cask**
> **firlot** *n* : **an old Scottish volume measure equal to ¼ boll or from ½ to 1½ Winchester bushels**
> **firmament** *n* : **the dome of the sky**

"Just the word I was looking for. Ah, here we are," said Mr. Birdsong, nodding toward the doors. The boys looked out as the train slowed enough for the flickering station signs to be read: 107TH STREET.

They left the station, climbing two flights of stairs to the street, then proceeded down three long blocks until they stopped before a tall, tapering apartment tower.

"You see before you the mighty Maestro Building, so called because the great orchestra conductor Puccilonino lived here. I am now fortunate enough to call it home."

Leonard and Norman tilted their heads back in an attempt to take in the mighty edifice; mostly, all they saw was the ribbing of bricks rising to the clouds, woven through with shimmering, square puddles of windows, many with air conditioners protruding like gray carbuncles.

"Built in nineteen twenty-nine," Balthazar Birdsong continued as he strode through the revolving door into the lobby, "just before the economic crash that mysteriously ate up all of the world's money, this building benefited from a decade of Art Deco experimentation and represents perhaps the apotheosis of that style in this city."

Leonard said to Norman behind his hand, "I have no idea what he's talking about."

"Never mind, Leonard," said Balthazar. "Think of this grand dwelling as a lady and take note of what she is wearing. Ah, here is the elevator. Hop in."

The three entered and duly took note of the polished metal surfaces all about them, which were etched with lines of entwining roses and tulips, everything sparkling under hidden lights.

"Unlike the other ladies I know," said Leonard, "this one seems to wear a lot of her jewelry on the inside."

"Ha-ha! Yes, Leonard, yes. This building is such a lady that she is clothed and bejeweled inside and out." Balthazar Birdsong hummed a counterpoint to the humming of the elevator as the floors ticked by. "Ah, here we are, twenty-sixth floor. Everybody out."

"Does this mean we are in the frontal lobe of the lady?" asked Leonard.

"Quite."

"You live on the twenty-sixth floor?" asked Norman.

"Not quite," said Balthazar. "I live on the twenty-ninth."

"Why did we get off, then?" said Leonard.

"Because the elevator only reaches the twenty-sixth. Use your frontal lobes! This way, please."

Balthazar led them a few steps down the short hallway, then turned left around a corner and left again into a steep stairwell.

"Does this mean we only made it to the medulla oblongata?" asked Leonard.

"Quite possibly," said Balthazar. "I see, Leonard, that what you lack in particular observation, you make up for in general information. I refer to your knowledge of neural anatomy. Now up you go, three flights."

"But how did you get all of your things to your apartment?" asked Norman.

"A man has arms to carry, has he not? And hands with which to grasp?"

"And thumbs, unless he is epollicate," said Norman.

"Quite so."

Up the three climbed, grasping the brass handrail with their fingers and thumbs, peering out of long, casemented windows on the landings, catching glimpses of a great city rather far beneath them.

"Here we are, floor twenty-nine," said Balthazar, "a prime number!"

"So is eleven, seven, five, and one, and I noticed the elevator goes to all of those," said Leonard, panting.

"But all of those do not have all of this," said Balthazar, opening a door before them. He waved the boys into a room filled with light; there was so much light that they could only blink and hold their hands before their faces.

"I should have warned you that there is always a bit of a visual adjustment to be made. Leonard, Norman, please make yourselves at home, so long as making yourselves at home means treating everything about you with great care and respect. I, meanwhile, will busy myself with the making of a coffee Viennoise. Would either of you two like one?"

"Ah, no thank you," said Norman, looking for a safe place to sit down, one without anything too tempting or delicate within elbow range.

"Suit yourselves," said Balthazar.

Leonard, on the other hand, tripped and scuttled to the nearest of the shelves lining the walls, where, after a momentary pause to take in its contents, he began to pick up and put down in very quick order every object he could reach.

"What's this, some kind of bomb?" said Leonard. "Is this a mousetrap? This is disgusting, where did it come from? How did you get this? What is it? Norman, come look at this."

Balthazar appeared in the kitchen doorway. "Let's play a little game of epoche. You describe something, an object from my shelves or maybe an object you make up, or you describe something you remember, and then I'll tell you what I think it is. Leonard, you first. Speak up, please. I'll be in the kitchen."

"Okay, it's white, hard, about the size of my fist. It's got two pieces, lots of holes, and where the two pieces come together, there are lots of sharp spikes."

"Elementary, my dear Watson. That does exist. And I have one: It is a cat's skull."

"From the Catskull Mountains?"

"No. No, the one in your hand dates from the last century and was discovered in the wild outskirts of the city of Chicago."

"Eeeeeyaaaah!" said Leonard, gingerly placing the cat skull back on its shelf.

"Norman? And please do not karate-chop the cat skull, Leonard."

"Right," said Norman. "It's the size of your hand. It's heavy, it's a short octagonal prism of glass mirrors faced inward. One of the walls is made of a two-way mirror."

"That's not on my shelves," said Balthazar.

"I know. It's not on any shelves. It's just in my brain. It's a perpetual light-motion machine. The light can get in, but it can't get out, it just rolls around inside for all eternity."

"Marvelous! Come, we'll take my coffee Viennoise and your hot chocolates, which I took the liberty of making for you, onto the terrace."

Balthazar emerged from the kitchen with a tray heavy with cups and dishes and whipped cream and cookies and chocolate bars.

Leonard and Norman followed him onto the terrace, which on this day was breezy but not cold, where, along with a metal table and chairs, they found two cages. The first housed a white rat; the second, a crow.

"May I introduce my companions? Watson, the rat, and Crick, the crow."

"Pleased to meet you," said Leonard, sitting down. Norman

stared happily at everything around him. The three—the five, including Watson and Crick—sat facing out over a corner of the building, the great stone-and-steel city of New York and the Hudson River before them. Norman and Leonard gazed upon a hundred buildings, with their thousands of windows, countless terraces and roof gardens, and water towers.

Balthazar said, as he passed around the chocolate and cookies, "My mission as your tutor, and I now include you, Leonard, in this as well, is to get your heads and noses out of your textbooks and back into the clouds where they belong. Toward that end, I have brought you here, to give you a leg up, if I may so put it, to offer you a little cloud remediation, to help you with strategies for how to look at clouds more clearly and easily, making this not a chore but a natural part of your day. I will increase your cloud aptitude by two hundred percent at the minimum. How will you succeed in life if your head is not in the clouds? Toblerone?"

Norman and Leonard stared in disbelief, and not just at the offer of Toblerone—delicious Swiss chocolate, if you did not know—to which, after a moment's hesitation, Leonard helped himself.

Norman said, at last, "You know, you're supposed to be helping me to pass the Amalgamated Academic Independent City Schools Test," himself now breaking off a chocolate triangle.

"Oh, yes, yes, yes, and yes, we'll deal with that when the time comes. But not now. Now is the time to look at the sky, or, if you prefer, the firmament."

This sky was indeed, in the truest sense of the word, marvelous. Above them drifted an armada of enormous, oblong, fluffy cotton balls. Nearer the western horizon, the cotton balls appeared to be piling up onto one another, while above and behind all of these, white wisps were smeared across the blue.

"Let us see what species of clouds we have today," said Balthazar.

"I thought 'species' meant 'animals,'" said Norman.

"I can tell we have not reached the *S* section yet, have we? 'Species,' as any third-grader with only a smattering of Latin knowledge could tell you, means 'kinds.' We are most used to this word when we speak of animal kinds, or plant kinds, due to the familiar classification system devised by Mr. Linnaeus, the great scientist and Swede. Just as a chef needs an overview of his pantry and spice rack before he bakes fabulous confections, we scientists need an overview of what is in the world before we bake our fabulous theories. Linnaeus chose the word 'species' because it means 'kinds.' Now let us consider the kinds of clouds we have today."

"Fluffy, normal clouds," said Norman.

"Yes. Fluffy, normal clouds, not too high up, looking like they just stepped out of a fairy tale, these are cumulus clouds. Moreover, if they are wider than they are tall, as are these, then they are cumulus humilis, the best-natured cloud there is."

"How humiliating," said Leonard.

"Well, yes, but perhaps 'how humble' is more apt. Now look at this." Mr. B. turned his head and pointed with his left hand. "To the east you can see these same clouds marching off to the horizon almost in formation, in lines. This is cumulus humilis radiatus."

Balthazar put down his coffee cup and passed an ancient pair of binoculars, which he had produced from under the table, to Leonard. "Here, have a look through these. Revel in the splendor of a cumulus humilis profile."

As Leonard, and then Norman, peered through the binoculars, a puff of breeze began to rattle the now empty cups on their tray and Crick looked up from gnawing his foot.

"Ho, ho, what have we over here?" said Balthazar, turning in his chair to look in the opposite direction. "You see there, cumulus no longer so humble—in fact, tall and beginning to bunch. These are cumulus congestus. And should they continue to bunch they may even become the mighty and sometimes terrible cumulonimbus, bringer of not just April showers but April thunderstorms."

Watson burrowed in his litter.

"I shall tell you much more, many grand things about the great cumulonimbus in good time, but not today. As I have no wish to return either of you to the bosoms of your families wet and bedraggled, we will go now. Leonard, will you please carry Watson, and, Norman, you Crick, please, and I shall carry in the coffee things."

The two boys, the rat, the crow, and the tutor prepared to move inside as the wind tickled and teased the yellow awning that hung along the wall above them.

As Norman picked up Crick's cage, he happened to glance directly across the narrow street at a terrace he had not noticed before. It was close enough for Norman to recognize, with a jolt, like the banging of your head on the bottom of a desk when you have just bent over to look for a dropped pencil, his own father, who—Norman thought—should have been somewhere on the other side of the world.

Norman set the cage down carefully and picked up the binoculars. He was not mistaken. There was his father, seated comfortably in a white deck chair, with a straw hat on, in a blue-and-white-striped shirt and black pants, with a large glass of something tan colored in his hand, presumably beer. He was talking animatedly with another man, who was partially hidden by a potted evergreen. Norman could see the other's gesticulating hands, which, as they at last came to rest, revealed something unique about themselves, something that created in Norman a condition of dread which he could not name. As for the condition of the bodiless hands, Norman could name it precisely, for they were not only without a body, they were both without thumbs.

Norman stuttered under his breath, "He's e . . . poll . . . i . . . cate!"

yabba dabba what?

Why was Norman's father not in Celebes and the Moluccas, nowhere near Celebes and the Moluccas, about as far away from Celebes and the Moluccas as you could get, drinking beer (presumably) with a man with no thumbs?

Norman sat, his dictionary in his lap, and brooded.

Maybe his father had come back early from his trip to have lunch with the man with no thumbs, the epollicate mystery man. Why no thumbs? Maybe this E.M.M. had lost his thumbs in a freak bowling accident. But why both thumbs? Norman did not know why both thumbs. He had been showing off, perhaps, demonstrating two-handed bowling with overweight balls, and both his thumbs had stuck and then just gotten yanked off by the tremendous force of the balls he was using. Norman thought that was it. And then maybe he was a world champion bowler in spite of having no thumbs, having heroically overcome his handicap, and was now a beacon of hope and courage for young bowlers all over the world. What was more, he was probably a motivational bowling speaker, which would explain why his father was having lunch with him: He was motivating his dad. Norman nodded to himself. His dad had lost his confidence in bomber salesmanship; he was no longer a bombastic bomber salesman but a diffident bomber salesman; and he had come back to the city for a quick, one-on-one, motivational meeting with the E.M.M. That was most definitely probably it, thought Norman.

Satisfied, Norman flew Alfred the Great around above his head, watching him through slit eyes.

"I can fly," said Alfred the Great. "Now I'm Super-Great! Wait till my archrival, Knut Knutson—King of the Danish assassins—sees this!"

"Norman!" shouted Emma. "Norman Normann! Stop playing with that stupid doll or staring into space or reading the dictionary or whatever you're doing and come over here. There's something I want to ask you."

Emma sat on a bench outside the dance studio where she and Norman awaited the end of Anna's tap-dance class. Leonard, spending the weekend with his father, was unavailable for any fun.

Norman jumped down from the high windowsill at the end of the hall where he was perching.

"What is it?"

"Listen," said Emma. "This is in the instructions on the box of my new fingernail polish: 'Brush on evenly from the eponychium to the tip of the nail.' Huh? What the heck is a epo-whatever?"

"Eponychium. The quick of the nail," said Norman.

"What's the quick of the nail?"

"The bottom part, toward your hand."

"How did you know that? And who thinks of these things?"

"I don't know, must've read it someplace. Maybe in the dictionary."

"Ooooh, must've read it in the dictionary. No more Looney Tunes cartoons for me, Mummy, I'd like to read the dictionary. Oh, Mummy, what have you there? *The Complete Archie Comics,* Volumes One through Four? No thank you, I'd rather read the dictionary."

"What can I say? It's my tutor, he makes me."

"Oh yeah, I forgot."

Norman sent Alfred the Great into a power dive. "When is my mom going to pick us up for lunch? I'm starving."

"After Anna's tap class."

"When's that?"

"When she's all tapped out."

"Ugh."

"Wanna know what she drinks when she's thirsty?"

"Tap water?"

"How'd you know? You know what they're gonna play at her funeral?"

"'There Is a Bomb in Gilead'?"

"No, stupid. 'Taps.'"

"Oh?"

"Forget it. It's 'balm,' not 'bomb,' by the way." Emma scrutinized her left hand, holding it close to her eyes and then out and up, and then rested it again in her lap. "You've got bombs on the brain."

Norman sat down next to Emma on the bench. He considered sharing his worries about his dad, but then realized she would answer something like "So? My parents are always gone and never where I think they are. Welcome to the club." Instead, he said, "I'm so starving I could eat a firlot of Ring Dings." Which was true.

"Firlot of Ring Dings? What's a firlot of Ring Dings?"

"About one and a half Winchester bushels."

"Winchester bushels? What's a Winchester bushel?"

"I don't know, I haven't gotten to the *W*s. Anyway, I could murder a firlot of Ring Dings." Norman crossed his legs and put his chin in his hand. "You will never believe what my mother was wearing this morning."

"Goody. Fashion news." Emma began to paint the nails of her right hand.

"Well, I'll start with her shoes. White sneakers. She always wears white sneakers, with lime-green footies. Then she's wearing pink sweatpants things, with elastic around the ankles. Then, and this is the beautiful part, she is wearing, I think it's called a twinset, a shirt and a sweater together, made from eponge—this weird stuff with fuzzy balls sticking out all over it. It's mostly pink, too."

"What else?"

"I don't know. By the time I had really studied the fuzzy balls, my mind was so overwhelmed I couldn't take any more in."

Just then Norma Normann stepped out of the elevator at the other end of the hall. She appeared to be covered in fuzzy pink balls.

Immediately behind her, the figure of a man appeared. Silhouetted against the light of the high window at the end of the hall, he looked, strangely enough, like he was covered in some kind of outlandish armor. At the same time, the doors leading to the dance studio were flung open and the sound of fifteen girls cavorting in tap shoes, like the noise of a million quarters dropping through a million soda-can machines, burst forth, not unlike one of the bombs on Norman's brain.

Mrs. Normann, the man, and Anna converged on Emma and Norman, and all spoke at once.

"Anna!"

"Norman!"

"Mrs. Normann!"

"Emma!"

"Anna!"

"Norman!"

"Emma and Anna!"

"Mr. B.!" shouted Norman.

For indeed, it was he. "Greetings, greetings," he said. "Anna and Emma, I believe? Lovely to meet you, I've heard such interesting things about you from my cousin Mr. Kreidewand. He can't recommend your charms too highly. I am Balthazar Birdsong."

He smiled and shook hands with the fidgeting and firking twins.

"And these," he said, removing the large, scalelike objects, now recognizable, hanging about him, "are our lessons for the afternoon: kinetic classroom aids, otherwise known as kites. Once more we bring our heads and noses into the clouds. I will explain further over lunch. Mrs. Normann?"

"Oh yes, yes. Girls, pack up your dance whatnots and we'll just . . ." But the others were already hurrying down the hall, Norman again muttering something about a firlot.

* * *

Over their plain (cheese), pepperoni, broccoli-spinach-and-onion, or eggplant pizza slices, Balthazar Birdsong questioned the girls about their classes.

"Anna, have you yet learned triple step in double time?"

"A little."

"Very good."

"Emma, how about you, can you triple step in double time?"

"I take ballet."

"*Ah, alors. Est-ce que tu peux faire le grand battement?*"

"*Oui, un peu.*"

"*Très bien.*"

"What can you do, Mr. B.?" said Norman.

"Norman, manners!" said his mother.

"No, Norman is quite correct. Fair is fair. I enjoy very much a regular *ardha baddha padma paschimottanasana.*"

"Abba dabba abba dabba yabba dabba what?" said Emma.

"*Ardha baddha padma paschimottanasana.* I am a practitioner of the ancient system of postures called hatha yoga. I have just alluded to the noble forward bend in half-lotus posture."

"Do you stand on your head?" asked Emma.

"Frequently, when appropriate. However, at this time, I prefer to point my head in another direction. With your permission, Mrs. Normann, I will accept your kind offer to drive us all to my preferred kite-flying venue, the Great Lawn of Central Park."

go fly a kite

On the grassy expanse of the Great Lawn, Balthazar Birdsong was distributing the kites, keeping the large red-and-white box kite for himself.

"The origin of the sport of kite flying is lost in the mists of time," he said, handing a kite to Anna. "Did it begin with the Egyptians? Some would say so. But not I, the noble Egyptians being too rooted to the earth in their great palaces and mausoleums. I believe it was more probably the Malays or Polynesians of the Pacific, people keenly attuned to the winds, winds that were sometimes mighty enough, after all, to blow away their towns."

Norman karate-chopped toward his green kite.

"Handle your kite with care, Norman. Remember, undoubtedly this practice began as a religious observance."

"It's just a paper kite," said Emma, "and it's wrinkly."

"My poor, cynical child."

"How come you and Mr. Kreidewand have different names?" said Anna.

"Our mothers did not marry brothers. But enough hobnobbing. We are losing precious time. We have a clear eight knots of wind with half a dozen cumulus

humilis clouds to keep us company. So please, observe."

Mr. B. held his kite aloft gently with his right hand, his arm extended, his head high, and faced away from the wind. He now opened his index finger and thumb, allowing the kite to kick up. Then, with the string running over his right palm, he whirled his arm above his head several turns, allowing the string to spool out rapidly, as the kite, nodding, as if in farewell to its friends, quickly climbed into the blue. Before very long, they all were squinting to see the tiny spots of red and white standing in the firmament.

"Circa one thousand five hundred feet. A nice height, I think," said Mr. B.

With the help of a stake pushed into the earth, Balthazar Birdsong secured the kite string.

"All right. Who's next?"

One by one the three attempted to launch their kites.

"Running is not necessary," cried Mr. B., cupping his mouth with his hands. He let them fall to his sides. "All right. Run if you must."

Soon four kites soared and fluttered quietly, high, very high above the earth.

Balthazar helped Anna, Emma, and Norman stake their kites securely.

"Norman. I've an idea. Let's send something up the string."

"How about Alfred the Great?" said Norman.

"I am familiar with the personage. However, I can't imagine that he is in your possession."

Norman pulled the small plastic figure from his pocket.

"Ah," said Mr. B., examining it. Now he attached a small sail with a fishing swivel to Norman's kite line, then attached Alfred the Great to the sail.

"Hold on to him until I say go." Norman held on. "All right, go!"

Alfred the Great rose smoothly and quickly up the line, finally reaching the kite itself, where he remained.

"I hope he's not scared," said Norman.

"Never!" said Balthazar B.

Mr. Birdsong stood with his head back, smiling broadly, his hands on his hips. "Marvelous," he said.

"Marvelous," said Emma. "What now?"

"What now?" said Balthazar Birdsong.

"Yeah, what now?" said Anna.

"We enjoy the afternoon!"

"But nothing's happening," said Anna and Emma together.

"Nothing's happening! What do these schools teach nowadays? Everything's happening! In fact, we are preparing for what will come next."

"By staring into the sky at a bunch of kites?" said Emma.

"Not just a bunch of kites. A bunch of kites and a small plastic action figure."

Anna and Emma crossed their arms. Even the normally chirpy Mrs. Normann pursed her lips and wrinkled her brow.

"Trust me, I'm a professional. An afternoon spent in the breeze upon the green grass beneath the tall trees is one of the very best learning methods known to humankind, a method which has been used successfully by human beings for thousands, possibly millions of years."

The twins crossed their arms the other way.

Balthazar Birdsong continued: "Perhaps you have heard the expression 'Go fly a kite'?"

Anna and Emma exchanged looks.

"I see you have. Yes, it is a favorite of my cousin's. Very loosely translated, it means 'Go think for yourselves.'"

* * *

Sometime later, if you happened to be strolling near the Great Lawn of Central Park, you might have seen four kites high in the blue sky; one girl halfway up an oak tree, singing, and another girl apparently tap-dancing on a tree stump; and a woman covered in pink, fuzzy balls, leaning back on her arms, with her face upturned to the sun; and a thin man in the middle of the lawn, standing on his head; and a boy with his back to a tree, a book in his lap.

Norman looked up from his dictionary for a moment and squinted at his kite. He looked down again and read:

> **gibberish** *n* **: confused, meaningless talk, utterance that is not understandable**
>
> **gibbet** *n* **: a gallows, especially an upright post with a projecting arm for hanging the bodies of executed criminals as a warning**
>
> **gibble-gabble** *n* **: senseless chatter**
>
> **gibbon** *n* **: the smallest and most tree-loving ape, with very long arms and no tail**
>
> **gibbosity** *n* **: a swelling or bump**
>
> **gibbous** *adj* **: rounded, bulging**
>
> **gibe** *vb* **: to taunt, to sneer**

gibbous

Norman looked at the sky and said, "Gibble-gabble."

He closed his eyes. "Gibble-gabble. Gibble-gabble. Gibble-gabble."

He opened his eyes and scrunched his mouth sideways a few times. "Ibbleg-abbleg. Ibbleg-abbleg. Ibbleg-abbleg."

He went on. "Blegab-blegib. Blegab-blegib. Blegab-blegib."

He went back to where he started. "Gibble-gabble. Gibble-gabble. Gibble-gabble."

"What's that, Norman?" asked Norma Normann.

"Nothing, Mom. Just gibble-gabble. It doesn't mean anything."

"All right, dear."

Nevertheless, it had given Norman an idea.

He took out the piece of paper he had kept in his pocket ever since discovering it in his father's study, now very crumpled and worn from all the unfolding and folding it had received over the past days, and smoothed it out on his knee. Once again he tried to read it.

```
ADO ZENE GGS
ALO AFO FBR EAD
ABO TT LEO FSE LTZ ERWA TER
THR EEO RANG ES
ACA NOFMU SHRO OMSO UP
```

"Now *this* is gibble-gabble, grade A," said Norman.

Norman tapped his forehead absentmindedly and sat up with a jolt. "Wait a second! ADO ZENE GGS. That's a dozen eggs!"

He jumped up, shouted "Hurrah," and then sat down again. "A dozen eggs?" he said. "Why a dozen eggs?"

Norman worked through the rest of the puzzle. He looked down. He looked up. He looked down and he looked back up, all the while recording his guesses on the piece of paper.

"Okay, here it is. Message decoded by ace code cracker, Norman Normann."

A DOZEN EGGS
A LOAF OF BREAD
A BOTTLE OF SELTZER WATER
THREE ORANGES
A CAN OF MUSHROOM SOUP

Norman nudged his mother, who had begun to doze. "Mom, I was wrong. It's not gibble-gabble. It's a grocery list."

great ear to great ear

Norman sat at breakfast, looking dreamily at Alfred the Great, who was perched on the top of a cereal box. Occasionally, Norman took a spoonful of cereal, but he continued to be off in his own world, as we have often heard his mother say.

Norman said aloud, "A dozen eggs, a loaf of bread, a bottle of seltzer water, three oranges, and a can of mushroom soup. Why would someone send Dad a grocery list in code? Why would he even need a grocery list? He can't even make toast."

"Who can't even make toast, dear?" said Mrs. Normann.

"Dad can't even make toast."

"Yes, dear, you're right. But he can buy toast."

"What a hero. I wish he would come home and stay home. I hardly ever see him."

"Now, dear, don't be snippy. You know Daddy works very hard for you and I."

"You and me, Mom."

"That's what I said. Now, haven't you got some lessons to finish for Mr. B.? You know we're meeting him with Leonard and Mrs. Piquant for a super-duper special lesson at the Bananical Gardens."

"You mean, botanical?"

"That must be it. I didn't think 'bananical' could be right. Sometimes I can't read my own handwriting. Finish your cereal, sweetheart, and let's take a look at your lesson together. We'll make it nice and cozy-wozy."

Norman carefully moved his cereal bowl aside and slid a large piece of blue origami paper into its place. He picked up the paper and then folded it carefully, this way and that, as Mr. B. had shown them all how to do on the way home from their kite-flying session, and after a few minutes of concentrated effort, he held in his hand a small kite. To this, he attached very light sewing thread. Norman got up from the table and switched on the fan on the kitchen counter.

"Thank you, dear, it is a bit close today," said Mrs. Normann.

Norman returned to his seat and attached the little blue kite to Alfred the Great, who still had the fishing swivel around his waist. He placed Alfred the Great onto a popsicle stick and taped his feet down.

"Now, Norman, stop playing with that little man and open your book."

"Right, Mom." Norman reached for his dictionary and paged through it until he came to the *H*s.

"Good for you, Norman dear," said his mother, absently paging through a home décor magazine. "Now read aloud to me."

Norman read, "'Hot, adjective, having a relatively high temperature.'"

"Everyone knows what 'hot' means, Norman. Today it's hot, for instance. Find something more challenging."

"Okay, Mom. How about this, 'hot air, noun, talk without meaning.'"

"'Hot air' is not 'talk without meaning,' it's what comes out of a hair dryer."

"Whatever you say, Mom. 'Hot brain, noun, hot head.'"

"Oh."

"'Hot buttered rum, noun, a hot drink made of rum and hot

water mixed with spice and sugar and served with a lump of butter floating on top.'"

"There is no need for you to know anything about hot buttered rum, Norman."

"Mr. B. just says I should read the dictionary, as much of it as I can."

"Well, all right, but not hot buttered rum, that's out."

"'Hotch, verb, to shake.' 'Hot dog, noun, from the resemblance of frankfurters to dachshunds, a cooked frankfurter served on a bun and garnished with mustard, ketchup, onions, or sauerkraut.'"

"That's fine."

"'Hotel, noun, a building of many rooms used for travelers on overnight stays,

with several floors reached by elevator, usually with a variety of rooms for eating, drinking, dancing, fitness training, business needs, exhibitions, and group meetings (as for conventioneers), sometimes with a pool, hot tub, or spa, with shops opening into the lobby and onto the street and selling T-shirts, gifts, candy, newspapers and magazines, and other things of special interest to travelers or with personal services like hairdressing, shoe shining, massage therapy, and with telephone booths, though these are now somewhat rare, writing tables, and washrooms.'"

"Well!"

"'Hoteldom, noun, hotels and hotel workers.'"

"'Hoteldom,' you mean, like 'kingdom'?"

"I guess so, Mom. 'Hoteldom.'"

"I think that's a bunch of hot air," said Norma Normann, getting into the spirit. She rose to refill her coffee mug.

"No answers in the dictionary today," said Norman to himself.

"What's that, dear?"

"I said, maybe Mr. B. will have some answers in the Bananical Gardens."

"That's right, dear."

"In the meantime," said Norman, under his breath, "it is time for Alfred the Great to try my new invention."

Norman set Alfred the Great, with his popsicle stick, on the rim of the cereal bowl.

Alfred the Great tested the kite strings and checked to see that his feet were securely strapped to the board.

"Well, here's how!" said Norman.

"For the Queen!" shouted Alfred the Great, and kicking himself off the edge of the great bowl, he yanked on his kite string, bringing the kite up and engaging the wind. The string snapped taut and the enormous kite shuddered, then pulled with tremendous power. Alfred the Great leaned back, allowing the force of the kite to pass through his waist, where he was tethered to it, down through his legs and into the board, which leaped up and began to slice through the milky liquid, the board squirting like a watermelon seed between two fingers.

"Eeeeeeyaaaaaa!" yelled Alfred the Great as the board rode through the waves, soaring over several large oblong shapes floating in the white sea. Indeed, with a little kick of his legs and a tug on the line, Alfred the G. found he could soar great distances before splashing down again, his silver locks streaming out behind him, his robes whipping and snapping.

This is like flying, rather exhilarating, thought Alfred.

But his robes were becoming a problem. They were getting wet and, royal velvet that they were, extremely heavy. Now the drag of the robes coupled with the fantastic pull of the kite were like two great locomotives going in opposite directions, trying to tear Alfred the G. in half. Suddenly, with a prodigious rip, the kite line tore from his waist, sending the kite pinwheeling wildly down as Alfred sent up a great rooster tail of milk as he careened into the side of the bowl.

"Norman!" shouted his mother. "Look at the mess you've made of your breakfast! Cereal and milk all over the table. Now stop playing and take a paper towel and wipe up this mess. And then get ready for Leonard and his mother. They'll be here any minute. Really! I thought you had more sense."

Alfred grinned from Great Ear to Great Ear.

jefferson oak

Norman, Leonard, Norma, and Mrs. Piquant entered the Botanical Garden through the great neoclassical gate, Norman and Leonard heeyahing and karate-chopping their way through the turnstiles.

"Norman, please, remember where you are."

"Where are we? We're outside!"

"Yes, but you are in a garden."

"Haaaawooooo," shouted Leonard. "Apparently, this must not be the Garden of Eden."

"Why not, dear?" said Norma.

"Well, first of all, the Garden of Eden was a paradise, and if it was a paradise, you should be able to do what you want, even if it's just goofing off."

"Well, dear, I'm not sure if you could goof off in the Bible."

"And another reason it's not the Garden of Eden is that we're all wearing clothes! Eeeyaaah!"

Norman and Leonard skipped and ran and hopped down the gravel path in a somewhat restrained way.

Norman said, "You know something I never understood about the Garden of Eden?"

"There's a lot of things I don't understand," said Leonard.

"Who did Adam and Eve's children marry to make the rest of us? You know, Cain and Abel. Did they marry their mom? Because if they married their mom, that's gross."

"That's not only gross, I bet it's against the law. In all fifty states!"

"Hiyaaaah! Do you know where we're meeting Mr. B., by the way?" asked Norman.

"He told my mom to go to the Jefferson Oak and look up."

If you have been to the Bronx Botanical Garden, then you know that after you enter through the great gate and have passed the buildings containing, on the one side, the palm collection and, on the other, the succulents, you walk along a pebbly path, coming quickly to a large, baroque, and filigreed fountain. From here out, the park spreads its wild acres, and to find the Jefferson Oak takes some careful planning and alert walking along the many crossing ways. Fortunately, Sarah Piquant knew the park well and strode onward purposefully, while the boys scampered in the grass where it was allowed and remained on the walkways where it was not, with Norma trotting along behind them, good-heartedly.

"Oh, this is beautiful, Sarah!" she said. "The leaves are all so freshly green."

Indeed, the leaves were the green they achieved only during the last weeks of April and the first weeks of May, nicely framing Norma's overall pinkness, as she breathed in their new-made aroma.

From a rolling meadow ahead of the mothers, Leonard called, "Mom, is this it?" pointing to a monumental oak standing a bit apart from the others.

"That's it. Now let's see if we can find Mr. B.," she called back.

Norman and Leonard ran to the great tree, Norman loping with long strides, Leonard skittering like a piece of paper blowing down a sidewalk.

At the base of the tree, they looked up. At first all they could see was the great spreading canopy of the oak, its heavy limbs like spokes of a wheel beneath the young, green, whispering leaves. Then Leonard spotted, high in the tree, two black boots at the ends of thin black legs.

"Mr. B.!" he shouted.

Mr. B.'s face, small but unmistakable, appeared above the boots.

"Ahoy!" he shouted. "I'm sending down a ladder."

"Righto," said Leonard. "Eeeeeyaaaah!" he added.

The moment the rope ladder reached the ground, Norman and Leonard began climbing it, which was really rather difficult, as you know if you have ever tried to climb one. Leonard had a bit of an easier time because Norman, behind him, secured the ladder; still, they both huffed and puffed. Rung by rung they clambered up to the juncture where the branches began, the ladder all the while swinging and bumping into the trunk.

"Boys!" Norman's mother bleated from far across the meadow. "Boys, really, I don't think you should!"

In between huffs, Leonard said, "I like your mom a lot, she's a very nice person, but she *is* a worrier."

The boys reached the first of the great limbs, which, if stood upright, would be a substantial tree in itself.

"Your mother is quite correct," said Balthazar from above them. "You should not be climbing this tree, as this is strictly against the rules here. However, I have an understanding with one of the upper gardeners. But don't stop now. Come along until you reach me, at which point your next lesson can begin."

The boys continued to climb, now more easily, since the surrounding branches gave them something else to hold on to and push against.

"Norman!" shouted Norma, now arrived below them. "How are your palms? Are they sweaty?"

"Palms are A-OK, Mom," said Norman.

Sarah Piquant called up as well: "Leonard, are you all right?"

"Fine, Mom," said Leonard.

At last the boys reached Mr. B.'s perch and hoisted themselves alongside him. The branches were narrower here, but grouped in an altogether comforting manner.

"Are either of you afraid of heights?" asked Balthazar.

"A little," said Norman.

"A little to a lot, actually," said Leonard.

"Fine," said Mr. B., "then this will be especially therapeutic for you both. I do appreciate your willingness to join me here because I have a very important lesson today."

"Okay," said Leonard, "but why are we going out on a limb?"

"Exactly," said Balthazar Birdsong.

observation
and imagination

Balthazar Birdsong began, "I would like you to observe this tree."

"Why, is it doing something?" said Leonard.

"Shh," said Norman.

"Exactly. Is it doing something?" said Balthazar Birdsong.

Balthazar Birdsong removed his sunglasses, began to polish them on his shirt, and said, "We are often taught that the world out there, including this tree, contains a certain amount, perhaps an endless amount, of facts, which are to be acquired as knowledge. Knowledge that must be gathered from out there"—he waved his glasses vaguely—"and put in here." He tapped each boy's head. "You follow me? *How* this knowledge is transferred is of no concern. What is of concern is that this knowledge gets from out there to in here," and he tapped Norman and Leonard on the head once more.

"My brain is already full," said Leonard.

"Quite possibly," said Mr. Birdsong, returning his glasses to the bridge of his nose. "All this suggests that the world of knowledge already exists, as if in an enormous warehouse. Whoever comes along and gathers the most knowledge, filling up his shopping cart the fullest, is deemed the smartest. Whoever, et cetera, the least, et cetera, the dumbest."

"Right," said Norman, who only ever felt that his shopping cart of knowledge had a couple of fifty-cent bags of chips and a small cucumber in it.

"Either way, the knowledge is sitting on those long, gleaming shelves whether you show up or not."

"Who is the stock boy and what color is his apron?" asked Leonard.

"Precisely," said Mr. B. "Now, there is a good bit of truth to this idea. After all, what is my trusty Ingmeister's Third New International Dictionary but a big storehouse of knowable words that I keep recommending to you?"

"Yeah," said Norman, wishing he had made this point.

"Yeah," said Leonard, "I was just about to say that."

"I'm sure you were," said Mr. B. "We will address this presently, but first let me suggest to you that there might be something more. Where does all this knowledge come from?"

"The knowledge farmers?" ventured Leonard.

"Why not?" said Mr. B. "We might say knowledge comes from an engagement of your mind with the world. Your mind must move out into the world."

"Gross!" said Leonard.

"I did not say 'your brain,' if you recall. I said 'your mind.' The movement of your mind is, of course, imagination. What I now want you to begin training your minds to do is to observe the world imaginatively. Observation performed merely on its own is no more than what a machine can do—a surveillance camera, for instance. And imagination alone, practiced by itself for too long, can cut you off from the world. You might wander away, like a hermit to a cave, becoming only a spirit to the rest of humanity. However, if you remain in the world, and you train yourself to combine observation and imagination in proper proportion, then, my boys, then you may change the world itself."

Leonard looked out from under his long eyelashes to see if Mr. B. was speaking seriously.

"How else," Mr. B. continued, "did Copernicus understand the true movement of the earth and stars, or Darwin the movement of species through evolution, or Madame Curie the movement of subatomic particles in her X-rays?"

He smiled. "That is why we are sitting in this tree."

"I was wondering when you were going to get to that," said Leonard. "I mean, I'm all for sitting in trees, but not necessarily with tutors."

"Leonard, you cut me to the quick."

"The eponychium?" said Norman.

"Verily, to the eponychium. Boys, we are here to observe this tree, imaginatively. And we sit so high up in this tree, which began its life in this spot before ever a street in the county was cobbled, or the city hall encrusted with marble—this tree being older than the borough itself—so that we may observe this unfurling leaf here in my hand, which we can see is as young and full of life as any baby's soft hands and feet. For as old as this tree itself is, its growing fringes are just as they were when it was but a seedling, the apple of its daddy's eye."

"Only it's an oak," said Leonard.

"The mightiest. Our goal should be to observe this leaf imaginatively enough so that we might know the essence of the entire tree without having seen it."

"I'm getting dizzy," said Norman.

"Ah, perhaps I let myself get carried away," said Mr. B.

"No, I'm just getting dizzy," said Norman.

"All right, down we go, then. Remember, down is always trickier than up. Just ask any cat."

The two boys scooched themselves back toward the rope ladder.

"Norman," his mother shouted up, "are your hands nice and dry?"

Norman wiped his hands on his pants.

Alfred the Great spat on his hands and tested the rope. It appeared to be plenty strong. Even if it feels like a wet noodle, he thought grimly, this is my only way off the face of this cliff. He began to ease himself slowly over the rocky ledge, keeping the rope entwined around his right leg, creating a sling that he could fix and unfix by letting the rope go or holding it fast. Alfred looked down. A thousand feet below him he could see the rocks and trees of the trailhead that would take him to safety; he also saw two members of his court, who had apparently packed sandwiches. Alfred the G. proceeded now, carefully but confidently, hand over hand, the fresh wind tugging at his long, velvet robes.

Alfred could hear hunting horns, somewhere down the valley. Darn it! The Danes! It sounded like someone had alerted the army. This time they might be arriving on horseback or with wild boars, he shouldn't wonder.

He placed one hand below the next, moving quickly now. Alfred the Great's palms began to sweat, and he was getting a cramp in one of his feet.

Horns again.

Alfred the G. reached out for a branch and was just about to grasp it when suddenly . . . he was falling.

a proper balance

"Norman!" cried his mother. "Open your eyes!"

Norman opened his eyes. He saw the tree above him, even farther above him than before, as he seemed to be lying on his back; he saw his mother's large face; then, slightly smaller, Mrs. Piquant's; then, much smaller, Leonard's, still up in the tree; and finally, very tiny, Mr. B.'s face, which, contrary to the worried aspects of all the others', still beamed merrily.

"Norman, you had your eyes closed and you just fell right out of the tree. I watched it all happen. I think my heart stopped," said Norma Normann. "Norman, why were your eyes closed? Why weren't you paying attention to what you were doing?"

"I was paying attention. I was paying attention to Alfred," said Norman.

"Norman! Really!"

But his mother kissed him and patted him and asked him if anything hurt terribly and if he could name the date and his middle name and did he want a cookie? And then she kissed him some more, which, if the truth be told here, Norman did not really mind.

In the meantime, Leonard and Mr. B. arrived at the base of the tree, Leonard shouting, "Heeeeyaaaaa! That was a little scary, but cool!" Mr. B. flicked some bits of bark from his trousers.

"Mr. Birdsong!" said Norma, turning to him. "You took our boys into danger, terrible danger!"

"Exactly," said Balthazar. "Remember, a good education is a risky thing."

102

"But he fell out of a tree!" wailed Norman's mother, now positively stamping her foot.

"Precisely. Norman, I must thank you for illustrating so energetically, so enthusiastically and wholeheartedly, indeed whole-bodiedly, my admonition in regard to finding the proper balance."

Mr. B. removed the cloth cap he was wearing, gave it a slap, and replaced it on his head.

"You see, my dear Mrs. Normann, I suspect Norman's admixture of observation and imagination was not properly adjusted, the infusion of imagination being a smidgeon too rich. A bit more observation, Norman," he said, helping him to his feet, "and you will be sailing like a schooner."

"Really, Mr. Birdsong!" said Norma.

"With its spinnaker flying!" said Mr. B.

"Mr. B., we haven't gotten to the *Ss* yet," said Norman, a little bent, rubbing his back.

"Yeah," said Leonard, "that reminds me. What about the dictionary! Why do we need it if imagination is so important?"

"Ah," said Balthazar Birdsong. "Mrs. Piquant, I think this might be an ideal time for the sandwiches." Leonard's mother began unpacking the lunch things onto the outspread blanket.

Hitching his pants up at the knee, Balthazar Birdsong seated himself comfortably on one of the great roots of the tree. He crossed his legs, cupping his knee with his hands, and continued: "The dictionary is here to make our acts of observation and imagination more acute, more perceptive, deeper, wider ranging or higher flying, more accurate, more daring, more correct, more exact, more adventuresome, in a word of two syllables, better."

Norman and Leonard sat down and helped themselves to sandwiches.

Through a mouthful of liverwurst on rye, Leonard said, "In a word of one syllable, how?"

"All right, how. If you walk through the forest with only the words *green*, *dark*, and *crunchy*, that is all that the forest will appear to be. Green, dark, and crunchy. Not bad, but not so good either. However, if you walk through the same forest with the words *olive*, *apple*, *oak*, *elm*, *hushed*, *cricket*, *aster*, *fern*, *still*, *mushroom*, *earthworm*, *screech*, *scuffle*, *itchy*, and *yellow-shafted flicker*, it will be a different experience altogether. A better experience altogether, full of possibility and further discovery."

Mr. B. gestured to the trees around them. Leonard and Norman bit into apples.

"Consider for a moment Charles Darwin," he said. "One day Charles Darwin sat upon a rock on an island of the Galápagos and observed the birds, in this case, finches, genus *Geospiza*. And he saw something which interested him. These birds had a great variety of beak shapes, large or small, or pointed or hooked, each one suited to the particular fruits or seeds or berries the bird ate. As he sat on his rock, his imagination roamed over these birds and their beaks, and an idea stirred within him, the idea that one kind of animal might change over time to fit different situations, thereby producing new kinds of animals. This was the idea of evolution, an idea that, believe me or believe me not, went on to the change the world. Where would we be if Charles Darwin had sailed to the Galápagos Islands and had not had in his mind the words *beak*, *finch*, *larger*, *smaller*, *intermediate*, *graduated*, *starling*, *parrot-shaped*, *chaffinch*, et cetera. Where, hmm?"

"Still swinging in the trees?" said Leonard, tossing his apple core away. "Eeeeyaaaah!" he added, jumping up and scampering off like a chimpanzee with a black belt.

"Quite possibly," said Mr. B., cutting a wedge of apple and popping it into his mouth. "Or in Norman's case, falling out of them. Eh, Norman?"

Norman crunched his apple and leaned back against his mother, who wrapped her arms around him.

Imagination and observation, he thought to himself. Well, he for one was going to subject his father to some serious observation when he got home, and then having observed him, he proposed to do some heavy imagining. Very heavy imagining.

In the meantime, he would read the *Is*.

infer *vb* : to deduce from evidence
infructuous *adj* : not producing fruit
infumation *n* : the use of smoke in drying
infundibular *adj* : funnel shaped
infuriate *vb* : to make very angry
infuscate *adj* : tinged brown
infusionism *n* : the belief that the soul exists before the body exists; it is poured into the body at or before birth

"Mr. B.?" said Norman.

"Yes, Norman?" Balthazar B. placed his hands behind his head and leaned against the tree. Stretching his legs, he turned his face, eyes closed, toward the May sun.

"That tree over there has a rather infundibular shape, in an upside-down kind of way."

"Does it? I see you have already dipped ahead into the *Is*. Very good, very good. The right spirit. Carry on, carry on. Summer vacation is just around the corner and we are not nearly halfway through the alphabet. Read on."

"Mr. B.?"

"Yes, Norman?"

"I have another question."

"I would be disappointed if you didn't."

"If a coded message turns out to be just an ordinary list, why put it in code?"

"If a coded message turns out to be an ordinary list, then we can infer only one thing."

"What one thing?"

"There must be another code."

* * *

Norman snuggled against his mother, pulling the dictionary into his lap. A soft "eeeeeyaaaaarrrrrg" floated over the meadow and then a quieter "Leonard, come and look at this beautiful Queen Anne's lace." Norman felt the warm sun on his cheek and a kiss on the top of his head. And he read.

dropping things on
other people's heads

When Orman Normann at last came home from his trip to the Pacific, the entire Normann family sat down together to a dinner of home-delivered pizza on nice, green paper plates, with cola beverages and pretty, yellow paper napkins. Orman was telling his family of the trials he had endured on his lengthy travels in a voice that was a smidgeon too loud and just a little uncouth, owing to the fact that for the past several weeks it had had to make itself heard in large meeting rooms, across ticket counters, over the din of noisy restaurants, and, you will remember, on a certain city terrace containing a certain mysterious man. Perhaps we will forgive Orman his manners, this time, as he has been out of reach of the civilizing influence of his wife and son.

"Darn it!" he said again. "That was a long trip. And what do I have to show for it? Nothing, zilch, nada, nix, zippo, bupkis, nil, null, a big goose egg."

"Dear," said Norma.

"Well, darn it, Norma. I've been to Tasmania, Wolfsbania, Kandicania, Rockbury, Kalamooga, New Kalamooga, Dixberg, Bulla Bulla, and even Houston, Ohio, chasing after the Alfurnian foreign minister and his underlings, who seemed to be doing business with everyone all over both hemispheres, everyone but me, and they still won't buy my bombers. They'll buy tanks from Tuscahassie, no questions asked, sign on the dotted line for a gross. But will they buy my bombers!

No! Darn it! I mean airplanes," he said, smiling at his wife.

"Dad, don't you think you ought to tell Mom the truth about what you really sell and where you've really been?"

"What you really sell?" said Norma Normann, squeaking.

"Norman!" said Orman. "What happened to our agreement? Oh, for heaven's sake, all right. Norma, I sell bombers—really, they're a *kind* of airplane, so I never was not telling the truth, honest Injun, Norma."

"Bombers, dear!"

"Don't think of them as bombers, honey. They're just nice, shiny airplanes, pretty as a picture, pretty as a picture on black velvet, airplanes that you can drop things out of. You could probably drop waffles or umbrellas or even pizzas out of them. That's probably what people use them for, I don't know, maybe folks use them for pizza delivery. Gosh, I'll bet that's what everybody's using them for." Orman poured himself some cola, drank, and after a rather well-sustained belch said, "Except that nobody is buying my bombers! Darn it!"

"Dear," said Norma.

Norman took a bite of his pizza and said, with his mouth full (Norman could use a little civilizing himself, let's face it), "Dad, why don't you try selling something else, like toothbrushes, or shopping centers or something?"

"Son, I got to tell you, and it's time I told you, as part of a good education, that, boy, there is nothing like selling bombers to make your small fortune. Hooooeeee! When you're selling bombers and certain foreign ministers are buying bombers—" Orman Normann's face took on a dreamy look, not unlike his son's when his son looked at clouds. "Did I mention the hats they wear? Weird. Tall and pointy and covered in fur. Anyhoozle. When you're selling and they're buying, the cash just flows like a house afire."

"That doesn't make sense, Dad," said Norman. "How can it flow like a house afire?"

"Son, pay attention! What I'm telling you is this. Since there have been people on this earth running around with the dinosaurs—"

"Not the dinosaurs, Dad."

"Whatever. Since the cavemen, then, people have dropped things on other people's heads, probably before they had toothbrushes, and certainly before they had shopping centers. Yes, son, the cavemen started with dropping things on other people's heads, and then after a little while folks threw spears and shot arrows, then it was cannonballs. Then it was exploding cannonballs. And now it's bombs. Progress, son, I'm talking about progress!"

"I got it, Dad. Progress."

"So long as there are people on this earth, they're going to want to drop bombs on each other's heads. And so long as people want—"

"Dear!" said Norma.

"Honey, don't interfere. This is an important father-and-son-type moment. Now, I never mentioned bombers before because I know how you don't like anything that explodes, though if you think about it, exploding is a kind of progress, too. You go from one big thing, a building, say, to lots of small things—say, a pile of bricks. Progress, see? Anyhoozle, so long as people want the kind of progress that only dropping bombs can get them, they're going to need—they're going to need what, son?"

"What, Dad?"

"What are they going to need, son?"

"Bombers, Dad?"

"Bombers, son! That's it, bombers! And that's where we come in," said Orman Normann, thumping the table with each invocation of the word "bombers," softly at first, loudly at the last, a crescendo that sent the plastic forks jumping in the air and caused half a glass of cola beverage to land in Norman's plate.

"Dad, there's something I don't understand."

"Wuzzat?"

"Where do you get the bombers?"

"Son, that's another inneresting story. I have this friend, my friend, and he gets me the bombers from someplace, call it someplace number one, and then I sell them someplace, call it someplace letter *B*, and here's the beauty of the thing. After I've sold the bombers from one to *B*, what am I left with?"

"A guilty conscience?"

"Cash, son! Heaps and heaps of the do-re-mi."

Orman smiled a thousand-dollar smile, took a gargantuan bite of pepperoni pizza, and pushed himself into the back of his chair with the air of a Roman senator who has just made an irrefutable case for sacking the Phoenicians.

Norman gnawed on a pizza crust. "But I thought only countries had bombers."

Orman shifted in his chair. "Well, sure, right. But sometimes one country might get tired of its bombers, you know, might want to spruce up the place with new bombers, so my friend buys the old bombers cheap, and we paint them up nice, put a few cool decals like skulls or shark teeth on them, stuff like that, and then sell them for loads and loads and loads of *dinero*."

Norman was beginning to wonder if this friend of his

father's might be missing a couple of digits, the particular digits for which human beings were so widely admired by the rest of the animal kingdom.

Orman pushed a napkin across his glistening chin, and his eyes rose up to the ceiling, indicating that Orman Normann was having a beautiful vision; that is, piles and piles of cash.

Norma, who of course knew this look well, nevertheless, or perhaps because of this—acting in her capacity as civilizing influence—broke into his reverie, saying, "Orman, I know how much you like to talk about money, and I don't mean to disturb you and I really don't mind a bit anymore about the bombers, since you explained all that about progress and pizza delivery and so on. But it will be summer vacation soon, and I know we haven't discussed any plans yet, but Sarah Piquant has invited us to meet her and Leonard for a few weeks in Europe, dear."

"Hot dog!" said Norman.

"Europe, eh?" said Orman, his eyes shifting down and to the left, eyeing the saltshaker.

"Yes, dear, Europe."

"I might be able to slip that into my travel plans. My special friend was mentioning something about Europe just the other day. Lotta countries there. Old countries. What I like to call little-old-lady countries. Countries that only flew their bombers on Sundays to church."

"They'd like to meet us in Vienna, dear."

"Hot dog with sauerkraut!" said Norman.

"Vienna!" said Orman. "Did you just say 'Vienna'?"

"Yes, dear."

"Vienna!" said Orman, pounding the table again. "Not only are there bunches of little-old-lady countries in Europe, but I happen to know that there's gonna be a conference of Polynesian states in Vienna, which means that quite possibly a certain Alfurnian foreign minister is gonna be there, too, heh heh. In Vienna!"

"Yes, dear."

Orman raised his glass to his lips, sipped, burped, and said, "Where is Vienna?"

"I don't know, dear."

"Son, where is Vienna?"

"I don't know, Dad. Dad, can I ask you just one more question?"

"Son, I'm your father and commander in chief and you can ask me anything, and I'll tell you or I won't. Shoot, son. Is it about bombers?"

"I'm not sure."

"Well, what is it?"

"What does this mean to you? A dozen eggs. A loaf of bread. A bottle of seltzer water. Three oranges. A can of mushroom soup?"

"Son, is this another one of your tutor's fruity ideas?"

"Not really. Does it mean anything to you?"

"Son, do I look like a pastry chef?"

"Kinda."

"Very funny, Norman. No, that grocery list means nothing to me, and I suppose it probably means nothing to any other sane person except the pastry chef what wrote it. Say, listen, maybe there's pastry chefs in Vienna. If there is, there'll be pastries. But we'll never know unless we first find out where in tarnation Vienna is. So come on, come on, come on! Let's go, let's go, let's go!"

"Where are we going, Dad?"

"To the Mega Bookstore! They'll know where Vienna is!"

* * *

Twenty minutes later, at the Mega Bookstore, Norman left his parents seated at a café table, up to their elbows in travel guides and more cola beverages, and wandered over to the humor section, discovering there, sprawled like two long cats before a fire, Anna and Emma, each with an enormous volume of collected comic strips on the floor beneath her nose.

"Hiyaaaaaa!" said Norman.

"Hi ya, yourself," said Anna, "What's up?"

"The cumulus clouds. My mom and dad are in the café reading about some place called Vienna. My dad wants to go there and see an old lady about her bombers."

"He's still selling bombers?" said Emma. "That is so last century. Nobody needs bombers anymore. It's totally uncool."

"Try telling that to my dad. What are you doing this summer?"

"We're going to camp," said Anna. "We're going to Camp Ess-Ay-Tee, the camp for intellectually superior boys and girls."

"I think I'm going to be sick," said Norman.

"Not on me, you're not, unless you want an intellectually superior kick in your intellectually inferior posterior," said Emma.

"Think they'll allow comic books at this camp?" Norman gibed, pulling out a volume and sitting down beside them.

"We've already got a plan on how to smuggle them in. We're going to cut out all the pages, then hide them in a secret compartment in our suitcases, then take them out one at a time,

113

hidden in our books. The pages will be rationed like water on a desert island."

"Brilliant," said Norman. "I bow before your intellectual superiority. That reminds me. I'm going to need some reading material for the trip." Norman began pulling out volumes of his favorite comics and became engaged in that most pleasant of tasks, perusing each volume slowly, in order to choose just exactly the right one.

let us consider watson

"Vienna!" said Balthazar Birdsong.

Norman and Leonard sat once again with Mr. B. on his terrace, sipping on the one hand a cup of coffee, on the other two hot chocolates, and contemplating the clouds. Watson, the rat, and Crick, the crow, sat in their separate cages, sipping, on either hand, water. Norman, as perhaps you have surmised, had just broached his and Leonard's summer travel plans.

"Vienna!" Mr. B. went on. "This is a bit of a how-do-you-do, is it not? Or is it more of a fine kettle of fish? Hard to say, hard to say. In fact, it is neither. It is in my estimation *etwas ganz anders*, something completely different."

Mr. B. beamed at the boys.

"Vienna, well," he said again, jumping from his chair to lean upon the terrace railing. "This simply means we shall have to compress our lessons, swallow them by the pitcher instead of sipping them by the glass. In a word, we shall guzzle our lessons." He looked at the boys, then looked out over the rooftops at the sky, and finally his gaze came to rest on his rat. He said, "Let us consider Watson, imaginatively."

Reaching into Watson's cage, he lifted him out gently and, sitting down again, placed him in his lap.

"Observe his wrinkled nose, his dirty brown tail, and here and there a lump beneath his fur. You can see that he is an old rat. A dear old friend who has shared his life with me. We humans owe much to rats. Millions daily give of their comfort and even their lives to assist us to new knowledge, new medicines, new

115

psychological insights. Think of the miles and miles of mazes they have run! To be sure, millions more eat our grain and rummage in our garbage, now and then bringing with them a plague or two. Still, on the whole, the rat has been a great friend to the human. And this rat has been a great friend to me. But now his life is coming to an end. He and I know this, but see, observe. Is his eye downcast? Never. It sparkles still." Mr. B. stroked Watson's nose.

"They're red like blood," said Leonard.

"They lack melanin merely. But they do not lack sparkle. Nor do the whiskers of his nose lack vim. I think they are especially full of vim. Perhaps they are vimful. Is there such a word as 'vimful,' Norman?"

"I haven't gotten to the *V*s yet."

"Ah, of course," said Mr. B., scratching Watson under the chin.

Norman held out a piece of peanut-butter cookie to the rat, who took it in his mouth and then, transferring it to his paws, nibbled it thoughtfully.

"Thank you, Norman," said Mr. B. "I mention Watson as an appropriate object for our consideration, for perhaps, if we observe him and his life properly—how his eyes sparkle!—perhaps we'll find something there. Perhaps the ideas we seek about life are all there within Watson."

"He's got a piece of cookie on his chin," said Leonard.

"Precisely!" said Mr. B. "Forget all the philosophers, starting with dear old Plato, who say objects are on one side of a great divide, ideas are on the other, and don't let objects sully our pure ideas. Life is good, or life is misery, life is a blessing or life is a curse. No! Ideas belong to objects like souls belong to bodies. Everything we need to know about the universe is right there in the morsel of peanut-butter cookie on this rat's chin!"

"He ate it," said Leonard.

"Exactly!" said Mr. B. "Which reminds me, there are a few things you need to know about Vienna, if in fact you are really going to Vienna and not merely conspiring in some kind of boyish ruse to slip the cords of your tutorial lessons, hmm?"

"No, we're definitely going," said Norman. "We've bought guidebooks. We even know what kind of money they use."

"*Wunderbar,*" said Mr. B. "Now pay attention, this is terribly important. When you are seated at your café table in the old city, or perhaps in one of the gardens of the palace, and the waiter asks you what you will have, you shall respond this way: *Einen grossen Braunen, bitte.*"

"Eeeeyaaaa, what's that?" said Leonard.

"Only the best coffee in the non-Mediterranean world," said Mr. B. smugly.

"But we don't drink coffee!"

"Heaven's sake, I keep forgetting. Difficult, difficult, you boys will insist on not drinking coffee. Well. Then in that case you are to order a hot chocolate with the following phrase: *Mit Schlag.*"

"Midd shlawg?" said Norman.

"*Mit Schlag,*" said Mr. B.

"Midt shlahgk?" said Leonard.

"*Mit Schlag,*" said Mr. B.

"*Mit Schlag,*" said both boys.

"Very good," said Mr. B. "It means 'with whipped cream.'"

his father's karma

Norman sat tucked into seat 34K on a ViennAir jumbo jet, his tray table open, his dinner upon it. Beside him, in seats 34H and J, sat his parents. Leonard and his mother, having departed a week before, would meet them in Vienna when they arrived.

Carefully, Norman folded back the hot tinfoil on the small casserole dish to discover something he had never imagined before: a mini–Wiener schnitzel.

Norman forked a fraction of a firlot and pulled out the entertainment controller from the armrest and pushed Power On.

"Norman," said his mother, "you've got to get some sleep. You'll feel miserable tomorrow otherwise, and tomorrow, according to your father, is going to be arriving sooner than you think."

"Okay, Mom," said Norman, now scrolling down the menu displayed. "Let's see. Arcade games."

"What's that, dear?"

"I wonder if I could get another ginger ale."

Twenty minutes later, a couple of top scores under his belt (which was fastened), his mother snoring softly beside him, Norman opened his Ingmeister's Compact International Dictionary, as he had dutifully promised Mr. B. to do, and read.

jaunt *n* : a quick trip
jaunty *adj* : stylish

118

jaw *n* : the upper and lower bones in the head of an animal or human being that form the mouth

jaywalk *vb* : to cross the street in a careless or prohibited manner

Jazyges *n* : a group of people whose ancestors came from the Black Sea

jazz *n* : American classical music, now practiced worldwide, originating in sacred and secular songs, the blues, ragtime, and marching-band music, often syncopated, always swinging, with contrapuntal or solo playing, usually featuring more or less improvisation, originally considered dance music, now principally heard in concert halls and smaller music venues

jazzbow *n* : a ready-made bow tie

jazzily *adv* : with real style

jazzist *n* : a lover of jazz

jazzbow

Norman skipped forward into the *K*s.

karma *n* : the force generated by a person's acts, which creates that person's destiny

katipo *n* : a small deadly spider of New Zealand

Katong Luang *n* : a nomadic small people of the mountains of Southeast Asia

katsup *n var. of* catsup *or* ketchup : a sauce, usually tomato, of many varieties, beloved of children and presidents

katuka *n* : Russell's viper, a snake

katydid *n* : a long-horned grasshopper

katzenjammer *n* : a hangover;
that is, the ill feeling caused
by drinking too much alcohol

katzenjammer

Norman closed the dictionary and looked at his parents; his mother slept with her chin on her chest, his father snored contented snores, still with a piece of mini–Wiener schnitzel clinging to his stubbly chin. Norman observed the Wiener schnitzel. His father heaved and grunted, but the Wiener schnitzel remained stuck. Would his father's eyes be as sparkly as Watson's when he reached Watson's age in human years? Would he still be full of vim? Or would his father's eyes slowly turn cloudy, permanently misted over by his constant dreaming of piles of cash, red-rimmed and watery like the eyes of a pig that has spent too much time rooting in slop?

Norman shivered. On the one hand, he wanted to learn all about his father, next to his mother the most important person in his life. On the other hand, he was not so sure he liked what he was learning. He couldn't shake the feeling that his own father's karma could use a sharp kick in the shins.

Norman, reaching up, switched off the light. He soon fell into a fitful sleep, unsettled by dreams of epollicate pastry chefs trying in vain to squeeze red whipped cream from golden tubes.

vienna katzenjammer

Early in the afternoon of the day after their arrival in Vienna, Norman and his mother strolled along one of the city's wide boulevards. The disorientation of the day before had somewhat abated. Indeed, Norman's wise mother had been correct in saying that Norman would feel miserable if he did not sleep on the airplane; on their arrival, Norman had felt as miserable as he'd ever felt, but not so miserable that he was unable to ask his father, "Dad, is this what a katzenjammer feels like?" To which his father, also feeling a bit shy of top notch, and no doubt anxious as to the fruits of his imminent labors with diverse customers, his little old ladies, had replied, rather peevishly, "Go practice your native lingo on some other Indian," which had not been very nice of him, not to Norman, not to the natives of Vienna, and not to the Indians either. But if Norman can overlook these failings in his father, as he can, then so, after all, should we.

The boulevard was a noble one, proceeding along the ground that had once carried a mighty wall, a moat, and a green space created during a time when the town citizenry were never sure if the approaching caravan was arriving to sell carpets or to carry off all the above-average children. Happily, the Viennese and we, too, believe those times are gone, and so the wall has been taken down, the moat filled up, and the green space planted with leafy trees, grand buildings, and the street itself.

Along the sidewalks, one café after another beckoned to the Normann pair, who nevertheless walked on, as they were to meet Leonard and Sarah Piquant, who were arriving that day

from Prague. With a great "Eeeee-yaaaah!" Norman announced that he had spotted them seated beneath one of the red-and-white table umbrellas at the Café Schmutzie.

"Norman!" said his mother. "Please, dear! Remember, we're in Austria."

"All right, then," said Norman. "Eeeeeyääääh!"

"Nörman! Oh dear, now you've got me doing it."

In the meantime, Leonard leaped up from his chair and then over the railing corralling the tables.

"Waaayargg!" he said, karate-chopping and hugging Norman simultaneously. "Look! I've already ordered. And the hot chocolate is fantastic!"

Norman looked. On the table stood a tall, pedestaled glass mug, still one-quarter full; around the mug, the splashes and spills of foam and chocolate told the story of unbridled delight; off to the side stood a simple metal tray holding a small glass of water, a plate of cylindrical wafer cookies, and a white napkin.

"*Mit Schlag?*" asked Norman.

"*Mit* very much *Schlag*," said Leonard. "Mom, call the waiter."

* * *

When Norman had drunk his hot chocolate, and his mother her small coffee, the four happy tourists caught a taxi to the Military History Museum (the Piquants having left their luggage for the time being at the train station), where they wandered the wide halls. This had been Leonard's choice. He had earned it by three days of dutiful visits, at his mother's request, to all the architectural wonders of Prague.

"This is more like it," he said, as he and Norman marched alongside great, raised tables, themselves the size of rooms. These carried proudly, though a little dustily, the meticulously detailed, handmade landscapes of all the battlefields of the last millennium that had been ennobled by spilled Austrian blood. Tiny companies and battalions and whole armies, re-created in tin and clay, marched and warred forever in silence.

"This is a bit overwhelming," said Mrs. Piquant.

"All of those mothers' sons," said Norma forlornly.

"Awesome!" said Leonard.

"I wish I could be in there," said Norman, peering at a miniature battlefield of some unlucky spot in France.

"I wish I could be sitting on that horse right there," said Leonard.

"Eeeeeeyääääää!" said Norman, holding his imaginary sword aloft.

"Norman and Leonard," called Mrs. Piquant quietly, "come look at these. They're marvelous."

Mrs. Piquant stood at the entrance to a long, wide hall lined on each side with glass vitrines enclosing the uniforms of all the ranks of Austrian soldiers, and even those of some of their foes.

"Leonard, look at these epaulets," she said, "and that helmet! Oh, and the gloves and sash. The workmanship is exquisite. Think of sending that kind of stitching into a war zone."

"Mom, there were people inside those things getting blown up. I think that's a little more important than the stitching," said Leonard.

"I know, dear, I know. That, I can't bear to think about. But I can still be upset at the thought of the waste of such fine human effort."

"Leonard! Mom! Mrs. Piquant!" shouted Norman from farther along the hall.

"Shh!" said his mother.

"You won't believe this!" whispered Norman as loud as he could.

"What is it?" said Leonard. "Exquisite stitching?"

"Much better. The uniform of a member of the Alfurnian Imperial Guard! And he's wearing the same hat as the old man in Dad's study!"

And so it was. All four stopped at the vitrine. Within stood an impressive figure in tall black boots with spurs; yellow breeches with a maroon stripe at the sides; a three-quarter-length, double-breasted, sky-blue coat with tremendous golden trimming and pink epaulets around a stiff, standing collar over a white ruffled shirt. A red sash, falling across the chest from shoulder to waist, carried the thin sword and scabbard. But the most stunning element of this martial ensemble, the item that topped it all, was the fur-covered, conical, or, if you prefer, infundibular, helmet with a red chin strap.

After drinking in this polychrome spectacle for several moments, Leonard said, "I guess they figured if they wore those hats, at least they'd have a pretty good chance of making their enemies die laughing."

* * *

"Goodn Morrgn!" said Orman Normann, sitting down to breakfast with his family at the hotel the next day. The Piquants, who had retrieved their luggage and checked into the hotel the evening before, would be joining them.

"It's *guten Morgen*, Dad," said Norman.

"Goodn Morrgn. That's what I said."

"*Guten Morgen*, Dad."

"Whatever. Have it your way. Irregardless."

He continued: "I feel good. I feel *gut*. Ha-ha. Pass me that coffee, son. Norma, I think I'm sitting on some fat and juicy bomber contracts."

"That's gross, Dad."

"Fat and juicy and oh so nutritious for our bank accounts. Ha-ha!"

"Terrific, Dad."

"Listen to this. I've been talking to my friend, who has been talking to some little old ladies, if you get my meaning, and I have been talking to some other little old ladies, and charming the pants off them—make that, charming the knickers off them—and it's been sell, sell, sell! Didn't I tell you the world loves bombers? I can't keep them on the shelves. Now, where's my bacon and eggs?"

"Dear, remember, they don't serve that here. Have a nice roll with salami, dear."

"For breakfast? Weird. All right, pass them over. Say, son. Howzabout a little wager? I'll bet you one Wiener schnitzel with mushrooms that I can get bomber contracts from as many different countries as the number of rolls I eat this morning."

"You're on, Dad."

"Dear, pass me six. Darn it, dear. I feel *gut*! So long's I keep an eye on the Alfurnians. Gotta make sure they don't try any funny business. Ha!"

So the morning proceeded, with many a hard roll and a sudden "Ha!" from Orman Normann, followed by a "Dear, not so loud, dear" from his wife.

When six hard rolls had been eaten, Mr. Normann rushed out to the street to find a taxi, with Norman following closely behind him.

"Why don't you take me along, Dad?"

"Son, maybe next time. Maybe on 'Bomb your kid to work day.' No, really, I couldn't take you along. 'Stoo grown-up. Look, if I can clear it with my buddy, when we get back to New York, I'll take you around. Oof Widderrrrsayin!"

"*Auf Wiedersehen*, Dad. It's pronounced *auf Wiedersehen*."

"Right, Norm," he said, opening the taxi door. "Nineteen Bombenhandler Strasse, and step on it. Bye, Norm!"

Norman watched the taxi merge into the quick-moving traffic, wishing he'd had some sort of homing device, like they have in the movies, that he could have attached to the trunk of the car.

He shrugged, took a look at the clouds—cumulostratus—and passed again through the revolving door to the breakfast room. Maybe Leonard was up.

fun house

As a matter of fact, Norman hadn't had any intention of accompanying his father, as he and Leonard had big plans for the day. His father's karma would have to wait. The boys had extracted agreements from their mothers to be taken to the Prater.

The Prater, for those of you who have not yet been there, is an old Viennese institution encompassing a grand park with ball fields, riding stables, an enormous Ferris wheel, and beautiful tree-lined allées, but above all, from the twelve-year-old perspective, an amusement park. It was a bit tattered and tawdry, but beloved by Viennese children and foreign children alike. Norman and Leonard had seen the great Ferris wheel rising above distant buildings, a huge thing carrying streetcars where its smaller cousins carried chairs for two, and had inquired about it at the desk. "Oh, that is the Riesenrad, the Giant Wheel in the Prater," the friendly desk clerk had said. "You must take your children there to the amusement park, Frau Normann." And that had been the beginning of the successful negotiations.

Mrs. Piquant insisted that they ride the Riesenrad first, which was exciting but slow, painfully slow, since Norman and Leonard could see all the rides they wanted to try but could not reach because they were swinging slowly back and forth hundreds of feet in the air. At last they burst out of the car doors and ran toward the colored bulbs of the target booths and the great papier-mâché monster heads of the haunted house.

Norman said, "Let's go on the bumper cars, then the haunted house, then the Alpine roller coaster, then the bungee jump, then the trampoline, then the spinning thing where the floor drops out, and then the bumper cars again, then the duck ring toss and then the fun house."

"No, no," said Leonard. "Let's go on the Alpine roller coaster, then the spinning thing where the floor drops out, then the bucket swings, then the haunted house, then the bumper cars, then the trampoline, then the go-carts, and then the fun house."

"*Nein, nein, nein,*" said Norman, "let's go on the—"

At this point, Norma Normann and Mrs. Piquant had caught them up, and Mrs. Piquant intervened. "I'll decide the order," she said.

"Mom!"

Nevertheless, this time there was no negotiation, Mrs. Piquant assuming emergency dictatorial powers.

In the end, with the summer sun slanting through the lindens of the park, their agenda included the following: the bumper cars, which, according to Leonard, were "pretty good, but a red-haired girl kept smashing into me from the side"; the bungee-cord trampoline, which Norman called "freaky, a bounce with turbochargers"; the haunted house, dismissed by Leonard as "hilariously lame-o, there were real cobwebs on the fake cobwebs!"; the go-carts, which intimidated Norman a bit, "fun, but I was a little afraid of the big kids"; the rug slide, which received a glowing response from Leonard, "awesome, proving the old proverb, sometimes simplest is best"; the Alpine roller coaster, which, on the other hand, Norman liked better, saying it was "jazzy—proving the old proverb that sometimes complicated, highly technical, shiny, and fast is better"; and finally the spinning thing where the floor drops out, which both Leonard and Norman found "totally awesome, epoch-making."

Seated at a café, Leonard took a last long gulp of his sparkling Almdudler, wiped his mouth with the back of his hand, and said, "Ah, now for the fun house."

"All right, last ride, boys," said Mrs. Piquant.

"Nööööö!" shouted the two critics, running from the table with their final tickets clutched in their hands.

The fun house was a grand fun house, four stories tall, festooned, oddly enough, with images and statues of American football players, the whole edifice under a tiara of naked lightbulbs spelling out these words: CHICAGO YANKEE FUN.

"Our kinda place," said Leonard, plunging through the turnstile.

Immediately he was buffeted by giant boxing gloves, his shouts of pain and delight soon joined by Norman's own.

"Ow! Ow! Ow! Ow!"

Then up the moving ladder (like a steep escalator split in two) they struggled, nearly falling back on each other, laughing and shouting over the thumping Yankee disco music.

"Eeeeyaaaa!" shouted Leonard.

"What?" shouted Norman.

"I said, Eeeeeyaaaa!" shouted Leonard.

"Oh!" shouted Norman.

Off they ran, down black-lighted hallways, over heaving floors, down hidden corkscrew slides, across rope ladders, dodging more giant boxing gloves and random blasts of compressed air. Other fun-house-goers bumped or crawled past them, in the light and in the dark, sometimes shouting to them phrases that were, to Leonard's and Norman's ears, only gibble-gabble, and nothing but gibble-gabble.

They reached the hall of mirrors, which occupied all of the top floor. At first the mirrors did no more than distort their images, making them hoot at each other. However, as they proceeded deeper into the labyrinth of mirrored glass, the mirrors seemed to close in on the boys, confusing them, moving them around, confounding them as they reached for each other but discovered that where Norman had turned left, Leonard had turned right.

"Leonard!" Norman shouted.

"I'm over here. Where are you?"

"I'm over here!" But this did no good for either of them, as it was impossible to tell where "here" was. All they could do was bump along farther into the ever-bifurcated and many-angled crystal heart of the dizzying hall.

Then the lights went out, all but a string of tiny bulbs hanging from the ceiling, which created a ghostly light reflected in all the mirrors, giving anyone groping through the dark the terrible feeling of having suddenly been pitched into deep space.

Norman got down on his hands and knees and began to crawl, feeling a twinge of desperation for fresh air and sunshine, guessing that Leonard was feeling the same. He crawled forward and bumped his head. He turned to the right, crawled forward, and bumped his head. He turned to the left, crawled forward, and bumped his head, but this wall budged a little, so he pushed through a kind of dark curtain into a dimly lit room, also mirrored.

Norman scampered on all fours like a puppy, blinking in the light, and bumped his head again, but not against glass or a curtain this time; he bumped his head against a pair of tall black boots. He tilted his head slowly back and let his eyes travel up. Above the black boots, Norman saw in the weak light a pair of yellow breeches with a maroon stripe, a sky-blue coat with golden trimming, pink epaulets, a stiff collar over a ruffled white shirt, and a red sash leading to a scabbard and sword. But this time past the stiff collar and out of the ruffled white shirt rose a pinkish face with beetle eyes, tremendous waxed mustaches, and terrible black eyebrows, beneath the now horrifying brown, furred, and infundibular helmet with a red chin strap.

"*Äääääääääääääääääääää!*" screamed Norman.

go fly a dragon

"Are you sure it really was an Alfurnian Imperial Guard?" said Leonard, sipping a lime soda.

"Am I sure it really was an Alfurnian Imperial Guard! Who else wears a two-foot-tall furry hat? And boots? And mustaches?" said Norman, searching for the letter *B* on the keyboard in front of him.

The boys sat at a computer terminal at the Zum Web Internet Café on the morning after their trip to the Prater. Norman was in the middle of writing a long and, he hoped, compelling narrative for Balthazar Birdsong, all about his close encounter in a fun house.

* * *

On the morning after the day after their trip to the Prater, they sat at the same café, at another computer terminal, and eagerly checked for a response from Mr. B.

Norman scrolled down through his inbox; Leonard was draped over his shoulder like a starfish on a seacoast rock.

Norman mumbled, "Buy Viagra cheaper, why would I want Viagra? Collect millions, nope. Enter our contest, forget it. Don't break the chain, I'm breaking it. Here it is, from Balthazar Birdsong, balthazarb@meistertalk.net, re: fun house no fun."

"Open it, open it!" said Leonard.

"I'm openiting it!"

Balthazar Birdsong's e-mail popped up:

```
Norman (and Leonard too, as I imagine you are
```

draped like a starfish over Norman's shoulder)—

"Weird," said Leonard.

"That guy has got one spooky imagination," said Norman. The letter continued.

> I commend you on the excellent description of the Alfurnian Imperial Guard's attire; it was comprehensive and well detailed; you are showing gratifying improvement in your observational skills. Bravo!

"He commends me on my improved observational skills," said Norman.

> Now add a dash of imagination, and carry on, carry on.

"'Carry on, carry on'? That's it?" said Leonard.

"There's more," said Norman.

> While you are carrying on, do not neglect your other lessons; it is imperative that you fly kites frequently.

At this point in his e-mail, Balthazar Birdsong wrote a rather lengthy and highly detailed description of how to procure kites in a German-speaking country. For instance, what to ask for at the store (*ein Drachen*, a dragon), where to buy them, and, once procured, what to do with them in Vienna: specifically, for instance, where to fly them (Schönbrunn Palace Gardens), how to get there, and many other things, including maps and drawings, etc., etc. We can skip these; it is enough that Norman and Leonard read them (and printed them out). However, we will take a look at Balthazar's P.S.

```
As ever,
BB
P.S.: Before you go fly kites, do cross the
square to the Stephansdom, Vienna's great
cathedral
```

Norman looked at Leonard and raised a bewildered eyebrow. "How does he even know where we are?"

```
and pay your euro to climb the north tower.
This is very important, for it is here that you
will see the bench built into the wall that made
more comfortable the work of the watchman as he
looked out for the advancing Turkish army, which
was famously turned back by the brave Viennese,
but not before an invader of a different sort
snuck past the city walls in the pockets of a
Viennese spy: what I mean is, coffee! After the
Turks had left in a hurry, the spy, Franz Georg
Kolschitzky, was rewarded for his bravery:
he could take what he liked and he chose the
coffee, soon opening Vienna's first coffeehouse.
In other words, had Mohammed IV not advised
Suleiman the Turk to capture Vienna, the Western
world would be a sleepier place.

Now go fly a kite!
```

"I'm being chased by a six-foot, sword-toting Alfurnian in a two-foot furry hat, and all he can talk about is kites and coffee!" said Norman.

"We're not sure you're being chased, are we? You said he was just standing there."

"I'm sure he's after me. I'm sure of it."

"But why, why would anyone in a two-foot furry hat want to chase you?"

"I know, it sounds weird, and it *is* weird, but then again, my dad is weird, and his bomber-selling is weird, and all that weirdness is starting to slosh over like a big weird bathtub filled too full of weirdness."

"You're starting to sound weird."

"I bet it's because I snuck into Dad's study, which was your idea, I might add."

"Yeah, but you didn't have to listen to me."

"And then I took that note, the grocery list. That must be it! He's after my grocery list."

"Why?"

"I have no idea. Maybe he saw me on the morning when I followed my dad out to the taxi. Come to think of it, I remember a big black car there with tinted windows."

"This city is full of big black cars with tinted windows. Listen, we've trusted Mr. B. this far, let's go meet our moms and climb the tower."

* * *

In the meantime, Norma and Mrs. Piquant strolled in the nearby cathedral mentioned by Mr. B., happy in their own artistic pursuits, but not happy for terribly long. With a jolt, they became keenly aware of elderly Viennese ladies and gentlemen shushing and frowning upon their own beloved

135

boys, who were running up the Gothic nave toward them.

"Mom," said Norman and Leonard together.

"Shh!" said Norma and Mrs. Piquant together. "What is it?"

"We want to look at the advancing Turkish hordes!" said Leonard.

"Oh dear," said Norma.

Two hundred and fifty-eight spiraling stairsteps later, Norma collapsed onto the very bench they were looking for, her back against the curving wall.

"Mom, you've become a part of history," said Norman.

"You'll go down in posterior!" said Leonard.

"Leonard!" said Mrs. Piquant.

As they gazed over the old city and its younger suburbs, Norman related all that they had learned from Balthazar's letter.

"Look!" shouted Leonard from the other side of the tower. "I think I see the summer palace." Indeed, Leonard was correct. He pointed to a large swath of green in the midst of dull apartment blocks, where among the trees rose a mighty yellow palace at the foot of a treeless hilltop crowned by a long, white-colonnaded monument.

Mrs. Piquant said, "Well, it's summer, and you two are our princes. Let's go fly a kite."

crazy garden

Schönbrunn Palace sits, as we have seen, at a distance from the center of the city. At the time it was built, it was far out in the countryside, but now it has been  swallowed up by the city, like a dandelion head in a mud pie.

Leonard shouted, "Yahoo!"

Two new kites—Norman's emblazoned with a green dragon, Leonard's with a mighty eagle—rode the breeze high above a wide lawn leading down to the palace.

"Yodelayee-hooooo!" sang Norman.

"Norman, do you think it's wise to yodel?" said his mother.

"Mom, if I can't yodel in Austria, where can I yodel?"

"Not in the U.S. of A.," said Leonard, tugging at his kite. "You can get beat up for that kind of behavior."

"You can get beat up for humming!" said Norman. "Yodelayee, yodelayee, yodelayee."

"Let's send Alfred the G. up," said Leonard.

"*Ja, mein Kapitän,*" said Norman.

Alfred the Great hung just below Norman's kite, looking down behind the enemy lines. Some say the Chinese were the first to send a soldier up on a kite on a reconnaissance mission; Alfred the Great did not know about that, he might not even have known about the Chinese.

"Mrs. Piquant," said Norman, "what is that cornery, spirally, puzzly-looking part of the garden down there?"

"I really don't know, Norman, but I'll check the map for you," she said. She looked down at the map. She looked up at the landscape. She looked down at the map. "It says *Irrgarten*. Whatever that might be."

She took out her well-thumbed German-English travel dictionary. A minute later she said, "*Irrgarten* literally means 'crazy garden.' It's a maze."

"A maze!" said Norman. "Let's go!"

"Mom," said Leonard, "it has just become abundantly clear that my good friend Norman and I must visit the *Irrgarten*."

"But what about the kites?" said Mrs. Piquant.

"Exactly," said Leonard, "you two hold the kites and we'll check out the maze."

"But, dears, what if you get lost?" said Mrs. Normann.

"You're supposed to get lost in a maze. But do not fear, we won't. So long as you keep the kites up, we'll be able to find our way back. It's like Hansel and Gretel or something."

"Correct me if I'm wrong, my young literary friend," said Mrs. Piquant, "but I believe Hansel and Gretel almost got themselves eaten by a witch."

"Mom."

"Oh, all right, if it's okay with Norma, you can go. But stay away from any Grimm characters."

"Not too long, dears!" Norma added.

"Eeeeeeyodelayeehööööööö!"

Skipping and running and yodeling down the sloping, graveled paths, they skirted the imperial woods. Norman said, "Leonard, guess what?"

"Chicken butt!" said Leonard.

"Besides that. I imagine that if some member of the Alfurnian Imperial Guard is after me or us, and if he's followed us to Schönbrunn, he'll know that sooner or later we'll be bound to go to the maze. That's where he'll be waiting for us."

"So that's where you want us to go? To be caught by the Alfurnians? That's crazy! That's *irr*!"

"I know. But I have to see if it's true. I have to check this out. Look, we'll stay together this time, we'll be on our guard, our super-guard. Maybe we'll chase *them*. Besides, an hour ago you thought I was weird to even think somebody was after us. And maybe you're right."

"Guess what," said Leonard.

"What?" said Norman.

"Chicken butt! Guess what else."

"What else?"

"Guess what 'chicken butt' is in German."

"What?"

"Hooner Po. I figured it out last night using my mom's dictionary."

"Hooner Po?"

"Hooner Po."

"Let's go!"

"Hooner Po!"

Passing the well-tended woods on their left, Norman and Leonard looked over a wide, graveled square with a fountain at its center, beyond which stood the entrance to the maze. In an instant, Norman was pointing frantically.

"Look!" said Norman.

"What? What? What? Wha . . . Oh my *Gott*! You were right! It's an Alfurnian Guard, and there's two of them!"

Standing at the entrance gate, rummaging in their deep coat pockets for something, perhaps change, stood two Alfurnian Imperial Guards, unmistakable in their boots and hats. Having found their money and paid the admission, the two tipped their head wear and entered the maze.

"That's it," said Leonard, "I now officially believe you. No need to go in. We know they're here. Okay, fine. Time to go back to the hotel, lock the doors, and order room service. For the rest of the vacation."

Norman looked over at the entrance, uncertainly. A man in a cloth cap leaned casually against a lamppost a few steps to the left of the ticket booth, his hands in his pockets, not rummaging. Norman watched as the man raised his head and appeared to nod at someone. A moment later, huffing and sweating, Orman Normann ran into view.

"Dad!" said Norman, "It's my dad! What's he doing here? And who is that guy?"

"I don't know and I don't know, but I do care, so let's get out of here," said Leonard.

"No, now we've got to go in!"

"Go in?"

"Go in."

"Oh, all right."

"Hooner Po, remember?"

"Yeah, yeah, let's go."

Leonard and Norman paid their one euro apiece and passed through the gate. Immediately, they plunged into green hedges about six feet high, perfectly smooth and flat, hard edged, with neat, squared corners; they looked rock hewn.

Norman glanced back over his shoulder nervously and was relieved to see the two kites still flying in the firmament far off behind them. Norman whispered over his shoulder, "Stay close!"

They walked ahead, with the hedge walls rising on either

side of them. They turned a corner. They walked ahead along the new alley. They ran a little. They turned at the second of three corners. They walked straight, then right. Right. Left. Straight. Right. Straight. Right. Right. Right. Straight.

And then they saw them: two pointed, furry hats rising over the hedge on their left.

Norman slapped his free hand over Leonard's mouth; Leonard slapped his free hand over Norman's mouth.

As they stood staring at the now stationary hats, a familiar voice floated over the hedge on their right, the opposite side, saying, "Right-o-rooni, N.T. Now what's this new protocol you think is so important?"

"Lissen, me ladd, try an' git tis intae yer nut, ye wee nitwit," said a voice that was unfamiliar and barely understandable. "We are bein' obsairved by cairtain atoorities an' possibly we are bein' follooed, an' it behooves us tae tek cairtain precautions."

"I think he called your dad a nitwit!"

"Shshshsh!" Norman put his ear to the hedge, shutting his eyes.

"Ye got me message, right? Me coded message?" said the unfamiliar voice.

"Was that a coded message? I thought it was just gobbledy-gook. Coded message. Right."

"Ye mean ye didnae decode it yit?"

"I told you I thought it was gobbledygook. Nonsense."

"Noo, why would Ah send ye nunsinse?"

"I thought you were just making conversation."

"Blimey, Ah tek it back. Ye dinnae be smart enoof tae be a nitwit. Ye be just a nit."

"He just insulted your dad!" whispered Leonard.

"Ix-nay!" Norman pressed his ear farther into the hedge. If only he could listen long enough, he thought, the second code would be revealed.

"Noo, lissen. Here be the message, decoded. Ah'll recite it slooly, like, an' clearly, like the wee bit o' poetry it surely is: A doozen eggs. A lowf o' brid. A boottle o' siltzer water. Tree oranges. A can o' mooshroom soop."

"Say, I've heard that somewhere before. But I still don't get it."

"Lissen, nit. Here's hoo it works. Ah've got two catalogues here, see? Two shiny L. L. Bomb catalogues. Noo, watch. Ah've marked the boot o' tem wit coot-oot pictures oov a doozen eggs, a lowf o' brid, a boottle o' siltzer water, ye ken?"

"Ah, no."

"Look. If ye say 'Two doozen eggs,' ten Ah open the L. L. Bomb catalogue an' Ah find where Ah've glued the picture oov a doozen eggs, see? Let's see wot it might be." The boys could hear the sound of pages flipping. "Here 'tis! 'Tis a Flieswitzer-Hassenfus 78. Ye ken? Noo, Ah ken ye need two Flieswitzer-Hassenfus 78s fer summon, Ah dinnae ken, mibbee the Katong Luangans."

"Not two dozen?"

"Nae, dummy. A doozen means just one."

"I thought I was a nit."

"Right, nit, if ye prefair it. The code is one doozen eggs means one Flieswitzer-Hassenfus 78."

"Why didn't you make it *one* egg means *one* Flieswitzer-Hassenfus 78? That would have been so much easier."

"Because tat would've ruined the code. Giddit?"

"Now, when you say one dozen . . ."

Norman did not hear the end of the sentence. Leonard, his lips pale and moving soundlessly, looking like a goldfish with something on its mind, was tugging at Norman's sleeve.

Norman glanced over his left shoulder and saw that the two furry hats had begun to move, gliding like hairy teepees, or fuzzy shark fins, above the hedge. The hats moved serenely away, but then turned, and one long boot began to show itself around the corner at the end of the hedgerow.

This was all Leonard and Norman needed. With the voice of Orman in their ears (saying, "Now, let me get this straight, one dozen eggs doesn't mean one dozen Flieswitzer-Hassenfus 78s, it means . . ."), they ran as quickly and quietly in the opposite direction of the Alfurnian boot as possible, this way, that way, right, right, left, straight, left again, until they came upon the tail end of a large group of English tourists, under cover of which they at last emerged from the *Irrgarten.*

Looking skyward, Norman saw that their two kites still flew gaily at the top of the hill.

* * *

At the Café Schmutzie, later that afternoon, Norman pushed his empty glass away and said, "Leonard, pass me a slice of *Kuchen* and the dictionary, I need strength." He read:

Lilliputian *n* : a resident of Lilliput, a country created
  by the British writer Jonathan Swift, visited by
  Gulliver, inhabited by tiny, tiny people

Lilliputian *adj* : very small

Lillooet *n* : a Salishan people of British Columbia

lilly-low *n* : a bright flame

lilt *vb* : to sing in a soft but lively way

lily *n* : one of many herbs of the *Lilium* genus
  from the northern hemisphere, generally
  with showy flowers with no aroma

lily green *n* : middle green

lily iron *n* : a harpoon with a detachable iron head

lily-livered *adj* : cowardly

Leonard draped himself like an especially-grateful-to-be-alive starfish over the back of Norman's chair.

"Hmm," he said. "Lily-livered. I could live with that."

since the age of
the neanderthals

"Now we know," said Norman.

He sat with Leonard at their regular table in the hotel restaurant, waiting for their three parents to come down.

"What do we know?" said Leonard, building a small pile of salt on the tablecloth.

"That my dad," said Norman, pounding the table and scattering the salt, "is obviously doing things that are, number one, over his pumpkin-shaped head; number two, creepy; and number three, probably against the law. My dad's going to wind up permanently a nitwit—"

"Or just a nit—"

"Right, or just a nit. Or permanently creepy or permanently in jail in some permanent dungeon. They may have torn down the city walls, but I bet they still have their old dungeons." Norman reached for the saltshaker, clenched it briefly in his fist, and put it down. "I've got to convince my dad to quit the bomber business and go into selling lawn-care products or something."

"N.G. No good," said Leonard, balancing two forks and a spoon together on the lip of his water glass.

"Why N.G.?"

"Has there ever been a single time in all of human history when a parent, especially a father, took advice from a son? About his business? His bomber business? When the son was only twelve years old? Since the age of the Neanderthals?"

"Maybe some Neanderthal dads listened to their Neanderthal sons, but we just don't know about it because they hadn't invented writing yet."

"Possibly. And look where it got them. *Nein*. No. *Nein*. If you're going to cure your dad, you're going to have to do it without him knowing anything about it."

"And how's that?"

"With psychology. Look, we're in Vienna, which, according to my mother, is the home of Sigmund Freud."

"Who's he?"

"Who's he? Only the greatest psychiatrist who ever lived. You know, the doctor who taught everybody about their inner urgings."

"So? I have no inner urgings," said Norman, smoothing a napkin.

"Maybe not, but your dad sure does. His inner urgings are telling him to sell bombers. We've got to get in there and tinker with his inner urgings directly. How? Psychiatry!" Leonard leaned across the dark table. "Here's my plan. You tell your dad that as a special treat he will have a surprise visitor in his room tomorrow at three o'clock. Then I arrive, dressed cunningly in a three-piece suit, glue-on beard, glasses, holding a big, realistic-looking fake cigar and a notebook. My name will be Dr. Otto Kopfschmerz, or something, and—"

"But you're too short to be a doctor. You're not even five feet tall!"

"So? Plenty of psychiatrists have been short. Why do you think they call them 'shrinks'?"

Leonard was unable to finish his argument because the unmistakable sound of a large American bomber salesman who has just smelled his dinner alerted the boys to the arrival of Norman's father at the other side of the room.

"Quick," said Norman, "pass me the dictionary! Pretend we've been studying."

Norman began to read aloud from the *M*s.

mayflower *n* : the trailing arbutus
mayfly *n* : a very short-lived insect with delicate wings
mayhap *adv* : an old form of *perhaps*
mayhem *n* : uncalled-for damage
mayonnaise *n* : a dressing made with
    egg yolks, vegetable oil, vinegar
    or lemon juice, and seasonings
mazard *n* : head
mazy *adj* : like a maze
me *pron* : the objective case of *I*

mazard

Orman Normann arrived and proclaimed, "Hooee, I'm glad to see you two so dedicated to your studies, but, darn it, Norman, I owe you a Wiener schnitzel."

"With mushrooms," said Norman, as Günter, their regular waiter, passed around the *Speisekarten*, or menus, with a friendly flourish.

"*Ein Bier, mein Herr?*" said Günter, who seemed to like Herr Normann.

"Yawull, ya, ya!" said Orman. "And two Almdudlers for the boys." The waiter smiled and retreated. "Darn it, I like it here."

"Dad, I think I'd like my prize to come without mushrooms," said Norman.

"Of course, my boy, of course. Five bomber contracts ain't bad. Six would have been better, but five ain't bad. So now as soon as I work out a teensy-weensy little miscommunicado with my old business partner-o-rooni, we'll be swimming in lettuce. That's cool-talk for money. I guess they'd say something like *salat*, here. Leastways, Goonder probably would." Taking a small notebook from his breast pocket, he went on: "Let's see, I sold bombers to the Moluscans, the Celebians, the Solomonians, the Jakartians, and the Blinesians, and almost, very nearly, to the Katong Luangans. At the last minute they backed out of the deal. Ah, thank you, Goonder."

Günter handed around two Almdudlers for Norman and Leonard and one tall beer for Orman.

"Why did they back out of the deal, Mr. Normann?" said Leonard, wiping the foam off his lip.

"Their legs were too short to reach the control pedals, son. Can't blame them, really," said Orman, taking a philosophical sip of his beer.

"Too bad, Dad."

"Goonder, Wiener schnitzels all around. Hold the mushrooms."

As Günter returned to the kitchen, Orman continued: "That was too bad, but I've got an idea about that. Boys, I've been thinking, we've all been working hard. How about a trip to the mountains?"

"You mean you're going to take a break from the airplane business?" said Norman, using the quote-mark finger waggle.

"You mean," added Leonard, "you've looked inside yourself and seen that your inner urgings were all goofed up like some kind of sloppy pile of bad spaghetti and now you're going to straighten that all up, even without a psychiatrist?"

"Leonard, you're talking gobbledygook. Gobbledygook! Norman, if you want me to take a break, then sure, I'll take a break. No more airplanes [finger waggle], no more catalogues, no more secret codes so certain organizations don't hear about what we're up to—I mean, forget about that last bit—no more foreign ministers. I promise. Leastways, until I change my mind. That's fair, ain't it?"

"You're my superhero, Dad," said Norman, shooting a glance at Leonard, as if to say, "Maybe he's beginning to see the light."

"Here's how," said Orman, tipping back a beer glass the size of a vase.

the sound of
mary poppins

A beautiful spot from which to see the mountains of Austria is the small city of Salzburg, and the train trip there is not a long one. After climbing aboard in Vienna, you soon find yourself humming smoothly alongside the Danube River, celebrated for its blueness, though you will find it somewhat brown. Gazing out their windows, the Normann and Piquant families found it somewhat brown.

"Mom, don't you find the Danube somewhat brown?" said Leonard. "I mean, for having the Blue Danube waltz named after it?"

"Yes, Leonard. But then maybe it was more blue when the waltz was written."

"Or *maybe* it's just another pack of lies served up by a bunch of soulless advertising men."

"Leonard, please don't use up all of your cynicism as a twelve-year-old. Save some of it for when you're sixteen."

"Just kidding around, Mom."

"The Blue Danube waltz," said Norma, turning from the window. "Do you remember when we used to go dancing, sweetie?"

"I do, my mountain dumpling, I do," said Orman Normann, patting his wife's hand. "But lissen, Blue Danube waltz, Blue Danube schmaltz! We're going to Salzburg, the home of *The Sound of Music*! What a movie! Julie Christie. Boy, I sure fell in love with Julie Christie in that movie. The way she arrives,

150

flying into the city on an umbrella. Fantastic! And then when they fly over the mountains in the flying car to escape the Nazis! I'll never forget it."

"Dad."

"I'll never forget a single detail."

"Dad."

"And when Dick Van Dyke sings 'Edelweiss'! Wow, that guy can sing and dance."

"Dad."

No train trip is long when ears and eyes are filled with engaging conversation and a beautiful landscape, even if the river is a little brown.

* * *

The first day in Salzburg was happily spent sightseeing. Norman began to imagine that their problems were over, that they would never hear of another bomber-contract signing again. It was not unheard of for a middle-aged man to suddenly try something completely new; it was practically a requirement. So Norman reasoned with Leonard as they climbed the steep and narrow streets of the old city, stopping to rest only when they had all reached the mighty castle, the burg, at the top of a high hill. Viewed from the castle's ramparts, the city was a haystack of steep, slated rooftops and blue-and-brown stones.

All around the city stood the first great mountains of the Alps. Orman Normann jovially suggested they climb to the top of the nearest one, the Untersberg; that is, he suggested that, since Sarah Piquant was outdoorsy, she would take the boys hiking up the mountain, and since Norma was indoorsy, she would stay in the hotel and have a bath, and since he, Orman, was outdoorsy but in an indoorsy way, he would ride the cable car and meet them at the top. "And," he said, with much emphasis, "if for any reason, any reason at all, the hike seems too hard for you, you three just turn around and go back to the hotel, where it'll be nice and cozy."

Accordingly, the following morning the three hikers rose early, ate breakfast, packed snacks and water, and then caught a Number 39 bus at the city square, which took them to the base of the mountain.

the under mountain

The first hour found them marching along a powerful stream, which dashed and shouldered its way past great boulders, all beneath a thick ceiling of elderly spruces. Three pairs of shoes scrunched satisfyingly along the thickly needled path.

"How is it possible that water can carve out rocks? I mean, if this water did, in fact, carve out these rocks," said Leonard. "Is it molecule by molecule? How does it happen?"

"I suppose it *is* molecule by molecule," said Norman. "I was just wondering more along the lines of 'Do you think there are such things as trolls? And if so, don't you think they probably live here?'"

"Just smell this air!" said Mrs. Piquant.

The second hour found the three beginning their ascent as the trail started a series of switchbacks, zigzagging back and forth across the side of the mountain, which had abruptly risen before them in folds like a draped blanket over the side of a bed. The trees were more widely spaced here and lofty; now the stream babbled and splashed below them.

"Eeeyah!" said Leonard, kicking through the dead spruce branches.

"Fairies. Real or unreal?" said Norman, puffing a bit, with his thumbs through the straps of his backpack.

"Breathe this air!" said Mrs. Piquant.

In the third hour they came out from under the trees to face what appeared to be a blank wall; it was the base of a great cliff, rising four hundred meters straight up. Moving closer they could see that it was not entirely blank, for there was a small metal sign fixed to the stone, which read: SCHWINDELFREIHEIT UND TRITTSICHERHEIT ERFORDERLICH.

"What does it mean, Mom?" said Leonard.

"I don't know," said Mrs. Piquant, "and I didn't bring my dictionary with me. I didn't think we'd need it. I just have the map."

"What does the map say?"

"Let's see, the map says . . ." She unfolded the green paper. "The map says the trail keeps going. Unless I'm completely confused about where we are."

"Maybe it's the wrong map?" said Leonard, squinting up at his mother.

"It's not the wrong map."

"Maybe it's the right map but the wrong mountain?"

"It's not the wrong mountain," said Mrs. Piquant, giving Leonard a look.

"Maybe it's the right map, right mountain, but the wrong galaxy?"

"Leonard!"

"I'm just going through the possibilities, Mom."

"Or maybe," shouted Norman, who was suddenly nowhere to be seen, "or maybe we just gave up looking too soon. I found the trail, it's around the corner here."

Indeed, turning the corner, the trail meandered diffidently along the base of the cliff. Then, seeming to pull itself together, it began to climb right up the stark face of the mountain by means of a narrow stone staircase.

When Leonard and Mrs. Piquant found their way around to where Norman stood calling, their eyes grew large as they took in the stairs, rising like a jagged scratch.

"Oops, I was right," said Leonard, "wrong galaxy," and he turned around.

"Oh dear," said Mrs. Piquant.

"We can't turn back now," Norman said, entreating his friend. "We've walked so far already! And we've got to meet my dad at the top. Come on, it's just walking up stairs. We've walked up millions of stairs before."

"The stairs I know and love have railings on one side and a wall on the other," said Leonard. "Some of them are even carpeted. This one has a creepy rock cliff on one side and air on the other. It'd be like walking up the Empire State Building—*on the outside!*"

"Look," said Norman, "these do have a railing."

A metal cable curving alongside the stairs was bolted into the mountainside.

"I guess we'll just have to take it one step at a time," said Mrs. Piquant. "If it gets too scary, we'll turn around. Norman, you go first. Leonard, you go next. I'll follow, and I won't let you fall."

"How are you going to do that, Mom?"

"I just will," said his mother. "Hold on to the handrail."

And so, after taking some deep breaths, they proceeded, step by cautious step. Though they went ever so slowly, in a quarter of an hour they were already high above the valley. After half an hour, they could no longer see the base of the cliff and the individual spruces and pines had become a thick green carpet below them.

As they steadily marched, the stairs crossed and recrossed

155

the cliff face, sometimes pushing their way into deep rock wrinkles, climbing ever higher. Sometimes the stairs stopped and a trail ran along a ledge where small flowers nodded their heads in the breeze, oblivious of any fear. These were the most frightening moments, because stairs, even when carved into a cliff, are still stairs, familiar, helpful, a friendly human invention. But a narrow ledge on a cliff face, suitable for alpine wildflowers if they are particularly hardy, is no place for a human being, especially not a twelve-year-old human being with his whole life ahead of him.

Thinking of this, and wishing he had not been quite so gung ho at the start of the day, Norman trudged ahead carefully, until he came upon a tall, rough-hewn ladder, aslant and fixed in the groin of another rock wrinkle.

Stopping behind Norman, Leonard said, "I can't go up that." Leonard turned around and looked back at the cliff faces they had scrambled up, cliff faces that plunged into bottomless mists, the valley from which they had come now completely gone. Then Leonard said, "I can't go back down that."

"Breathe this air!" said Mrs. Piquant, smiling determinedly. "Up you go, it's just a ladder, you've climbed hundreds of them before."

In the fourth hour, they arrived at the end of the fourth ladder, poking their heads up and over its top as you do when you climb into an attic, only in this case the attic was an endless, sloping meadow of the most exquisite yellows and greens, and its rafters were pillows of lily-white clouds in a ceiling of blue, untainted by the meanest smudge. For at the end of that last ladder, they had reached the top of the cliffs and come to the bottom of rolling meadows leading gently to the summit of the mountain.

"Breathe this air!" said Mrs. Piquant.

"Thank these lucky stars! We're alive! Feeeeyaaaa!" said Leonard, running like a young goat in the long grass.

Butterflies skittered over the meadow.

"How did these butterflies get here?" said Norman. "Can butterflies fly so high?"

"Leonard, come on over here, we've earned ourselves some M&M's," said Mrs. Piquant.

As she rummaged in her backpack, the two boys sat on the side of a wide slab of sun-warmed rock. Had it been an overstuffed sofa, it could not have been more comfortable.

"I'll tell you one good thing about being scared half to death," said Leonard. "It kind of takes your mind off everything else, even members of the Alfurnian Imperial Guard."

"I know, it's true, although for a while I kept thinking I saw pointy furry hats between the trees."

"Probably just trolls."

"Or fairies."

"Hairy fairies."

"Boys," said Mrs. Piquant, handing round the goodies, "I'm so proud of you."

Beyond the narrow valley below them, now far in the hazy distance, Salzburg's hill stood out against the blue of a distant mountain range.

Norman said, "It's positively Lilliputian!"

The last hour of their climb was, on the one hand, easy, as it was a stroll through a gently rising meadow. On the other hand, it was extremely difficult, as it came at the end of their long march and seemed as if it would never end.

"My dad is not going to believe we made it," said Norman proudly. "I bet the whole time he thought we'd give up and he'd have it nice and quiet on the top of the mountain by himself."

At last, when they all felt they could not go another step, they reached the gentle peak, where they could see, just below the summit, the last pylons of the cable car and the skiers' mountaintop restaurant. Even at a distance, they recognized the large shape of Norman's father, slightly sunburned, on the terrace. As they switched back and forth down the path to the restaurant, however, they became slightly confused, for it appeared that he was not alone. He seemed to be sitting with two very small gentlemen in dark blue suits and wraparound sunglasses. Coming closer, they saw cups of coffee, a large beer, and stacks of paper strewn on the table between them.

Stepping onto the terrace, Leonard let out a whooping yodel, which caused Orman Normann to leap from his chair, his bulk twitching like a jelly.

"Leonard! Sarah! Norman!" he said. "You! Here! But didn't you read the sign? I didn't think you'd—"

"Dad, we made it!" said Norman, sprinting over to give him a hug around the middle.

"Er, Norman, Sarah, Leonard, I'd like to introduce you to my Katong Luangan friends, Ronny and Rinny."

The two tiny men stood and offered their small hands.

Orman Normann spread out his arms. "I've convinced them that they really do want to sign those contracts. Norman, you owe me a schnitzel!"

can you sell bombers on pluto?

It is always uncomfortable when you have allowed tentative hopes to grow into certainties, only to find the certainties, from one moment to the next, cough twice and expire. Balthazar Birdsong might suggest this was the result of imagination and observation being out of balance—too heavy on the imagination. Where Leonard and Norman saw certainties, more careful observation might have told them these were merely hopes. Now the boys felt just this kind of uncomfortableness, their dream of ex-bomber salesmanship for Orman Normann deflated and defunct.

Norman and Leonard were home again, sitting gloomily at the kitchen table of the Normann residence in Buddingdale Heights, planning their next move. The hot chocolate the boys sipped tasted like it had come from a little plastic bag, which should not have surprised them, because it had.

In New York City, August was asserting itself, making the city and its suburbs hot, loud, sticky, smelly, and unpleasant in many other ways. While the Austrian mountains had been cool and slightly thrilling, August in Buddingdale Heights was warm and very boring.

Norman said, "Katzenjammer."

He picked up his mug of hot chocolate, swirled it around, and set it back down.

"How do you like that dad of mine telling us he was taking a break from airplane selling, two-finger-waggle" (the boys had now taken to adding the spoken phrase "two-finger-waggle" instead of actually waggling their fingers), "and then grandly taking us on a vacation, two-finger-waggle, and then actually sending us on a life-and-death struggle on a mountain, thinking we'd definitely turn around when we read the sign, but the sign was in German, so how could we read the sign? So that, right under our noses—"

"Over our noses, actually," said Leonard.

"Right. Right over our noses he's making some kind of deal with two more shady characters."

"Wearing shades."

"Wearing shades. By the way, did your mom ever figure out what the sign at the bottom of the mountain meant?"

"Oh yes."

"What did it mean?"

"Sureness of foot and freedom from dizziness required."

Norman poked a moody spoon into a cantaloupe wedge. The telephone rang, humidly.

"Mom! The phone's bombilating!"

"What, dear?"

"The phone, it's bombilating!"

"It's what, dear?"

"Bombilating! Loud bombilation! Never mind, I'll answer it."

Norman crossed the kitchen and lifted the receiver. "Hello, Normann residence. Norman speaking."

"Hello, Norman. It's Balthazar" came his voice loud enough for even Leonard to hear.

"Mr. B.!" said Norman.

"In the electronically noncorporeal voice, yes."

"What?"

"Norman, how are the clouds where you are?"

"What?"

"The sky, Norman, the sky. Have you looked at it yet?"

"No."

"I guessed as much. I imagine you've been sitting around feeling bored, nursing your jetlag katzenjammer, and poking a moody spoon into the dregs of your breakfast, hmm?"

"Yeah," said Norman, rubbing his nose.

"Well, I can tell you it has been a marvelous altocirrus-with-just-a-couple-of-cumulus-humilis-on-the-horizon day here. Now the sun has set and I'm looking forward to the rising new moon."

"What?"

"Is our connection bad? I said, it has been a marvelous alto—"

"Mr. B., where are you?"

"Northern Australia, my dear boy. I've come in hopes of witnessing that fabulous species of stratocumulus, the Morning Glory. Haven't seen it yet, but hope springs, et cetera."

"Northern Australia?"

"Yes, northern Australia, and the concern I hear in your voice is touching. But do not fear. Remember, Australia is the continent without indigenous mammalian carnivores. Think of it. It's the first vegan co-op on a massive scale."

"What?"

"Never mind. I'll explain all when I get back."

"When? When are you coming back? I think my dad's karma is kaput."

"Quite possibly. However, there is nothing I can do about that here. But to answer your more immediate question, I shall be home soon. In the meantime, keep your nose in the air. Toodle-oo."

And just as suddenly as Balthazar Birdsong was present, he was gone.

"He's still no help," said Norman, grumpily replacing the receiver. "So anyway, we need a new plan. Got any? If so, shoot. Fire. Bombs away."

Leonard rocked back on his chair and then let it fall forward. "Okay, listen," he said. "What do we know about your dad that he doesn't know we know?"

"That he wears too much aftershave?"

"No. He knows we know that. What do we know about his airplane business, finger-waggle, that he doesn't know we know?"

"The code!"

"Exeeeeeeeyaaaaaaaactly. And not only do we know the first code, thanks to you, we know the second code, thanks to the unfamiliar voice, the sinister, unfamiliar voice, let's call it the S.U.V., in the *Irrgarten*. I refer, of course, to 'one dozen eggs equals one Flieswitzer-Hassenfus 78, with plenty of cup holders.'"

"Yes!"

"So now do you get it?"

"No!"

"All we have to do is get hold of your dad's copy of the L. L. Bomb catalogue and then switch around the picture codes. That way, when your dad sends the orders to the man with the sinister, unfamiliar voice, S.U.V., the order will be all screwed up. For instance, when the Lilliputians ask for three Flieswitzer-Hassenfus 78s, they'll get, I don't know, something completely different, like, say, a Hopper-bopper Overdropper 39, which might not have nearly enough cup holders or something. And then the buyers, the Lilliputians, will be mad, demand a refund, ask to speak with the manager. Same thing will happen with the Blinesians, the Katong Luangans, the Jakartians, and so on."

"So?"

"So when everyone is screaming at once, your dad will get fired. Bound to, when he messes everything up completely. Boom, problematic-dad-karma fixed, blown up."

Norman gazed into the middle distance—at the family blender, actually—in a dreamy way, until with a fist thump to the formica tabletop, he blurted, "Leonard, it's brilliant! It can't miss. And you know why it can't miss? Because it plays to our strengths. What are our strengths? My dad's weaknesses. I mean, he can't ever keep anything straight anyway, so Mr. S.U.V. will just think my dad has lost more than his usual share of marbles and fire him."

Leonard basked in his friend's admiration like a happy canary.

"So what you have got to do is sneak into your dad's office and—" Leonard stopped and sniffed. "Do you smell aftershave?" A moment later, a humming Orman Normann entered the kitchen.

"Norman!" said Orman. "Oh, hello, Leonard. You here?"

"Yup," said Leonard.

"Norman," Orman said, filling a massive coffee mug with the words WORLD'S MOST EXTRA SUPER DAD emblazoned on it, "I'd like to speak with you. Come into my office. Excuse us, Leonard."

"Yup," said Leonard, giving Norman a wink and a silent (mouthed behind Orman Normann's retreating back) "NOW!"

* * *

"Norman, come on in, and shut the door behind you," said

163

Mr. Normann, sidling around his desk before dropping into his chair with a bilious whoosh.

"Whoo, boy!" he said, holding his coffee mug above him. "Nearly spilled my java, ha-ha! Sit down, son."

Norman sat.

"Son, I just wanted to chat a bit because, well, with school coming on again, I just wanted to check in with you like a concerned shareholder would. How's Norman Normann Enterprises doing on the big board? Is the stock I hold in you going up or going down?"

"I don't know, Dad. What big board?"

"The big board of the marketplace of life, where how much you're worth is up in lights for all to see. How's your net worth, son?"

"I still don't get it, Dad."

"It's a metaphor, boy, a metaphor. What I mean is, are you learning stuff? When January rolls around, will you be prepared to hit your target on the next Amalgamated Schools Test? Will your air strikes be laser-guided missiles ripping apart that test booklet answer sheet?"

"I guess so," said Norman, shifting in his seat.

"Let's look at the big picture for a minute. I'm not just talking about the next test, the next school, I'm talking about your life, son, your career. When the time comes, will you be ready to join me as a partner in my beautiful bomber business? We'll call it Orman Normann and More!"

Norman fidgeted.

"I'm not sure that's what I have in mind, Dad. I think I'd rather sell things that people really like."

"Really like? Really like? I'll tell you what people really like: bombers! No, I take that back, people don't like bombers.

164

No. People love bombers! People love dropping heavy metal exploding objects on other people's heads. How many times do I have to tell you that? They love it! Especially men. Men will spend millions of any kind of money you can name for the simple pleasure of dropping heavy metal objects on other people's heads. Hooee! Ain't it a grand world?"

"It sure is, Dad."

While his father was talking, Norman allowed his eye to roam over the pile of papers that covered his father's desk like a raised topographical map, scrutinizing each bit of paper surface in order to spot the L. L. Bomb catalogue.

"Where else can a guy make a living selling bombers? Mars? I don't think so."

A yellow capital *L* and the unmistakable tip of a Flieswitzer-Hassenfus 78 magnetized Norman's gaze. *Gotcha!* The L. L. Bomb catalogue lay in the upper layers of the paper mountain, sandwiched beneath a Big Ricko's pizza box and a stack of three-ring binders.

"Venus?" said Orman, getting up from his chair. He began to pace the room.

Norman could feel his father working up his bombast like steam in a boiler.

"Saturn? Can you sell bombers on Saturn? Well, I don't rightly know," said Orman, turning now to look out into the garden.

Norman eased himself onto the edge of his seat and, pretending to yawn, stretched his arm forward.

"I'm not boring you, am I?" said Orman, turning around.

"No, Dad, no," said Norman, pulling his

arm back hastily and scratching his elbow. "Go ahead. What about Pluto?"

"Pluto? Pluto! But Pluto's not a planet anymore, is it?" Again, he turned to look out of the windows into the garden.

With a quick and silent motion, Norman lifted the pizza box. For a moment, Norman blinked, for it seemed that the L. L. Bomb catalogue had vanished, but then he realized that it was merely stuck to the underside of the pizza box, glued there by a paste of oily cheese. Norman hesitated for just a second, then, yanking the catalogue off the box with a horrible tearing sound, he dropped it neatly to his feet and kicked it under his chair.

Orman Normann turned at the noise, saying, "Plu—" He looked at the pizza box in Norman's hand. "Did you want to order a pizza? That's not a bad idea. After all, it is ten forty-five on a Saturday morning in mid-August. And that seems to me as good a time as any. Let's order! What do you want on your half?"

"No, Dad, I'm fine. I just had breakfast, actually."

"No pizza?"

"No, Dad, thanks."

"All right, suit yourself. Now, where was I?"

"On Pluto, Dad."

"On Pluto, right, and can you sell bombers on Pluto? No, you cannot. Which is why I say, for my money, drop bombs right here on Earth. Why travel to outer space when you've got a whole world to bomb right under your own two feet?" With his last words, Orman stamped his two feet on the floor, heavily, one after the other. The ensuing tremor of the floor, coupled with Norman's disturbance of the desk, caused the uniquely balanced mountain of paper to wobble and then, giving up all its ambition to remain a mountain, dissolve into foothills and cliffs and mesas of paper, and then slide to the floor.

"Hooeee!" said Orman.

"Let me get all that, Dad," said Norman, dropping to the floor to grab the L. L. Bomb catalogue. But Orman was already bent double, scooping up armfuls of paper.

He was not bent for long. With another whoop, Orman Normann jumped up and cried, "The L. L. Bomb catalogue!" He held it aloft. "I've been looking for this for a week! This is a very important document!" He performed a quick little dance, possibly called the Bacon Fat, which he had danced in his youth on the prairie. "I can't afford to lose this again." He walked around his desk, crouched next to the safe, and punched in some code letters on the keypad. The safe emitted a soft chime. Orman swung open the heavy door, placed the L. L. Bomb catalogue carefully within, and then, with a gentle push, let the door swing shut, listening for it to lock with a confident, multiple click. It chimed again.

"That should just about do it. Norman, let's have another chat again soon. I think they do us both a world of good. It certainly did me. I was nearly in deep doo-doo without that catalogue—a certain business partner of mine would not have been happy, nae, sir, nae. But, in the meantime, I think I'll order a pizza after all."

It was a very droopy Norman Normann, whose chat with his father had possibly done him a world of bad, who returned to the kitchen to report on these events to Leonard.

Summing up the entire mission neatly, he said, "I bombed. Pass me the dictionary. Maybe it'll have something about safecracking."

nip *vb* : to grab hold of and squeeze tightly, to pinch or bite

nip and tuck *adj or adv* : very close

nipcheese *n* : a miser, someone who will not spend money

nipperkin *n* : a container with a capacity of half a pint or less

nipcheese

nippily *adv* : quickly

nippiness *n* : the state of being nippy, agility

nipple *n* : a conical protuberance on top of the mammary gland all higher mammals possess, from which the young animals draw milk and first receive sustenance

the key to unlock
any door

The next morning Norman sat brooding at the kitchen table, when his mother entered the room, carrying her handbag.

"Norman, I'm just going to my exercise class, and then I'm going to buy groceries. There's not a thing to eat in this house. And then I'm going to the bank. And I may stop by my hairdresser's and see if she can squeeze me in."

"Okay, Mom, I'll be fine right here, alone by myself, finding plenty to do."

"Will you be fine right here alone by yourself? Will you find plenty to do?"

"I'll be fine right here alone by myself finding plenty to do. I'm absolutely positively sure."

"Are you absolutely positively sure?"

"I'm absolutely positively sure. I love you, Mom."

"Do you love me?"

"Bye, Mom."

The next days passed fruitlessly for Norman, in regard to his father, his father's study, and his father's study's safe. Orman Normann had been in and out of the house, allowing Norman plenty of chances, but affording no solutions. Apart from thumping his head gently against the wall over and over, there seemed to be practically nothing to do.

* * *

The days dragged on, as they so often do in August. Leonard was traveling again with his mother, who was inspecting various projects around the country; Norman was on his own.

On a particularly bland Tuesday, Norman found himself contemplating mayonnaise.

"Mom," he said, "is mayonnaise really made out of eggs?"

"No, dear, it comes in a jar," she said.

"I think it is made of eggs, Mom."

"Fine, dear. I'll see you after my exercise class."

"Okay, Mom."

On a similar, remarkably hot yet dull Thursday, Norman contemplated mayflies.

Mayflies spend their entire adult life, which, as he had read, is about one day long, without a mouth. Norman was revolted. How could you live your life without a mouth? What kind of a world is this, thought Norman, that includes a creature that spends the most important time of its life without a mouth?

In between musing about such matters, Norman continued to check the safe. It remained locked.

* * *

On the last boring day of August, when Norman thought he couldn't stand even one more, the twins returned from camp and Balthazar Birdsong returned from Australia and Leonard returned from Kankakee, Illinois, bringing back all the color that was lacking in Norman's pale cheeks.

The Normann telephone nearly bombilated off the hook.

"Eeeeyaaaa!" shouted Leonard.

"God, camp was boring," said the twins.

"Norman, it is vitally important that we meet," said Balthazar Birdsong. "Tomorrow I shall be upon your doorstep at eleven a.m. sharpish. Alert your mother and your friends."

As a result, and after much further phone calling, they all—that is, Anna, Emma, Leonard, and Norman—assembled

170

in the Normann living room, with their parents' permission to spend the day with Norman's tutor, which, frankly, had been granted speedily and gratefully on all sides. Balthazar Birdsong found them there, gabbling like young geese starved of honking partners. He found he had to practically nip at their heels like a sheepdog as he steered them out of the house, onto and off a couple of buses, and then into a Q subway train, where they sat in a row opposite him, hooting and nearly quacking, utterly unheedful of the other travelers on the train. Occasionally Mr. Birdsong admonished them to mind their impulses and not to overvocalize, but mostly he allowed them to revel in their reunion. Even when Leonard leapt up and down to dramatize some individual moment of terror or joy, or when one of the twins stood up and pressed the sides of her face with her hands to mock some especially odious fellow camper, Mr. B. refrained from scolding them much.

It is a little difficult to record any of what was said; even the four themselves sometimes had trouble understanding one another over the rattle and shrilling of the train wheels. Nevertheless, a bit of their conversation could be heard over the din.

Leonard said, "I looked out across open space, thousands of feet in the air, across to another cliff exactly like the one we were on, and I thought: Eeeeeeyaaaaaah! My mother's trying to kill me!"

Emma said, "Anna tried to kill me. She made me pair up with Tiffany Simpleton for the trust walk in the middle of the woods at night, which was horrifying enough. But what was worse was the next day the Tiffikins was my lab partner. I mean, the way she says 'Oh, the difflugia in my sample are exquisite' is enough to give a person heart palpitations. I don't know what difflugia are, but I'm sure they aren't ever exquisite."

"They're a kind of protozoan," said Norman, "a single-celled animal."

"A what?"

"A bug."

Anna said, "I saw her difflugia. They were awful."

"Awful?" said Leonard. "This is awful: Imagining myself falling over a cliff, helplessly clawing the air, my whole life flashing before my eyes. What if, on my way down, there wasn't even enough time for the year I turned five? That was a great year!"

And so their subway trip passed pleasantly, full of their loud conversation, tales and gossip about everything and nothing, on a train to they-knew-not-where, under the watchful eye of Balthazar Birdsong.

* * *

At the end of the line, they walked to a boardwalk along the beach, opposite the city's famous amusement park at Coney Island. They squeezed themselves onto a bench, the twins on one side of Balthazar Birdsong, the boys on the other, Mr. B.'s long legs stretched out before him, his arms draped over the back. Balthazar smiled and gazed at the small dirty waves beneath the hot sky. Gulls, children, and teenagers called to one another; jets moaned overhead and subways rumbled nearby; the air blew gently but stickily, and Balthazar sighed a heavy sigh of contentment as the four friends looked at him expectantly.

"Er, Mr. B.," said Norman, "what was it that was of vital importance to us all?"

"This moment," said Mr. B.

"This moment?"

"Precisely."

Four pairs of eyes turned away from Balthazar Birdsong and began skeptically to gaze about.

"I still don't get it," said Norman.

"What could be more vitally important than simply spending time with your friends? I'll tell you. Nothing. That is, to be with those whom you hold most dear is the great key which will unlock any door."

Balthazar Birdsong pushed his hands into his pockets.

"And the other great key to unlocking any door, as Norman's father is always ready to tell us, is cash, which your dear parents have sent along with me to dispense as I see fit. So here's some cash for each of you to squander in trivial amusements."

"Fa-whammm!"

"Groovalicious!"

"Awwwwwwwwww yeah!"

Only Norman said nothing and did not move. Balthazar Birdsong had just given him an idea for how to open his father's safe.

celestial domes

The start of a new school year is a good time to pause, to take a look at where we all stand, how far we have come, where we might be headed, and to consider the state of our affairs, their phases and moods, pluses and minuses. While Norman contemplates domestic safecracking, let us take a moment to contemplate him and his friends.

Norman and Leonard were each entering the eighth grade, although in separate middle schools.

Both boys had grown taller in the last year, of course, though Norman more so than Leonard, Norman's Norse heritage exerting itself. His boy's round face was slowly revealing the adult within, as his freckling cheekbones spread, perhaps attempting to keep up with his shoulders, which were broad, though they tended to fall forward; Norman, at ease, resembled a soft *S*. Had Norman been a bit more active he would just about qualify as strapping. But he was not strapping. Pleasant to look at, certainly. However, if we are to be honest, we must admit that, under his untucked T-shirt, he was a bit flabby.

Leonard, by contrast, could have benefited from his best friend's avoirdupois, and if you cannot imagine what that means, it is suggested that you yourself peek into a dictionary. Leonard over the past year had just grown thinner. As he grew thinner, his deep-set green eyes appeared to grow larger and ever more reptilian, in a good way.

Leonard and Norman faced the new year with equanimity; that is, neither dreading nor looking forward to it. For one thing, they had Orman Normann's soul on their minds.

The twins, on the other hand, both dreaded and looked forward to the new year, eager to assert their dominance over all and sundry, whether in math, volleyball, or the general-studies area called style. Though they were required to wear uniforms, the twins had the ability to express all the style in the world simply by how they rolled their socks. Anna and Emma had always been tall. Over the summer they mastered a number of retorts to stupid questions concerning their altitudinous physiques, such as: "Q: Do you play basketball? A: No. Do you play miniature golf?" Their three sets of school uniforms, complete with headbands and stockings, were purchased, ironed, and ready.

So much for Norman and his friends. What about the significant grown-ups? Norma Normann had become slightly more petite, having lost a bit of weight over the summer. She took enormous, though silent, pride in this, knowing as every good Scandinavian does—though she was only one by marriage—that to speak of good fortune was not only in bad taste but was courting doom. But we may take note of her achievement and be happy for her, though we all liked her just as much in the larger version.

Energized by her recent travels, Mrs. Piquant returned to her architectural firm with fresh ideas from Prague.

And what of Balthazar Birdsong? It is a little hard to say, as rather little is known about him. Norma was under the impression that, apart from tutoring her son, he wrote important and probably impossible-to-understand articles of some kind, but for whom and where she had no idea. It is probable that he was a writer of some sort, since he could come and go as he pleased, lived in a tiny abode filled with books, and seemed to

175

have no responsibilities other than to Norman. Suffice it to say that after his Australian travels he returned a shade browner overall, with the end of his long nose a little more red. Also, he needed a haircut.

We come to Orman Normann. While his son grew taller and his wife grew smaller, he had grown slightly larger and, if possible, even more boisterous, full of more jokes and always hoping for even more cash. His cheeks were pinker, like bubble gum straight from the wrapper. The lines around his eyes were deeper and more hilarious. His lonely chin was growing a double to keep it company.

And beneath this good-natured, pink and sweaty, boy-grown-large, there was a good-natured, pink and sweaty, boy-who-sold-bombers. In other words, and as was becoming only too obvious to his son, Orman Normann's karmic levels were dangerously low.

This worried Norman. He was desperately eager to test the idea that had come to him on the beach at Coney Island; he was only waiting for another chance to sneak into his father's study alone.

As it happened, Norman did not have to wait long.

But first, whatever else the new school year brought, whether unexpected fun or unknown stress-makings, it always brought a very special occasion: Norman's birthday. Norman Normann was born on 9/9, the ninth of September. His party was to take place on the coming Saturday, and true to his usual form, his father would be absent.

On the morning of his departure, Orman handed Norman an envelope.

"Here, son."

"What's this, Dad?"

"It's your present, dodo! Go ahead, open it."

Norman cautiously opened the envelope and pulled out a goldish and rectangular paper. He looked at it.

"This is a check for five hundred dollars, Dad."

"That's right, son. How do you like it?" Orman Normann beamed, with a face as shiny as the knees of a four-year-old's corduroy pants.

"What am I going to do with a check for five hundred dollars, Dad? I don't even have a bank account."

"Well, I'll take care of it, then," said Orman, taking the check from Norman's fingers and sliding it into his wallet. "I'll just put this into my checking account until you need it. For college or something. Heck, maybe you won't even need to go to college."

"But then why did you even bother to write it?"

"It's the thought that counts, son. Now eat your breakfast. I've got to catch a plane to Cincinnati."

* * *

The party was to be held at Balthazar Birdsong's apartment. On Saturday, Norman, his mother, Leonard, Mrs. Piquant, Anna, and Emma stood shoulder to shoulder in one of the elevators of the Maestro Building, rising to the twenty-sixth floor.

"What time is it?" asked Norman.

"Two minutes to eight," said his mother.

"Why did he want it to be so late?" said Leonard. "If the party had started earlier, we could already be playing with your presents by now."

"He said eight o'clock," said Norman. "I don't know why."

The elevator doors opened, and Leonard and Norman leapt off and ran around the corner to the stairs.

"This way!" shouted Norman.

"Let's go! Hooner Po!" shouted Leonard.

"What? What? What? What?" shouted the four behind them.

"We're not there yet?" said Anna.

"Just three flights of stairs," Norman called back.

"What kind of a building has an elevator that doesn't go all the way to the top floor?" said Emma, puffing.

"A tapered one," said a voice from above them. Looking up, they saw Balthazar Birdsong's sharp face peering down at them from over the railings.

"Just keep coming up. You'll find it well worth your while. I go to fix the beverages."

Stepping into the short hallway at the top of the stairs, they beheld an eerie blue light falling through Balthazar's open doorway. Norman and Leonard waited for the others to arrive, and then all six peered inside; they saw a large black bird silhouetted against an enormous silver moon.

"Eek!" squealed Norma, turning to flee.

"Mom, Mom! It's just Crick, Mr. Birdsong's crow. He's very friendly."

"Come in, come in, come in," said Balthazar, emerging from the kitchen. "Now you see why I asked you here at this time. Isn't the full moon marvelous? You won't see it quite like this for at least a year, perhaps even more. Who knows?"

The four friends rushed onto the terrace as Balthazar returned to the kitchen followed by Norma and Mrs. Piquant. Soon his murmurings mingled with their exclamations.

Leonard and Norman led the twins back inside to give them a tour of the room's best treasures.

The lights in the kitchen went out, and Balthazar, Norma,

and Mrs. Piquant stepped into the living room, each carrying a tray, bearing, in Norma's case, a large chocolate cake lit nicely with thirteen candles; in Mrs. Piquant's, various sparkling ciders; and in Balthazar's, a large pot of rich hot chocolate and a large pot of richer hot coffee. Balthazar, as he set the table with the goodies, led them in singing "Happy Birthday to You," the second time through whistling like a bird.

"Eeeeeyaaaah!" sang Leonard.

"Eeeeyoooo!" shouted Norman, attempting to blow out the candles.

The presents were passed around. Norman received two volleyballs from the girls, one hot pink, one lime green.

"Fantastic!" said Norman. "But I don't play volleyball."

"That's okay," said the twins together, "we do."

Leonard's present was a small rubber pig, which, when squeezed, produced very realistic-looking feces, coming out of its rear end.

"It's a pooping pig," said Leonard.

"Now this I can use!" said Norman.

"I, too, have something for you, dear Norman," said Balthazar, placing a thin box into Norman's hand. "I hope it's useful, too."

Norman removed the wrapping paper and held the cloth-covered box. Opening this, he found, nestled in red velvet, a compact brass telescope, a monocular: a bit longer than a pair of powerful binoculars, but single.

"Awesome," crooned Leonard.

"Let us observe the moon imaginatively," said Balthazar. "As you see, I took the liberty of inviting the moon to your party, and as she could not arrive until now, I planned the hour accordingly. I hope you understand."

Indeed, though presumably shining on the entire city, the moon did appear to be looking directly at all of them, now gathered on the balcony.

"If we attach this small tripod and set it on the table, thusly, we will be able to invite the moon even closer. So. Yes. Ah," said Mr. B. "Now take a look, take a long look."

Soon each in turn had peered through the telescope, with many an "Eeeeyaaa!" or "Wussome" or "Don't bump the table!"

*　*　*

Balthazar invited them back inside and asked those who were willing to sit for a few minutes holding Watson, who, as you will perhaps remember, was nearing the end of his life.

"Let us give him a bath and then fluff his piney nest, as best we can, to ease his journey," he said, lifting the rat carefully from Emma and cupping him in his long-fingered hands. He supported Watson in the washbasin, gently scratching him behind the ears. Watson's eyes had grown cloudy over the summer, but he seemed to enjoy the warm bath and happily nipped and nibbled the slice of banana Norman offered him after Anna had toweled him dry.

In this way Norman spent his thirteenth birthday, the moon all the while becoming a little more silvery and high. When Norma Normann began to doze—it was nearly eleven o'clock—Balthazar stood up from his chair, placed Crick (who had been sitting on his shoulder, sampling chocolate cake) back in his cage, and said to the others, "Before you leave I shall give each of you a party favor. To receive it, you must all return to the balcony." They stepped back outside, where it was now rather chilly, and stood in a row, prepared to duck if the party favors looked iffy.

"Now look above you at the night sky, letting your eyes roam from horizon to horizon, from north to south, from east to west, and back up to the top. This is your very own celestial dome."

"You mean, we have to share our party favors?" said Anna.

"No, you need not share your favors. What kind of a party-thrower do you take me for? No. Now each of you, point straight up. The point directly above your outstretched finger is the zenith of your celestial dome, so, you see, each of you has a different zenith. Therefore, each of you has a unique celestial dome, which will travel with you and remain unique to you wherever you go. The great astronomers of the past had their own slightly different celestial domes. Take your celestial domes home with you. Cherish them. Study them. And let's see which of you turns out to be the next Copernicus."

At home after midnight, Norman peered out of his bedroom window to check on his celestial dome, a small piece of which was visible past the trees in his backyard. His new telescope, tucked in its box, sat upon his desk. Norman was too tired to read his dictionary, but would check the Os in the morning.

obtuse *adj* : dense
obus *n* : an artillery shell
obviate *vb* : to make unnecessary
obvious *adj* : easily seen
ocarina *n* : a small, potato-shaped flute
Occaneechi *n* : an extinct people of Sioux ancestry
occasion *n* : a time for something to happen

obtuse

The next morning Mr. B. called to say that Watson had passed away.

theory of the air terminal of the afterlife

On Sunday afternoon, the two boys lay belly up and belly down on Norman's bed.

"I already miss Watson," said Leonard.

Norman said nothing.

The events of the birthday party and the coming of fall had put them both in a philosophical mood.

"I didn't even know him that well, but I miss him," said Leonard.

"Maybe he'll come back," said Norman. "Maybe he'll come back as a new rat."

"Hmm, that's possible. Maybe he'll come back as a wild rat, a rat ruler, father of a rat dynasty! He didn't have any kids, did he?"

"I don't think so."

"He was a male, wasn't he? I mean, we're sure of that, right? I never really checked."

"I didn't either, but Mr. B. always called him 'he.'"

"Maybe Watson will come back as a human being."

"Maybe. But how long will he be gone? Does Watson step out of his rat self and immediately into some new self? Or does he go to some waiting room somewhere?" said Norman.

They were silent again.

Then Leonard said, "Maybe he has to go to some enormous ticket counter and stand in line with all the other rats who have died recently, which must be a lot, thousands, maybe millions, and they stand in a line that zigzags back and forth, and it takes

182

nearly forever, and then he gets to the ticket counter, and the lady there, maybe a starfish or a guinea pig or a mynah bird or something, hands him his ticket, and he looks at it to see what gate, and the gate says something like 'Feather-duster worm,' or 'Weeping willow,' or 'Human being,' even, and then he goes there and he waits at the gate until his name is called, and then he walks down the ramp into whoever has the next baby whatever-it-is for that particular gate."

"Hmm, we could call this the Theory of the Air Terminal of the Afterlife," said Norman. "Do you think they have frequent-flier points?"

"Frequent-dier points."

"Right, frequent-dier, do you think they have frequent-dier points, and if you get enough points, you could ask for an upgrade from, say, one of those horrible fish that live their whole lives in the dark at the bottom of the ocean, eating rotting whale carcasses next to hot sulfur vents, to, like, a Baltimore oriole or something?"

"I think so. But what if they overbook?"

"What's that?"

"It's when they sell more tickets than they have places for. What if you have to give up your chance at being a dolphin or an eagle or something cool, and you have to go back and wait?"

"Well, you can always kill time in the gift shop."

"I bet that's where Watson is right now."

The boys looked at the ceiling and at the floor.

Norman hoisted himself up and said, "I nearly forgot! Watson pushed it right out of my mind. I think I know how to crack the safe."

Leonard bounced up. "Tell, tell, tell!"

"Okeydoke. Listen. Remember at Coney Island, Mr. B. said

183

something like 'Keep in mind, my young misguided juvenile delinquents—'"

"Did he say that?"

"Something. Anyway, 'Keep in mind, my unevolved lumps of protoplasm—'"

"That sounds more like it."

". . . the key to any conundrum is being with those you love."

"Did he say that?"

"I think he said that. Anyway, it got me thinking. What code would my dad choose for his safe?"

"Cheeseburger?"

"Possibly. But I think maybe even he is smarter than that. Let's just suppose that what he loves most is us, his family."

"For the sake of argument."

"For the sake of, as you say, argument. And let's say his family is me, Norman; Mom, Norma; and him, Orman. So let's write that out like this."

Norman crawled over Leonard to his desk and wrote at the bottom of a sheet of old math homework:

NORMAN
NORMA
ORMAN

"The common letters are *A*, *M*, *N*, *O*, and *R*," said Norman.

"Brilliant."

"Okay, when my dad opens the safe—I've heard it a couple of times—he always punches in five letters."

"Brillianter!"

"But here's the thing. When he punches in the code, it sounds like this: Beep boop bap boop brrr."

"Beep boop bap boop brrr, so?"

"Listen. Beep boop bap boop brrr."

"Yeah?"

"Don't you get it? There are two boops. That means that two letters are the same, the second and the fourth. Now, it's safe to assume that the code spells a word, because otherwise my dad could never remember it. If it's a word, then the second and fourth letters are most likely vowels. So they must both be either As or Os. All yesterday afternoon, I tried to find a five-letter word with two As. Zilch, as my dad would say. But then, when I looked for a word with two Os, the answer was obvious."

"Brilliantest! What's the answer?"

"Moron."

Leonard sat up on the bed, bounced a few times, and then stopped. "Moron?" he said.

"Moron," said Norman.

* * *

Five minutes later, Leonard and Norman were in the study, contemplating the violation of the integrity of Orman Normann's safe.

"Let's go," whispered Norman.

"Hooner Po," whispered Leonard.

Norman pressed the letters M-O-R-O-N into the keypad, pausing carefully between each letter.

The safe chimed merrily, and the door lock clicked.

"Eureka!" whispered Norman.

"Eureka!" whispered Leonard. "What does 'Eureka' mean?"

"It means the safe's unlocked."

"Unlocka!" whispered Leonard.

Norman eased open the door, and both boys peered inside. The safe was empty.

a three-year-old
with a stick

In October it rained. It was a rain that had come on slowly, the low clouds trailing veils of mist. But now, on this first Saturday of the month, the clouds delivered plush downpours, making the city streets shimmer.

The disappointment of finding the safe empty, the onset of school with its attendant—to use Leonard's phrase—horrible and useless homework, and the frequent absence of Norman's father had stymied any further attempts at direct karmic intervention on his behalf. Norman's elation at cracking the safe had soured. His hope fizzled.

"I feel like a baseball team that's just lost an eight-game lead going into the play-offs," said Norman to Leonard one day.

"Do you even care about baseball?"

"Nope. But that's how I feel."

* * *

Norman stood at a large table in Balthazar Birdsong's apartment, assisting his tutor with sticks and string, paper, scissors, and a variety of glues and tape.

Balthazar Birdsong was saying, "As in any stable situation, a high-flying stationary kite is the result of a variety of opposite forces, each exactly balancing its counterpart, thereby achieving stasis, steadiness, stillness. The kite stays up because the blowing air, which it deflects downward, pushes upward, exactly as much as the combined pull of the earth's gravity on the kite's mass plus the tension of the string. If any one of these forces changes, one or more of the others must also change if we want the kite to stay up. For instance, if the wind blows harder, all the extra push up and away must be countered by the pull of the string down and back, which we will feel as the string becomes more taut. The mass of the kite won't change and neither will the force of gravity, so the string must do more pulling, and possibly our own arms as well."

Norman shook his head a little and wiggled his nose, hoping this would shake what he had just heard into a spot in his brain that could understand it.

Then he said, "I thought some kites flew like airplanes."

Balthazar Birdsong cut a short length of thin stick.

"Ah, you refer, of course, to Bernoulli's principle. Yes, indeed, some kites do. But most, like our box kite, have flat faces which primarily divert the air downward. It's just a case of Newton's Third Law: For every action, there is an equal and opposite reaction. The air goes down, the kite goes up. This pushing up is called lift, by the way."

Norman wiggled his nose a bit more.

Balthazar Birdsong lashed two short sticks together, creating an X.

"If we can induce enough lift in our kite, and if we make some clever triggers, we can send up objects to drop. For example, parachutes or paper airplanes. Or leaflets, as did the poet Shelley, spreading his hotheaded views over chilly Wales. Perhaps our leaflets should advertise 'Karmic Cleansing' or 'Call for Free Celestial Dome.'"

Balthazar placed the rigid box-kite skeleton upright on the table.

"So. Our frame is ready for the paper. What color would you like? In order to bring the sometimes overwhelming blueness of a clear sky into balance, might I suggest one of the warm tones? Yellow, orange, red, perhaps?"

"Orange, please," said Norman.

"The complement of blue. That will be fine."

Balthazar began the measuring and the cutting of large rectangles of tangerine-orange paper from a roll.

Partly to give his brain a break from lift and gravity, and partly because he really wanted to know, Norman said, "Mr. B., why do people like bombers so much? My dad sells them."

"Yes." Mr. B. lowered the kite frame. "Well, we might ask the question like this: Is our attraction for bombers primarily utilitarian? That is, is it a means to an end, a way of getting something we might not have otherwise, not unlike two kittens scrabbling over a piece of meat, the kitten with the sharper claws being the victor? Yes? Or is there actually something alluring in the power of destruction itself, hmm?"

Norman fingered a pair of scissors.

"Perhaps it is just a phase we human beings are going through. Human beings, like house cats, are a manifestation of neoteny—that is, the holding on to childishness in adulthood. In many ways we are childish, hairless apes. And within our own species, we celebrate full-grown immaturity, everywhere. Think for a moment how much we pay people to throw a ball or hit one with a piece of wood. I'm sure you have seen and perhaps even met many childish adults? Yes. And goodness knows, children are ruthless and adore weapons of any kind. There is nothing so terrible as a three-year-old with a stick. One shudders! The human family as a whole, I should say, is still a three-year-old with a stick."

"But that's horrible!" said Norman, dropping the scissors.

"Well, yes. And yet, by some miracle, three-year-olds do,

sometimes, grow up. And if they grow properly, they learn to play nicely. They observe, they study, they imagine."

"But three-year-olds have teachers and parents. Who is going to teach the adults? Aliens from Mars?"

"Not at all, not at all. The objects already in this rich universe possess within them all the teaching we need. Mother Earth herself will teach us. And don't misunderstand me, Norman. I would not reduce the world merely to a series of causes and effects, mere materialism. Some who have studied the world conclude that we, even you and I, are merely the end product of millions upon millions of these causes and effects, and that there is really no such thing as a personality, a unique you or a unique me. Even a thirteen-year-old knows this is nonsense. It remains a fact that I am I and you are you, and we each think and move and feel out of our own I-ness."

"I-ness?"

"I-ness. For instance, consider me for a moment. I know that I am composed of thousands of millions of cells. I have seen my own cells with my own eyes, which are themselves made of cells. By careful observation, I have seen that these cells have lives of their own, living and dying within me. I have seen them and I know them. But they do not know me. The I-ness of me, though made only of them, is more than them, it is I. You see? And it may be that we are even more complicated than this. It is common to speak of body and soul—perhaps you know the lovely song by Johnny Green—which would indicate an I-ness made of two parts, but there may be more. Perhaps we are divided into three parts, or four or seven, each functioning with and separately from the others."

"Doesn't anybody know?"

"Oh no, not yet. Remember, we're all more or less still

a three-year-old with a stick. Maybe we will know when our human family has grown, when it becomes more interested in the joys of conversation and study and less in beating one another over the head. When will this happen? Who knows, maybe when we all get a little more sleep. Look at cats, they sleep eighteen hours a day."

"I feel tired," said Norman, sitting down.

"Yes, that's the problem, isn't it? We're all staying up too late," said Balthazar, looking at Norman. "And we're not making any progress with this kite," he said.

"I think there's not much chance of getting enough lift for any kite when it's raining like it is right now," said Norman.

"Too true, too true. Let us put aside our physics project for the time being. I know of only two sources of sufficient lift for a day like this one."

"What are they?"

"One small cappuccino and one large hot chocolate."

"*Mit Schlag?*"

"*Mit* most definitely *Schlag*. Until I return with the heavily laden tray, you may keep your hands from any weaponry by reading your *Ps*."

* * *

Balthazar Birdsong returned not only with hot beverages but with sweet bakery items as well, thinking perhaps that this very dreary day called for special mood reinforcement. Sitting down, he began to distribute the sundry items from the tray, saying, "What have you learned?"

"'Pelf' and 'pell-mell,'" said Norman.

"Two most excellent words, both managing to indicate their meanings by their very sounds. 'Pelf,' noun for stolen goods. One does not even like to say it. 'Pelf.' Phooey. And 'pell-mell,' adverb for chaotically. Is it possible to say this word, 'pell-mell,' in a stately manner? No. You try it. To say it is to be it. By the way, let me ask you

pell-mell

something, so that an unexpected phone call does not send us pell-mell into a state of upset and confusion. When does your mother intend to pick you up today?"

"She's not. My dad is."

"Is he? He has returned from his peregrinations? Another fine *P* word, meaning travels, by the way."

"Yup. And he's probably packing pelf."

"Tut-tut. Is he? Do tell."

Before Norman could tell, a buzzing came from the house phone by the door.

"Not your father already?" said Mr. B. on his way to answer it.

Norman quickly finished what remained of his hot chocolate and his *Schlag*, while listening to Mr. B. say, "Yes, yes, yes, he shall be down presently."

He hung up the phone. "Your father awaits. 'Presently,' another fine *P* word, which, contrary to popular usage, primarily means 'soon,' though the use of it for 'now' is not, technically, incorrect."

Norman stood up from the table as Mr. B. lifted Norman's jacket from its hook, saying, "I fear you must go. Until next week, be conscious of your I-ness and please be punctual— adjective, on time."

obushead

In front of the Maestro Building, the rain streamed across the sidewalk. Pulling his jacket over his head, Norman raced across the pavement and grabbed the handle of the rear door, which his father had pushed ajar. Safely inside, Norman was a bit surprised to find his father hunched over the steering wheel, making bomber and machine-gun noises. But only a bit.

Accustomed to most of his father's childishness, Norman just buckled his seat belt.

"Ehnnnynaaaawww. BABOOM! Eh eh eh eh eh eheheheheh. Bch. Bch. Bch! Babababbabbababbabba. Pich pich pich pich— kaFWOOM!" said Orman Normann, all the while turning the steering wheel left and right.

"Dad?"

"Pf, pf, pf, pf, pf. Kakakaka ba. Baba BOOM!"

"Dad?"

"Pppppppppp. Mpmpmpmpmp! Mmmmm meh meh mmmm meh meh maow maow!"

"Dad?"

"Hello there, boyo! I see you're already strapped in, which is good—we're going for a ride."

"Could we just go home? I kind of have a lot of homework."

"Sure, Norm, sure. But why rush? You still have Sunday. Heck, you still have Sunday night. Sunday night's the time for homework. Now's the time for you to learn a little something about the bomber business," said Orman Normann, putting the car into gear.

Orman Normann eased the Normann sedan away from the curb and out through the puddled streets toward the river. As he drove, he regaled Norman with tales of his recent super-duper bomber-business salesmanship.

"Hooey, when it rains it rains. Now everybody wants bombers. Well, almost everybody. The Alfurnians are still holding out, but everybody else, everybody else is going crazy, acting like, like, like . . ."

"A three-year-old with a stick?"

"A three-year-old with a stick! Hot jimjams! I love three-year-olds. I love sticks!"

Orman Normann sped up as he approached a lakelike, corner-curbside puddle, sending an enormous spray across the sidewalk.

"Dad, I think you just soaked a nun."

"Nunsense!"

"I gct it," said Norman, wishing his father would get it—the fact that he was turning into an obtuse obushead.

They crossed the George Washington Bridge, which carried them into suburban New Jersey, and entered an expressway, which headed them south along the other side of the river. Norman vaguely recognized that they were traveling toward the Newark airport, skimming over the slick pavement at high speed, a ragged layer of low stratocumulus clouds drifting across their path. All the while, his father sang along to the overwrought squawk of the classic-rock radio and occasionally drummed the dashboard with his right hand to its rhythm.

Just before the turn to the airport, Orman Normann steered the car down a ramp off the highway, bringing them around and under railroad trestles into a bleak neighborhood of anonymous warehouses, many with large trailer trucks protruding from open garages like gargantuan caterpillars, or medium-sized dragons, their great grimacing grills towering above the car's windows as Norman looked out forlornly. Along this parade of giants they crawled for several blocks, Orman leaning this way and that, apparently trying to find an address. At last, with a grunt, he pulled the car over to the curb in front of a single-story, buff-brick building with glass-block windows. Shutting off the engine and pocketing his keys, Orman said, "Norman, wait here. I'll be back in a minute."

Norman's father trotted off across the pitted pavement and banged on a battered black metal door, which some seconds later opened an inch or two wider than he was thick. He slipped inside.

The rain no longer hammered but pinged diffidently on the roof. Norman peered out the front and rear windows at the neighborhood; it was blank wall fronts or idle trailer trucks and cars, empty of any human life, or any other life that he could see.

Norman settled back in his seat, undid his seat belt, and thought about his I-ness. "My I-ness is definitely alone on this miserable street. I would rather my I-ness were in my own house and room and bed. I know I'm me, and I'm right here, but I wish I were there."

The rain dripped on the horribly still car, the air in the car itself seeming depressed and bored.

Norman Normann pulled Alfred the Great out of his pocket and imagined himself and Alfred far away.

Alfred the Great stood alone at the end of a long, cobbled alley, somewhere in the dreariest part of dreary medieval

London, where several Danish assassins looked forward to making him miserable. Alfred the Great silently drew his sword from beneath his robes and placed his left leg one step in front of his right, keeping both knees slightly bent, with his back foot turned out and bearing most of his weight. He inhaled deeply. Suddenly one of the assassins leaped out of the shadows and . . .

Even the Danes got boring.

The rain thrummed a little louder on the roof.

Norman scanned the street again. "'Back in a minute,'" he grumbled. "More like back in an hour."

A jet flew overhead, unseen in the darkening sky, but low and loud.

It was funny, thought Norman. When he was with his friends or at school, he never really thought about his parents. He could be away from them for twelve hours and never think about them once. Maybe it was just because everyone was where they were supposed to be. But if they were not where they were supposed to be, like now, Norman missed his mother and his father with all the energy his I-ness had.

What would his life be like without them? Now that Norman thought about it, possibly exciting. He would be on his own, ready to meet the world's challenges by himself. No more would anyone be fussing about his clothes or his hair or whether he paid any attention to his teachers. He would be Norman the Great, Norman the Conqueror.

He would be miserable. Norman was wise enough to know that he would be miserable. He wondered how it was, anyway, that we get our parents? He knew about sex and everything, how babies were made. Theoretically, anyway. But who says you get your particular parents? Because of all the parents Norman had seen, only his own seemed somehow the right ones, even if his father acted like a three-year-old with a stick. Much as he loved Leonard and his mother, Mrs. Piquant, if ever he stayed overnight with them . . . It was strange, there were too many strange things. For instance, Leonard slept in his socks. How could you sleep in your socks? And Mrs. Piquant smelled wrong, not bad, but wrong. And the bathroom was mysterious. How was each child assigned to his or her parents? He would have to remember to raise this question with Leonard himself, next time they were together. Perhaps the answers could be worked into their Theory of the Air Terminal of the Afterlife.

The day had grown darker and the streetlights had come on. The rain was again a little louder.

Speaking of the afterlife, what if he, Norman, contracted a terrible illness and was about to die? That would be cool. Everyone would come to see him and give him absolutely anything he wished for. He could say, weakly, "Mom, all I want is my own hot-air balloon, just to ride around in for one last weekend." Bingo. Norman would get a hot-air balloon.

Of course, at some point, Norman acknowledged to himself, he would have to die, and this was maybe not so great. On second thought, maybe it was not worth the hot-air balloon.

He missed his father. Where was he? Why was he not selling something—anything—besides bombers and not leaving him alone in this awful place in this awful car? Norman peered out the side window; the night had settled into its full darkness, the clouds were now black, the branches of the few rotten trees blacker.

Norman looked out at the street again, now yellow in the harsh sulfurous glow of the streetlights. He thought he heard a bang. Maybe his father was finally coming back.

Norman jumped. Something was scuffling on the other side

of the car, in the back. Hesitantly, jerkily, Norman turned his head to see.

Framed by the opposite window, he saw a hand reaching out of a rough brown sleeve, moving toward the door handle.

The hand was missing its thumb.

no thumbs mcsweeney

Wop weep woop. The key-chain remote sounded and the door locks popped open.

The thumbless hand began to pull the door open.

How did he open the door without a thumb? thought Norman. Will this be the last question I ever ask myself? Norman thought next.

Before either of these questions could be answered, Norman's father appeared at the front of the car and, sidling around and opening his door, let himself fall into the driver's seat, just as whoever was attached to that thumbless hand did the same in the back.

Orman Normann hiked himself up, craned his two chins around, and, beaming a wide smile, said, "Sorry about the delay, Norman. Business, you know. Never mind. Norman, I'd like you to meet my good friend and partner." He shot a glance at the man and continued in an aside, "It's all right, I don't keep anything from my son." Then he looked back at Norman. "N. T. McSweeney, Norman Normann. Norman, N. T. McSweeney."

Norman looked at his father's good friend and partner. Besides a rough brown corduroy jacket, he wore a floppy leather cap. His face, shiny like Norman's father's, presented a large nose, deep-set eyes, and a broad chin covered with stubble. He placed a briefcase between his feet.

"Pleased as poonch tae meet ye," said N. T. McSweeney, holding out his right, epollicate hand.

Norman took it in his, with a weak smile, carefully sliding himself farther into his own corner of the backseat. Hearing this voice, Norman knew now that his father's good friend and partner, or G.F. and P., was the E.M.M. and the S.U.V., the epollicate mystery man and the sinister, unfamiliar voice.

"Aye, ye've nowticed me wee loss o' me wee tums, have ye?" Norman smiled more broadly, yet more weakly, if such a thing is possible.

"Ah'll tell ye hoo it coom tae pass tat Ah lost me wee tums. Ye see, 'twas a booling accident."

"Booling?" said Norman.

"Booling, aye, wit nine pins, an' all. Aye, 'twas a terrible day tat Ah lost me pur tums, but tair's nae need tae gae intae it, noo, is tair noo?"

"Nae, noo, nee, na, noo, ni," said Norman, sliding ever farther into his corner.

"Norman," said his father, "No Thumbs here and I have just a couple more stops to make along the way. You just sit tight and we'll be home in a jiffy-jam. No Thumbs is going to sit with you in the back because it makes him nervous to ride in front, him used to driving on the left and all. He's got a million stories. No Thumbs, tell him the one about the little old lady and the M-37 tank."

As N. T. McSweeney told the tale of the little old lady and the M-37 tank, and the car retraced its route back to the city, Norman reviewed the situation. First of all, the E.M.M. or the G.F. and P. (or the S.U.V.) was not, as he guessed when he first glimpsed him on a terrace opposite the Maestro Building, a motivational speaker. That was right out. And as for a bowling accident, it was probably more likely a TNT accident, or a deadly dagger accident, or even a crocodile accident. All Norman knew for certain was that he would prefer to put as much space between himself and N. T. McSweeney as possible. But at the moment he was trapped by four car doors and about ten lanes of traffic.

After they crossed the Hudson River, Orman Normann bypassed Buddingdale Heights and took them, instead, to the upper east side of Manhattan, where the clean streets were lined by spreading trees and the sidewalks reposed neat and gumless in front of elegant mansions.

Some of these mansions had a national flag hanging above the front door. Orman Normann double-parked—that is, parked the car in the middle of the street next to an already parked car—at a house with a flag of orange, black, and yellow stripes.

"Norman," he said, "I want you to slide up here into the front seat and pretend you're the driver."

"But I'm only thirteen years old!"

"I know, I know. Here, put on these sunglasses. No one's gonna ask any questions. We'll be back in a minute."

"You said that last time," said Norman, but both doors had already slammed.

Norman climbed into the front seat. He looked around. At least it's a better neighborhood, he thought warily.

This time Orman was as good as his word, nearly, for a few minutes later both men descended the front steps and opened the doors as Norman jumped into the back.

"How do you manage to . . ." Norman began to say to N. T. McSweeney, who was buckling his seat belt.

"Hoo dae Ah . . . ? Oh, tat. Ah've me ways."

"Just one more stop," said Orman, starting the car.

No Thumbs turned his wide face toward Norman again, leaned across the middle seat, and said, "Wot dae ye call summon wot's got nae legs an' nae arms an' sits in froont o' the door?"

"I dinno," said Norman, wishing they could get off the subject of limb loss.

"Mat."

"Oh boy," said Norman.

"Ye git it?"

"I git it."

Norman smiled his by now trademark weak smile and made a show of being terribly interested in the passing street life out his window.

The flag hanging in front of the next mansion they stopped at was overall green with a blue moon and orange stars.

Again, his father asked Norman to sit in front.

"Dad, I hate this. What if someone comes? My feet don't even reach all the way to the pedals."

"Just like the Katong Luangans, ha-ha!" said Orman. "You'll be fine. Here, chew some gum and look bored but sort of dangerous."

Norman did his best to look bored but sort of dangerous, but was not fine. Still, nothing unpleasant happened before the two again descended the front steps.

Orman Normann pulled the car up to the red light at the end of the block.

Once more, N. T. McSweeney took this as an opportunity to lean across the middle seat and say to Norman, "Wot dae ye call summon wot's got nae arms an' nae legs an' flowts?"

"I dinno," said Norman, doing his best to shut his ears from the inside.

"Bob."

Norman said, "Dad, I've really got to get home now. I've got tons of homework."

"Last stop, Norman," said his father, parking in front of a mansion with a flag that was half yellow and half blue and showed the black silhouette of a two-headed eagle.

Norman climbed into the front seat a third time. He chewed gum and felt bored but even less dangerous.

Back in the backseat, as the car pulled away and N. T. McSweeney rummaged among many papers in his battered briefcase, Norman thought he spotted the shiny cover of an L. L. Bomb bomber catalogue.

N. T. McSweeney said, "Noo, last one. Wot dae ye call summon wot's got nae arms an' nae legs an' works fer the Sanitation Departmint?"

Norman smiled his weakest smile of the evening. "I give up."

"Chook."

* * *

"Chook?" said Leonard.

"That's what he said."

"Chook? But that makes no sense and is repulsive all at the same time!"

"I know. I know. But that's what he said."

Norman, Leonard, and the twins were making final adjustments to their Halloween costumes in the Normann kitchen.

Halloween, every right-thinking person's favorite holiday, was still taken very seriously by our four friends, with much planning and costume making. Anna and Emma had proposed this year to appear as a knife and fork; it was traditional for them to go as a paired set.

Leonard and Norman, too, had decided to go as a set, which

was unusual for them, as Norman generally went as some sort of invertebrate—a worm, perhaps, or an oyster on the half shell—while Leonard favored the more active roles, such as mad scientist or undertaker. However, this year they agreed that the only choice for them was to wow the public as two members of the Alfurnian Imperial Guard. Their costumes would include the works, from furry infundibular hats to shiny black boots. Both opted for long mustaches as well.

In the city, a cluster of blocks on the Upper West Side always hosted a boisterous Halloween street party and parade. In past years, Orman Normann had taken the boys trick-or-treating. This year, however, he said, "Scare the city without me, boys. No Thumbs and I have got something a-cookin'." Therefore, it would be Norman's mother who would take them and the twins into the city in the car.

Anna placed another strip of duct tape on the back of her fork. "So you think your dad's a spy or something."

"A used-bomber salesman," Norman corrected her.

"Whatever. A used-bomber salesman, then."

"Up to his double chin in trouble."

"Up to his double chin in trouble. And the reason you think your dad is in trouble is because you managed to open an empty safe and then rode around with him to some place in New Jersey and someplace else in the city, with a guy with no thumbs."

"Or sense of humor, apparently," said Emma.

"And a lot of other things besides," said Leonard. "Tell them about the codes, and about the maze, and the Katong Luangans and the Alfurnians."

"Right," said Norman, "there were Alfurnian Guards chasing us around Vienna."

"It just sounds like your run-of-the-mill kerfuffle," said Emma.

"Where did you get that word?" said Norman.

"Found it in the dictionary, so there."

"That reminds me, I should be reading the Qs. Well, maybe it *is* just a kerfuffle, but I think my dad's in trouble and he needs my help."

"There's only one thing to do when you find yourself in a kerfuffle," said Emma.

"What's that?" said Leonard.

"First gather, and then consume, tons and tons of candy."

giant pixies

The day of Halloween was crisp and cool.

By evening, the air was a little cooler, but not so cool as to discourage the already hundreds of costumed revelers milling about the streets. The houses were bedecked with every variety of skeletal ghoul and lumpish fiend. One long-windowed house even provided an enormous spider, which dropped from a tree out front. Here and there, smoke and steam rose ominously through the groupings of living monsters, Freddys, cowboys, X-Men, and princesses, all looking slightly sinister, appropriately or inappropriately, in the half-light.

Norma, Norman, Leonard, and the twins, having parked the Normann car, proceeded into the slowly churning cauldron of costumed people.

"Look! Look at him!" said Anna under her breath, pointing discreetly at a large, red-haired, middle-aged man, fat cigar in his alfiona lips, who was dressed in pink tights, a shimmering bodice, and gauzy fairy wings.

"He's a big, hairy, blotchy, pasty, smelly-looking, overgrown pixie," said Emma.

"Spooky," said Anna.

The twins made a fine cutlery set, their long torsos neatly hidden within the handles, their faces showing through oval cutouts in the knife blade and below the fork tines. The tines over Anna's head looked like four, fat, silver hairs.

Leonard and Norman began to march up the sidewalk in step. They came to a halt, clicked their heels, and saluted.

"What are you two again, nutcrackers?" said Emma.

"Alfurnians! Members of the Alfurnian Imperial Guard. You know, the ones we keep telling you about," said Leonard.

"Oh yeah, those guys. Well, I like your mustaches."

They began to move along with the crowd.

"Oh dear," said Norma. "This is a little too much for me. I think I'll just wait for you back at the car. All right? Now don't lose anybody. We don't want to come home without a complete set of utensils, do we, ha-ha!"

"Good one, Mrs. Normann," said Leonard.

"We don't want to be accused of walking off with the spoons!" said Norma.

"None of us are spoons," said Norman.

"Well, you know what I mean."

"Okay, Mom. We'll see you a little later."

Norma left them as they reached the end of the first block, treat bags slowly filling.

"Guess what?" said Anna.

"Chicken butt," said Emma and Norman together.

"Exactly. I think I just saw a man dressed as a chicken butt."

"Eww," said Emma.

"Wow, look over there!" said Leonard. "It's Thing One and Thing Two, eeeyaaaa!"

And so the evening went. After an hour, all of our friends' eyes began to glaze over and generally looked the color of candy corn, so our little troop commenced the return trip to the parked car. The four were shuffling along, examining their candy loot, when Norman suddenly pointed wildly, his mouth open, nearly losing a sucker.

"What is it, Norman?" said Anna.

"It's the Ah, Ah, Ah, Ah, it's the Ah, Ah, Ah," said Norman, still pointing, the others looking but seeing nothing remarkable.

"Look!" Norman tried again. "It's the Ah, Ah, Ah." Leonard whacked him on the back with the side of his sword.

"Ow! It's the Alfurnians, the real ones!"

Over the heads of the paraders, the two, tall, furry hats, like upside-down ice cream cones, couldn't be missed. Though seen from the back, the tall hats were unmistakable.

The taller of the two began to turn around.

"Duck!" said Norman.

"I'm ducking!" said Leonard.

They all quickly hid behind a small flock of young mothers in devil horns who were pushing huge perambulators with babies in devil horns, the group offering substantial cover.

"What? What? What? What?" said Anna and Emma together.

"It's the Alfurnians we were telling you about," said Norman. "They're the ones that were chasing us in Vienna, and now they're here!"

"Come on," said Emma.

"No! Yes!" said Leonard. "It's definitely them. Anna, stand up slowly and see if they're coming this way."

The points of the tines of Anna's fork costume rose like antennae, until she stood on tiptoe, weaving back and forth a bit, like a fork that has just lost its appetizer.

"What do you see?" hissed Leonard.

"Nothing. Just a lot of people—ohmygod, it's them! Yes, they're coming this way!"

Anna dove back down.

The devil moms with their devil babies began to perambulate.

The four duckers perambulated with them, only, being bent double, they perambulated like crabs, or ducks.

"This is stupid!" said Emma. "This is ridiculous." And she stood up.

"Eeeeeeyaaaa!" she shrieked.

The two Alfurnian Imperial Guards—for Norman and Leonard were quite correct—were striding forcefully toward them and were only a couple of houses away. Cameras flashed, ghosts moaned, and all around them haunted music thumped its bass.

"Oh boy," said Emma, slowly stepping back onto Norman's foot.

"Ouch! What do we do?"

"I don't . . ."

A moment later, the Alfurnian Guards were running at them, their monstrous mustaches streaming behind.

Just as the Alfurnians were almost within lunging range, our friend, the overgrown pixie, began hooting and waving, making the Alfurnians stop and stare, aghast at this spectacle. The large pixie continued to hoot. And then, when the Alfurnians seemed to remember that they had other things to do, a dozen more big, pudgy, pasty, white-and-pink, middle-aged pixies, who were apparently part of some pixie reunion, surged forward, laughing and shouting and shaking hands all around. The Alfurnians were corralled and unable to move, fenced in by tubby arms and legs and clasped hands. There were pixies on all sides of them, hugging and high-fiving. The Alfurnian hats bobbed in the thicket of arms and legs.

"Run!" said Emma.

Anna, Leonard, and Norman thought this sounded like a good idea, and they all ran pell-mell for the open spaces and the avenue where the car was parked, with Norma presumably inside it.

Rounding the corner, and in sight of the car, Norman shouted, still running and clutching his furry hat to his head, "We're ready to go home now, Mom. We're really, really, really ready to go home now."

Norma Normann, sticking her head out the window, called back, "All right, dears, climb in," and started the car.

Norman wrenched open the back door, and all four scrambled into the backseat. At last, with the door slammed convincingly and locked, Norma pulled the car away from the curb. Looking back, they could clearly make out the Alfurnians coming around the corner.

"Did you have a nice time?" said Norma, over her shoulder.

"Sure did, Mom," said Norman, turning from the back window.

"Fantastic," said Leonard, panting.

"Very educational," said Anna, wiping her brow.

"We were saved by a troupe of giant pixies," said Emma.

"That's nice, dears," said Mrs. Normann, pressing down on the accelerator. "I always think it's nice to be saved."

Ps and Qs (and Rs)

Just above the tower of the Maestro Building, a thick layer of stratocumulus opacus hung gloomily and determinedly, allowing, as the name suggests, very little light to pass through its featureless blanket. Sometimes, on a day like this, you can just tell where the sun is as it passes behind the clouds, a bit of lighter grayness in the gray. Not so on this day. The city's face was ashen. An occasional cold mist wet the roofs, but so little light reflected from the oily puddles left by the meager precipitation that they failed to glisten. Norman sat in Balthazar Birdsong's old armchair as its owner busied himself with the coffee and hot chocolate.

"This should cheer us up," said Mr. B., placing the trayful of hot beverages on the small table next to Norman.

"It won't."

"Drink."

Norman drank.

"I'm worried," said Norman.

"What about, dear boy?"

"Well, I'm worried about my dad. I think he's in some kind of bad business. And I'm worried about the Alfurnians, who are part of the bad business. And I'm worried about the test I have to take in January, which is not that far away. Darn it!"

"I see. I imagine your concern for your father is spilling over into everything else. And this story of the Alfurnians, and their apparent interest in yourself, is indicative of something unwelcome, though I'm uncertain as to what. However, I'm not sure that we can actively undertake steps regarding your first and second concerns. On the other hand, your last concern, as to the impending test, well, we've been preparing for that all year, haven't we? You have been reading the dictionary, I trust? You know my creed: Welcome to Pennsylvania. Now read the dictionary."

"What? We don't even live in Pennsylvania."

"What of it? 'Pennsylvania' is a wonderful word. You have read your *P*s?"

"Yes."

"What about your *Q*s? Taking a squint at the calendar here, I would say you should be done with your *Q*s by now, hmm?"

"Um."

"Yes?"

"I haven't read my *Q*s," said Norman, resting his cheek on his fist. "I've been meaning to, but I guess I've been distracted."

"In other words, you've minded your *P*s, but not your *Q*s."

"I suppose so. I mean, I suppose not."

"Never mind. As a matter of fact, I have been remiss in my duties and have nothing planned for us today, so what better way to pass the time than to sip hot chocolate and coffee and read our *Q*s? Here." Balthazar rose from his chair to fetch and place in Norman's lap the enormous dictionary.

"Ooof," said Norman.

"Yes, we've done the *O*s. Now the *Q*s. Just read a sampling to me."

Norman heaved the pages over slowly until he reached the *Q*s, then cleared his throat.

He read, "'Quack, verb, to make the sound of a duck.'"

"Very, very nice. An onomatopoeic word and one of the best. A word that means as it sounds. Quack. Cast your eyes farther down and see if English-speaking humanity has made any more of this word."

"'Quack, noun, doctor.' 'Quackster, noun, a fraud,'" said Norman. "Also, 'quackish.'"

"Now we're really getting somewhere. Quackster, excellent. I'm curious to know why the sound of a duck has implied to our ears untruthfulness. Why not, say, the sound of a cow? Why 'quack' and not 'moo'? Let us shelve this inquiry for the time being. Go on."

"'Quadrumvirate, noun, a foursome, a group of four men.' Hey, that could be Leonard, Anna, Emma, and me! Except that none of us are men."

"No matter. You may rest assured that, in this case, 'men' means all of humanity. The four of you make a perfect quadrumvirate. Did I mention that the letter Q is one of my favorites? The Romans were fond of it as well."

"'Quaestor, noun, a Roman official in finance.'"

"You see?"

Norman took a long swallow of hot chocolate.

"Hey, I like this one: 'quaff, verb, to drink deeply,' or 'quaff, noun, a long drink.'"

"Splendid suggestion," said Balthazar. He quaffed.

Norman quaffed.

"Ouch!"

"Stick to the Qs, please."

"I mean, 'Ouch, I burned my tongue.' Okay, 'quagmire, noun, soft ground, a swamp.'"

"Let us avoid them. Here, let me browse a bit," he said, standing and lifting the heavy tome from Norman. "You quaff your cocoa."

Mr. B. read with the dictionary cradled in his left arm.

"Ah, here is a favorite of mine. 'Quirk, noun, a groove separating bits of molding in carpentry.' Or, 'a peculiarity, an odd trait or twist.' Again, like 'quack,' here is a word that began its life describing one thing and now describes another, from the particular to the general. In fact, our English language is full of funny little quirks. Scanning farther, we come to someone of your Scandinavian heritage. Quisling. Poor man, his name now lives ever on as synonymous with 'traitor.' One thing I'm sure you will never be, my dear Norman: a quisling quack."

Norman smiled and quaffed.

Mr. B. continued, "And here's one we all know and love. 'Queen, noun, loosely defined as the king's better half.'"

Norman quaffed and dreamed.

Alfred the Great, with head bowed, knelt on one knee before a woman. She looked tall, even though she was sitting down. Her long, curling red hair cascaded over her shoulders, its mellow scent of chilly mountain streams diffusing in the air. Her diaphanous gown shimmered over bare feet. Gazing at Alfred the Great, she said, "Well, Alfred?"

queen

Alfred, summoning all of his great, medium-great, and super-great powers, said, "Princess Theodosia"— for this was her name—"will you be my queen?"

Princess Theodosia parted her lips and—

"Norman. Norman, you seem to have dozed off. The lesson is concluded," and Balthazar Birdsong closed the great book with a thump.

* * *

Sitting at the kitchen table that afternoon, Norman continued his studies in the dictionary, chin solidly in both palms.

His mother floated past him, lifted the hot glass carafe from its parking spot in the coffee machine, and poured the odiferous brew into her pink mug. Returning to the doorway, she paused behind Norman's chair and said, "Watchadoin'?"

"Reading the dictionary," said Norman.

"I wonder if you shouldn't be playing video games or looking at the Innernets or listening to your eye-pot or something, like other boys."

"I'm fine, Mom."

"All right, dear," she said and, with a slurp of coffee, scuffed out of the room.

Norman read.

roupy *adj* : **hoarse**

Norman cleared his throat and read on.

rouse *vb* : **to stir up**
roustabout *n* : **a handyman**

"Nice word," said Norman quietly to himself.

route *n* : **the way to go**
routine *n* : **a regular course of things**
roux *n* : **a flour and butter mixture used to thicken soups and sauces**
rove *vb* : **to roam or ramble**
rover *n* : **a wanderer, a pirate**

"I thought it was just a dog's name."

row *n* : a quarrel
row *vb* : to move using oars
row *n* : a line of things
rowboat *n* : a boat for rowing

"Duh."

rowdy, rowdyish *adj* : rough, noisy
rowel *n* : a little spiked wheel on the end of a spur
rowen *n* : the second growth, aftermath
royal *adj* : of or about kings and queens; magnificent,
    grand

rowel

Norman leaned back in his chair and said, "Of course, *Royal Wedding*."

royal wedding

Ever since they all were small, a routine had developed between the twins and Norman, in which they would meet in the Normann living room, once or twice a month, for a movie night. Besides featuring a film, these evenings included plenty of buttered popcorn and one tall mug each of root-beer float. Leonard joined the routine when he became Norman's official best friend at school, sometime during the third grade. After the movie was shown, it was discussed. For instance:

Its Merits: "Good scary bits"—Anna
Its Faults: "Boring fight scene. I mean, how many lives
  is this guy supposed to have?"—Emma
The Acting: "Lousy—all she ever did was scream"—Leonard
The Plot: "I didn't get it when they stole the parrot—
  why'd they do that?"—Norman

And so forth. Sometimes these discussions took place during the movie, of course, and sometimes the discussion had no bearing whatsoever on the movie they were watching.

Such was the case one night, during the viewing of *Royal Wedding*, when Anna and Emma expounded at length upon a particularly difficult social situation—this was in the fourth grade—involving Chastity Ziegenhals, a half-eaten tuna melt, and Benjamin Franklin's famous experiment with the kite, the key, and the lightning storm.

Ever afterward *Royal Wedding* had become the code

words for calling together a gathering of the foursome—or Quadrumvirate, as Norman now liked to say during which, as the film played, matters of special difficulty or urgency could be addressed and discussed by all.

* * *

Norma Normann chugged into the kitchen, bearing down on the coffee machine.

"Mom," said Norman, "I think you and Dad need a night out. Dad's been traveling so much, you hardly ever get a chance to see each other, you know, just to be together by yourselves."

"Why, Norman, what a nice idea. And so, so thoughtful," she said, stopping to put a hand on Norman's shoulder and her cheek to his.

"Right, Mom. How about tonight?"

And so it was arranged, the great call going out: "*Royal Wedding*, tonight at seven-thirty."

* * *

"The stove's off and I've put the big pot in the sink to soak," said Norman, standing at the front door, speaking to his mother, who waited on the walk for Norman's father to bring the car around from the alley, the chilly late-fall air slowly crawling over Norman's stockinged feet.

Norma Normann said, "Make sure the stove's off, and please, put the big pot in the sink to soak."

"The big pot's in the sink to soak, and I promise we'll all just have one root-beer float each."

"Please, darling, promise me you'll all just have one root-beer float each."

"One root-beer float each, and I know you love me oodles and oodles."

"Oh, Norman, do you know how much I love you? Oodles

217

and oodles," said Norma Normann, blowing her son a kiss almost kittenishly and nipping out to the car.

"Bye, Mom, bye, Dad," said Norman, shutting the door.

"Next time I've got to wear my slippers!" announced Norman to his friends as he hurried into the living room.

"All right," called Emma, through a fistful of buttery popcorn, "place the beloved DVD into the beloved DVD machine and press the revered Play."

"Pressing the revered Play," said Anna.

The large television flickered to life and turned everything in the otherwise-unlit room blue, even the popcorn. The four were in their accustomed places, like senators in a Senate, only here the discussion was sometimes, but not always, more immature. Anna lay on her left side on the sofa, knees tucked up and her head on the armrest; Leonard sat on the floor, with his knees pointing forward and his feet pointing back, as close to the screen as he could get without blocking the others' view; Emma sprawled in the large leather recliner, tilted back; Norman sat on the back of the sofa, with his feet on the seat cushions, a pose to which his mother, had she been in the room, would have objected. Munching their popcorn, they watched as the credits came on during the overture, displayed like elegant invitations to a grandiose affair. As some of you no doubt know, in the film Fred Astaire and Jane Powell play a brother-and-sister, show-biz couple who, in the first scene, perform the wonderful song-and-dance routine "Ev'ry Night at Seven," with Fred Astaire's character, Tom Bowen, playing a king and Jane Powell as his sister, Ellen, playing a housemaid.

"The reason I—" said Norman.

"Shhhhhhhhh!" said the twins.

Norman had violated the first rule when calling for a *Royal Wedding*, which was that there be no discussion until after this first dance number—in fact, not until Tom and Ellen Bowen's agent, Irving, says the line "Who's da square?"

At last, Irving the agent said, "Who's da square?"

"So," said Emma, "what's the hubbub, bub?"

"I've called this meeting of the Quadrumvirate—"

"This meeting of the what?" said Anna.

"The Quadrumvirate, noun, a group of four men or, in our case, four human beings," said Norman.

"Pass me that dictionary," said Emma, stretching toward Norman, "because I suppose that's where you got that one from."

Norman reached down to the end table where the dictionary lay and passed it to her.

"Be my guest. Maybe you'll find something to help me with my problem. Read the *S*s."

"What's the problem?" said Anna.

"My dad, of course. He's traveling too much, I hardly ever see him, he just got back from who knows where last night and I think he's already leaving who knows when, and when I do see him, I always check to make sure he still has all his fingers. What if something happens to him? I don't want my dad to be called No Toes Normann or Earless Orman."

"Or Four Fingers Orman," Leonard suggested.

"Or just Scarface," offered Anna.

"Stop!" said Norman. "Thank you, we've all got the picture."

"Shirty," said Emma.

"What?" said Norman.

"Shirty," said Emma. "Norman, you're being shirty, it says so right here in the dictionary. 'Shirty, adjective, ill-tempered.' Don't be so shirty, Norman."

"Be socky," said Anna.

"That's right, say you're socky, Norman," said Leonard.

"All right, all right, I'm socky—I mean, I'm sorry," said Norman. "What I want help with is what to do with my dad. How to save him from the bomber business. Leonard had some good ideas before—thank you, by the way, Leonard, for those. But . . . they didn't work. We need a new plan. Something that's a sure bet. Something foolproof."

"How about we keep him here by, say, breaking both of his legs somehow," said Leonard. "That way he won't be able to travel and he'll lose all of his bomber buyers and have to quit."

"Shish kebab," said Emma.

"No, break his legs!" said Leonard. "Not shish kebab."

"'Shish kebab! Noun, roast meat broiled on a skewer.'"

"No, no, no, no," said Anna, standing up on the sofa and twirling once, then jumping lightly onto the ottoman. "No leg breaking. You watch too many spy movies, Leonard, that James Bond stuff doesn't work in real life. Forget James Bond, it's time to try the Miss Marple approach, more subtle, more wise. We will consider the psychology of the individual."

"Shit," said Emma.

"What?" said Anna.

"'Shit.' It's actually in the dictionary."

"What do you mean, 'shit'?" said Norman. "I think Anna might have a good idea."

"Look. 'Shit, shat, shitting, shits, verb, to defecate.'"

"Wow," said Anna, "no shit."

"I didn't know you could say 'shat,'" said Leonard.

"Who knew 'shit' has a past tense," said Anna.

"It also has a history," said Emma. "'Shit, noun, from the Old English, shite, usually vulgar, excrement.'"

"Vulgar, oh really?" said Leonard. "I had no idea."

"That reminds me," said Anna, sitting down again, "once, our social-studies teacher, Mr. Tattlesmith, was trying to impress us girls or something and he was saying that the word 'shit' came from exploding manure on boats, or something, so they stamped 'Store High In Transit, S.H.I.T.' on boxes, and that's how it got its name or something."

Leonard said, "Sounds like Mr. Tattlesmith is full of—"

"'Shitten, adjective, covered with excrement,'" said Emma.

"Wait, wait, wait, wait, wait, wait," said Leonard.

"What?"

"What do you get if you clean the litter box in your winter clothes?"

"I dunno, what do you get when you clean the litter box in your winter clothes?"

"A shitten kitten mitten."

"Can we *please* get back to the subject?" said Norman.

"What? Shish kebabs?" said Anna.

"Why do you want to talk about shish kebabs?" said Leonard.

"My dad!" said Norman.

"Your dad likes shish kebabs?" said Leonard.

"Leonard!" said Norman.

"Norman, don't be shirty," said Anna. "And Leonard, please be quiet, and I would appreciate it, Emma, if you would keep your Old English filth to yourself. I was talking about the psychology of the individual. Behavior modification, you know. It works with kindergarteners and it'll work with Mr. Orman Normann. We have to get him to associate selling bombers with 'bad' and selling something else with 'good,' see?"

"How do we do that?" said Norman.

"It's a two-pronged approach," said Anna.

"You mean we're going to stick him with a fork?" said Leonard.

"No. Listen. We start with the bad. What doesn't your father like?"

"Well, besides anything that doesn't make him a lot of money, um, he doesn't like being disturbed during a nap. He hates that," said Norman.

"Good, that's good," said Anna.

"No, I said that's bad. And I thought of something else. He's always looking for omens, good and bad, he's kind of superstitious. Like, the first unusual thing he sees in the morning will be a big deal for him. You know, like if he sees a teddy bear being thrown into a garbage truck, or mushrooms popping up in the yard, or if he sees a dog limping. Stuff like that really gets to him."

"Very, very good. Now, we just need to figure out some way to use this," said Anna.

"Shock therapy," said Emma.

"What?" said Anna.

"'Shock therapy, noun, applying a strong jolt to a person or system in order to change unwanted behavior.'"

"You mean . . ." said Leonard.

"Yes," said Anna. "Here's what we do."

"Wait, wait," said Emma. "Fred is about to dance with the hat stand."

"All right," said Norman, "we'll watch the hat-stand routine."

When Fred Astaire was done dancing with the hat stand and several other inanimate objects, Anna continued: "Here's what we do. We start by lulling your dad to sleep."

"Not hard to do," said Norman. "Just put him on any couch and turn the TV on for two minutes."

"Okay, that'll do nicely. Now we need to insert bombers into the situation."

"A war movie!" said Leonard.

"My dad has tons of them!" said Norman.

"Yes!" said Anna. "Then the last thing he sees before he falls asleep will be bombers, and then he'll dream about bombers. And then, when he's sound asleep, really asleep, happily dreaming about bombers, we pop three balloons right next to his ear."

"How about firecrackers under the sofa?" said Leonard.

"I like the way you think, kid, but maybe it's too dangerous. We don't want to burn the house down."

"Right," said Norman.

"We just want to shock him. Now, and this is crucial," said Anna, "once we associate loud bangs and disturbed nap with bombers, which he will be dreaming about, we introduce something new, something good, to replace the bombers."

"Shoe," said Emma.

"What?" said Anna.

"'Shoo'? Like 'shoo away'?" said Leonard.

"No, like 'shoe, noun, an outer covering for the human foot, usually

shoe

made of leather, with a thick or stiff sole and an attached heel.'"

"A shoe salesman!" said Norman. "That's it! I would love to have a father who sells shoes. Shoes are good! Shoes are healthy, shoes are wholesome. Where would we be without shoes?"

"Florida?" said Leonard.

Norman jumped up and began to dance around the room, then on the sofa, balancing on the arms, shimmying along the top, and sliding into the seat, then collapsing into a heap on the floor.

"I'm going to start putting this plan into action immediately," said Norman. "I'm going to wear every pair of shoes I own, I'm going to polish them and buff them. I'll polish my dad's shoes, too. I'll . . . Wait a second. How are we going to get him thinking that shoes are good?"

"Yeah, how are we going to get Mr. Normann into shoes?" said Leonard.

"With a 'shoehorn, noun—'"

"No. Norman's already got it," said Anna. "First, Norman starts a campaign of shoe promotion. Like, Shoes Now! And The Beautiful Boot. You know, you'll mention how nice your mom's shoes are, and say things like 'Wow, I wish I were a shoemaker. Think how rich I'd be. Everybody I know wears shoes.' Then, when your dad's totally immersed in shoes, we spring the shock therapy on him. And then, when he wakes up, we make sure the first thing he sees is one big beautiful shoe."

"It's got to work!" said Norman.

"But when?" said Anna. "How do we do it without making him suspicious?"

"'Shoestring potatoes, noun, thin-sliced potatoes fried—'"

"Quiet, Emma," said Anna, "we're trying to think."

"'Shoofly pie—'"

"Potatoes, pie—that's it," said Norman. "Thanksgiving! We'll have an entire day to carry out the plan."

"All right," said Anna, "In the meantime, everyone bone up on shoes, what they're made of, who makes them and where, how much they cost, styles, shoe stores, everything."

"We'll do some sole-searching," said Leonard.

"I don't know," said Norman, suddenly sagging. "What if it doesn't work?"

"It's bound to," said Emma. "I'd call it a 'shoo-in, noun—'"

"Operation Shoo-in," said Norman quietly.

Fred Astaire quietly danced on the ceiling.

operation shoo-in

Every year since Norman could remember, the Normann family celebrated Thanksgiving with Anna and Emma, their parents being busy with one holiday show or another. This year, Norman made sure that Mrs. Piquant and Leonard were invited as well.

Always an all-day event, the day began with watching the big parade on television as Norman's mom made pancakes, this time with help from Sarah Piquant. The Quadrumvirate had agreed to use the parade event as the first wave of attack in Operation Shoo-in; any opportunity would be used to introduce the glory of shoes, thereby planting shoes firmly in the department of Orman Normann's brain where the sign over the door read GOOD. They assumed that this department was full of thoughts of bombers at the moment, and they wanted a change of occupancy. The Quadrumvirate knew that thoughts of bombers would not vacate without a fuss and a fight, but it was time to start knocking at the door.

Believing that Orman Normann was within earshot in the kitchen, Anna began the campaign with "Ohmygod, look at her! Look at her! Look at her gorgeous shoes!"

"Ohmygod," said Emma, "look at him! Look at him! Look at those loafers!"

"Look at the to-die-for, red-and-white, hand-tooled leather boots on that majorette!"

"They must have cost a fortune!"

"I wish I were her shoe salesman," said Norman, overly loud.

"How can they dance like that, holding trombones?" said Leonard.

"Do you suppose they're really playing those instruments?" said Anna. "Maybe they're just faking it, and someone is blasting a CD on a big boom box."

"No," said Leonard, "they're playing for real, and you know how I know?"

"How?" said Anna.

"Because it would be un-American for them to be faking it!" said Leonard. "And if something like that ever got out, it would destroy every nine-year-old boy's faith in his country!"

"What about the ten-year-olds?" said Emma.

"Well, that's maybe a different story."

"Ohmygod!" said Anna. "Look at that balloon. What is it?"

"It looks a little like a giant lime-green alfiona," said Norman. "Notice the rubber lips."

"It's wearing clothes," said Anna.

"And fabulous shoes!" Leonard shouted, getting back to the point.

"Wow," said Anna, "I think those are ostrich-leather slingbacks!"

"They must have cost a fortune!" said Emma.

"I wish I were her shoe salesman," said Norman, megaphoning his mouth with his hands.

"Hey, wouldn't it be great if there were two ginormous Alfurnian Guard balloons?" said Leonard.

"Complete with enormous furry hats and mustaches," said Anna.

"They'd probably have to fly them sideways like Superman," said Leonard.

"The first thing you'd see is two hairy mountains flying sideways down the street," said Anna.

"Then we could take them down with peashooters."

"Yeah!" said Norman.

"No more fear of unwelcome attention from a large, hairy man with boots," said Anna.

"And what wonderful boots they would be!" said Emma. "Mongolian yak leather with silver toe tips and traditional mythological designs. Reminds me of the legend of the wealthy shoemaker and the elves, who just got richer and richer and richer."

"I love that legend!" said Norman, shouting.

Emma continued her description of the Alfurnian boots. Meanwhile, Leonard stood up from the rug and slipped into the kitchen to see whether the first wave of attack was having any noticeable effect on its object. A moment later, he was in the living room again.

"Emma," he said, "you can skip the sales pitch. Norman's dad is in the alley, messing with the car. Judging by the amount of stuff lying around, he's been there the whole time!"

* * *

After the parade had ended, and the breakfast dishes were cleared and washed, the Quadrumvirate retreated to Norman's room to prepare the next stage of the operation.

Anna and Emma lay head to toe on Norman's bed, hands behind their heads, facing the ceiling; Leonard reposed deep in a green-corduroy beanbag chair; and Norman paced on the carpet between them.

"Darn that dad of mine. The first stage of Operation Shoo-in was completely wasted. His bomber mania remains unscathed."

"If only we could have scathed it a little," said Leonard.

"What's that supposed to mean?" said Emma, rising up on one elbow.

"The opposite of unscathed, obviously," said Leonard. "Ununscathed must be scathed, right?"

"Listen, troops, this is no time for argument. The Quadrumvirate must remain as one—a mighty force," said Norman, still pacing, eyes downcast, but with his fist pumping the air. "There's still Stage Two: The Meal. And then Stage Three: The Leather Recliner."

"Right!" said Anna.

"Right," said Norman. "Let's review our plans." He cleared his throat. "Ahem, feeling a bit roupy. Ahem. During dinner, remember to keep the dishes moving back to my dad, keep them moving. We want my dad full and sleepy. Generally, you can count on him eating himself into a stupor, but I don't want to take any chances. If he hesitates over the mashed potatoes—"

"Shoestring potatoes," said Emma. "We brought some frozen this morning."

"Right. Shoestring potatoes. If he hesitates over the shoestring potatoes, then pass him the stuffing. If he doesn't want the stuffing, pass him the turkey. If he . . . you get the idea. Main thing is, he eats, but I don't think that'll be a problem."

"Sir, a question," said Leonard.

"Yes, Piquant?"

"How do we maneuver the subject into the comfy recliner? What if he takes evasive measures like this morning, sir?"

"That contingency is very remote. Nevertheless, you are right to raise the issue. Should the subject show any tendency to deviate from his normal flight to the recliner, it is imperative, men—and er, women—that we use any and all force to achieve our objective. Everything's on the table."

"Even shoving and pinching?" said Leonard.

"Shoving and pinching are not ruled out. Shove and pinch him if you must, but we've got to get him into that chair. Now then—"

"Sir, once he's in the chair, what next, sir?" said Emma. "Do we go straight to the movie *Bomber Parade*, starring Henry Wingnut and Ernestine Truejoy, or do we lead up to it with something else?"

"Yes, this is a question I've spent much time over. If we start with something as good as *Bomber Parade*, starring Henry Wingnut and Ernestine Truejoy, 'the story of romance on a short fuse,' he might just get too interested in the movie and stay awake. In other words, he won't fall asleep. This, of course, would render Stage Three completely useless. A big flop. No, men—and er, women—we can't take that chance. I think we'd better start with the football game on TV. Then, when he's very nearly asleep, we quickly pop in *Bomber Parade*, starring—"

"We know, we know!"

"Right, and then fast-forward to all the best bomber parts. Then we let the sound of hunks of exploding metal work its magic."

"Aye, aye," said the twins.

"Righto, Sarge," said Leonard.

"It is now eleven hundred hours. Dinner is at fourteen hundred hours. Piquant, pass me a comic book."

* * *

At twelve hundred hours, not being able to stand the waiting any longer, Norman put down his reading and departed the room on a reconnaissance mission. He found the subject in his headquarters, with the door half open, already eating some of the first batch of shoestring potatoes, his feet comfortably at rest on the large metal desk.

"Norm, buddy!" said the subject when he noticed Norman lurking in the hall. "Come on in and sit down!"

Norman, though at first stricken at having been so quickly discovered, pulled himself together, entered the study, and sat down opposite his father.

"How's life treating you, son?" said Orman Normann through a mouthful of spuds. "Emvrifg alrieh?"

"Everything's great, Dad," said Norman.

"This is cozy, isn't it?" said Orman, after a weighty swallow.

"Yup."

"How's your mom?" Orman chewed. "Workin' in the ol' kitchen? With Dinah? Har, har. No, seriously, son, she works hard."

"I know, Dad."

"Heck, I work hard."

"You bet, Dad."

"But we both work hard for you, son."

"I really appreciate it, Dad."

"Sure you do. And I appreciate it that you appreciate it. Ha-ha!"

Orman took another bite of potatoes, settled himself back in his chair, and crossed one foot over another on a pile of papers.

"Have you noticed the trees, Norman?" Orman waved some potatoes vaguely at the window. "Wintry! The leaves—gone! Crisp and cool, cold sometimes! Baseball season, over. Heck, the football season's almost over. Do you like football, son?"

"Not really, Dad."

"But you're happy? Right? Right! Have some shoestring potatoes."

"Thanks, Dad."

"Norman, you look kinda pale. Kinda stressed-like. Nervous. Anything bothering you? Anything on your mind?"

"Well . . ."

"Norman, how's the tutoring going?"

"Really well, Dad. Mr. B. is great."

"Good, good. Because, you know"—Orman swallowed and dropped his voice a bit—"with the football season almost over and all, the big test is coming up again. The big bangeroo!"

"What big test, Dad?" said Norman.

"What big test? Your big test! The big Amalgamated Schools Test. Heck, it's only what you've been preparing for all year, ain't it?"

"Uh . . . oh yeah, right, Dad. The test. Sure, Dad."

"I'd be real proud of you if you did all right on that test, son. I mean, if you got a ninety-five on the verbal and an eighty-five on the logical and a ninety on the mathematical and an eighty on the astronomical. Or a ninety on the verbal and an eighty-seven on the logical and a ninety-eight on the mathematical and a seventy-nine on the astronomical. Or even a seventy on the . . . Darn it, what if you got all ninety-fives on everything, you could have your pick of any school in the city! Any school you wanted. Or any school I wanted!"

"That would be really great, Dad."

"Are you learning a lot, son?" he said, placing his hands on the armrests and recrossing his feet on the desk. "Is Mr. B. teaching you some good stuff?"

"He is, Dad."

"But is he teaching you the right stuff? Stuff that will really help you get the things you want—you know, help you acquire the important things in life, like what I got here?" Orman waved his hands airily over his desk, which was covered in papers, a couple of cell phones, an electronic date book, plastic cups, and food wrappers, his piggish eyes big.

"I think he is, Dad."

Orman Normann wiped his hands on a paper napkin and settled himself in his leather chair.

"Hooooeeeeee! That was just about what I needed!"

"Were you hungry enough to eat a firlot of Ring Dings?"

"Huh? Where do you get expressions like that?"

"Never mind, Dad."

Orman sighed. He looked above Norman's head at his toy bomber, which, for once, hung limply.

"Gotta change the batteries on that thing. You know, Norman, this may come as a bit of a surprise to you, but I'm thinking of getting out of the bomber-selling racket. I'm tired."

"What! Hey, that's great, Dad!" said Norman, sitting up. "That would be really great!"

"You think so?"

"Yes! Selling bombers is a childish thing to do."

"What? Well, I wouldn't say that. But I *have* had some second thoughts lately. I've even sometimes got this weird feeling that I'm being followed. That I'm being watched. Maybe I'm just being paranoid."

"It's definitely time for you to quit, Dad." Norman reached across his father's desk and grabbed the last shoestring potato, which he brandished like a general rallying his troops. "That would be really, really great."

Orman tilted his chair back, folding his hands behind his head, and contemplated his large feet.

After a moment he said, "What about shoes?"

"What about shoes?" said Norman, sitting up even farther.

"Yeah, what about selling shoes? People must need shoes as much as they need bombers, right?"

"Right!"

"I like shoes. What's more, I've worn shoes all my life! I like all kinds of shoes. Shoes have interesting parts to them, too, don't they? Uppers? Tongues. Soles. Thick soles. Hard soles. Crepe soles."

"Immortal soles!"

"Immortal Soles! Immortal Soles. I don't like it, no, I don't like it—I love it! That'll be my new business name." He looked at his shoes again, yawned, and stretched. "Naw, I'm just kidding. I've been a bomber salesman all my life. Why should I change? No, son, I'd need a real sign, a true omen, before I jump this ship."

"But—"

"All right, son, that's enough. This father-son-type moment is now concluded. More later when we watch us some football. Now skedaddle."

* * *

Fourteen hundred hours rolled around, and with it all the wonderful aromas of the day. Norman's mother was not the most gifted chef; still, she ordered well. The turkey, which had just required an hour of warming up, and the other ordered items, along with the several Mrs. Piquant and the twins' parents had provided, created the smells that had lured the foursome down from Norman's room long before the appointed dinner hour.

Leonard announced, "I could eat a firkin of turkin, a firkey of turkey—I mean, a firkin of turkey!"

"What's that, dear?" said his mother.

"A lot."

* * *

"Dad, how about some more shoestring potatoes?" said Norman.

"Well, a couple more won't hurt. They're awfully skinny,

ha-ha," said Orman Normann, reaching for the large bowl of deep-fried spudlets, which Norman passed to him.

"Stuffing, Mr. Normann?" said Emma.

"Don't mind if I do," and he was handed the dish of stuffing as well.

"Speaking of stuffing," said Leonard, wiping his mouth, "did you know that one of the oldest frozen people ever found was wearing shoes?"

"What does that have to do with stuffing, dear?" said Norma Normann.

"Well, they were made of straw and hay and stuff. He came out of a glacier. It's true."

"Speaking of frozen, how about some more steamed frozen peas and corn, Mr. Normann?" said Anna.

"Why, thank you, Anna, there's always room for peas and corn. They're pretty small already."

"Mrs. Piquant, would you please pass me the gravy shoe?" said Emma.

"It's called the gravy boat, actually. Here you are."

"Oh, I always thought it was called the gravy shoe. Mr. Normann, how about some nice gravy for those peas?"

"Okeydokey."

"Say, doesn't this turkey skin look kind of like those super-expensive boots you see in the stores on Madison Avenue?" said Leonard, who began to push and pull a piece of turkey skin.

"Leonard, please stop making food sculptures, and I don't think we want to hear about what the turkey, which is delicious, by the way, Norma, reminds you of."

"Okay, Mom."

The assembled diners were quiet for a moment and chewed.

"Mmmmm."

"Delish."

"Yummy."

Leonard lifted his turkey leg and began flying it toward Norman's plate. "Bzzzzzzzzzzzzz, Turkey Leg Bomber 29 and a half requests permission to drop payload of sweet baby onions into mashed-potato gravy lake, over."

"Leonard, please."

"You're right, Mom," said Leonard, putting down the turkey leg. "Bombing is not polite. It is impolite to bomb."

Orman Normann grunted.

"What's ruder, would you say, or more impolite," said Emma, "bombing or burping?"

"Let's see. *Uuuuuuuuuurrrrrrrrrlllllp!* That was a burp," said Leonard. "Now I'll bomb."

"Children, please, this is a holiday meal!" said Mrs. Normann.

"Just trying to understand the order of things, Mom," said Norman. "You know, where things go in the great scheme of things, like what's good and what's bad."

"Like bombing," said Emma.

"Bad," said Anna.

"Bad," said Leonard.

"Yup, bad, yup," said Norman.

"Shooey, I'm getting full," said Orman Normann, dropping his hands in his lap.

"Good!" said Leonard.

"Good," said Emma.

"Good," said Anna.

"Right, like shoes are good," said Norman.

"Good enough for that guy frozen in a glacier for thousands of years," said Leonard.

"Good," said Emma.

"Good," said Anna.

"Good, right!" said Norman.

"Leonard, why are you sticking out your tongue?" said Mrs. Piquant.

"Oh, sorry, Mom, I didn't notice."

"Shoes have tongues," said Emma.

"Right, good," said Anna.

"And they never stick them out," said Norman.

"Good," said Leonard.

"Very polite," said Emma.

"They also have soles," said Anna.

"Good," said Norman.

"Very deep," said Leonard.

"Not like bombers," said Emma.

"Nope," said Anna.

"Shallow," said Norman. "No souls."

"Children, really what are you all going on about?" said Mrs. Normann, passing the cranberry sauce to Emma.

"Just making conversation, Mom. Mom, everything is really delicious, really delicious and good. Shoobedooby doo."

"Thank you, dear."

"More shoestring potatoes, Dad?"

"Sure, couple more can't hurt," said Orman Normann.

"Did you know that every president of the United States of America, including our current president, has worn shoes?" said Leonard.

"How about that!" said Emma.

"And did you know that every member of the Supreme Court wears shoes, especially when they're handing down some kind of important decision?" said Anna.

Norman began to count ostentatiously upon his fingers. "That's nine times two, that's eighteen shoes!"

"So long as none of the judges is missing a leg or something," said Leonard.

"Don't people sometimes put a shoe on the bottom of the thing they wear instead of their missing leg?" said Emma.

"What's it called, a pro . . . pro . . ." said Anna.

"I'll go get the dictionary," said Norman.

"Norman, stay right where you are and eat your dinner," said Mrs. Normann.

"All right, Mom."

"I'll have the other leg if no one wants it," said Leonard. "Mr. Normann?"

"Help yourself, Leonard," said Mrs. Normann.

"In the Miss America contest, they even wear shoes during the swimsuit competition," said Emma.

"Really?" said Anna.

"Really," said Norman.

"Weird," said Leonard.

"Very," said Emma.

"On the other hand, it's good for shoes," said Anna.

"On the other foot," said Norman.

"Right, on the other foot," said Leonard.

There was a silence.

"How about some more shoestring potatoes, Dad?" said Norman.

* * *

Orman Normann dozed peacefully in his leather recliner. The television emitted the only light in the hushed living room, a soft shimmering in the dimness. Henry Wingnut murmured the details of his next mission into Ernestine Truejoy's cheek.

The room was warm, not from any fire in the roomy fireplace, as the Normanns were not that kind of a family, Mrs. Normann being too nervous for it, Mr. Normann not having a knack for axes, and Norman being up until now too powerless to prod his parents to act against their natures. It was a warm room, because the house had central heating and Mr. Normann possessed the finger that set the thermostat.

All was still.

Apart from Henry's and Ernestine's loving murmurs, the only sounds were the gentle breathing of Mr. Normann, which sounded like a stuck wheel on a tea trolley being intermittently pushed across linoleum tiles, and the whoosh of the hot air emerging from the heating ducts, which sounded like, well, hot air emerging from heating ducts.

A casual observer would have perceived nothing but peace, the peaceful result of a happy family dinner. However, a more careful observer would have noticed Leonard's left foot protruding from behind the couch—Leonard's designated station—where he hid, balloon in one hand, pin in the other. Another observer might have found something odd in a pair of fine brown loafers resting on a red-plush pillow facing Orman Normann's recliner, and in regard to this, another observer with a heightened olfactory sense might have noticed the smell of freshly applied shoe polish. No observer, however, would likely have seen Anna, Emma, or Norman, all holding filled balloons and pins at the ready, as they were well hidden in back of the china cabinet, behind the drapes, and in the linen closet.

The four waited almost breathlessly for the agreed-upon signal—when Henry Wingnut shouts to his copilot, "I don't care *if* the weather looks bad, *or* our starboard motor is on fire, *or* that the wings are icing up! We've got to complete our mission!"—

when they would step silently to Mr. Normann's chair and pop their balloons by his ears, on the quiet count of three.

Orman Normann snored like a stuck tea-trolley wheel on linoleum tiles. The air whooshed like air whooshes. From across the street, very softly, came the sound of a football, punted.

When Norman thought he couldn't stand one more second in the stuffy linen closet, he heard Henry Wingnut say, "I don't care *if* the weather looks . . ." With a gentle exhalation of breath, Norman began to ease open the closet door, but then stopped when he heard something else: something not in the script, not in *Bomber Parade*, and not in Operation Shoo-in. It was the sound of the living-room door opening quietly and two slippered feet shuffling across the deep shag carpet.

Then came the unmistakable voice of his mother.

She said, cooingly, "Wakey, wakey, honey-bunchum-munchum-lunchum. Time for cakey-cake and pie-ee pie and nice black coffee-woffee."

Orman Normann snorted once, yawned, and said, "Thanks, darling. You know, there's nothing I like better than waking up from a nice nap with my favorite movie on and hearing you say it's time for cakey-cake. Give me a smooch."

Norman cringed at the sound of smooching.

Orman Normann continued, "You know, with Norman this morning, I was thinking maybe I ought to get out of the bomber business, but now, watching *Bomber Parade*, I think it's the best job in the world!"

"You bet, dearie. Now come have some cake. I wonder where all the kids are. It's been so quiet. And I have a telephone message from Mr. B. for them."

"That's nice, that's nice. Good for him." The recliner creaked and then chattered as Orman Normann stepped out of it. He slipped into his polished loafers, saying, "Lead me to the cake."

The living-room door shut.

The four members of the Quadrumvirate emerged slowly from their four hiding places, each holding a large pin and a large balloon, one yellow, one red, one pink, and one white with a smiley face in blue.

From the television came the sound of a tremendous explosion, and then the voice of Henry Wingnut sang out, "Mission accomplished!"

the great little india walk

Balthazar Birdsong's message had summoned them all to the Maestro Building at nine o'clock the following morning. You may imagine that a good bit of the Quadrumvirate's oomph, regarding Mr. Normann's karma correction, was knocked out by the debacle of Operation Shoo-in. This was so. Anna, alone, remained undeterred.

"Maybe Mr. B. will give us an idea," she had said, as the dejected Quadrumvirate was eating dessert.

Norman, shoveling up a listless forkful of pumpkin pie, had merely responded, "Hah!"

* * *

Nevertheless, the foursome stood the next morning, disconsolate and knock-kneed, on the terrazzo floor of the lobby of the Maestro Building. Mrs. Normann, who had brought them, checked to see if they all had their mittens.

A gentle ping announced the arrival of an elevator, the doors rolling open to reveal within a man dressed in a checked raincoat, ankle-high leather boots, and a brimmed sailor's cap, holding a black umbrella beneath one arm and a canvas knapsack over the other: in short, Balthazar Birdsong, dressed for fun. He strode out, arms extended, singing, "My children, my children!"

"Here they are, Mr. B.," said Mrs. Normann, "bright-tailed and bushy-eyed, ready for their adventure," not altogether sure that they were, or she was.

"Splendid! Splendid! And I might add, swell!" said Mr. B., still beaming his smile all around. "I've been peeping over the balcony with Crick this morning and the weather is cooperating: cool with no sign of rain on any horizon. Nevertheless, I trust you followed my instructions and have brought along either an eight- or sixteen-ribbed *parapluie* or a garment of the aqua-impermeable variety?"

"A what or a what?" said Emma.

"Exactly. An umbrella or a raincoat."

"Oh yeah. We've got those," said Anna.

"They've got everything you requested," said Mrs. Normann. "Rain gear, extra socks, peanuts, and chocolate."

"Splendid, swell. Splendid, swell."

"All right, then," said Mrs. Normann, "I'll be off, then. I'll see you all later, then."

"Should it so please God," said Balthazar Birdsong.

"Ha-ha," said Mrs. Normann, uncertainly.

"Bye, Mom. I'll remember the sunscreen," said Norman.

"Bye, sweetums! Remember your sunscreen."

"It's November, Mom."

"I know it is, dear. Bye!" she said, and she walked out through the revolving door.

"Well," said Balthazar, grabbing his wrapped umbrella by the waist and giving it a twirl, "off we go, then," and he pointed with the handle, "to the mysterious East, lunch in Little India."

"But why are we going now? We all just had breakfast," said Anna.

"Exactly," said Mr. B. "Then you should last till we get there."

"But you just said we're going now."

"Yes, certainly, we are now going to begin our journey to the mysterious East and Little India. The trip will take us, at the very least, three hours."

"What?" said Leonard. "Are we going by rickshaw?"

"Very amusing, Leonard. But, no. We walk."

"What!" shouted the Quadrumvirate.

"We walk. Like so," said Mr. B., and he strode to the lobby door, his umbrella swinging.

The four hurried after him, remonstrating.

"But isn't Little India miles and miles from here?" said Norman.

"Approximately seven," said Mr. B., pushing the revolving door, then breathing in the crisp air as he reached the street.

"Seven miles! But we could get lost," said Anna.

"Possibly," said Mr. B., now marching up the street toward the midmorning sun, "but not permanently."

"We could get run over by a deranged delivery truck," said Leonard, "possibly delivering flowers, which we can then use at our own funerals!"

"Also possible," said Mr. B. cheerfully, "but unlikely. Most flower deliveries have already been made. Especially the deranged ones."

"Norman's mom is good at flower deranging," said Emma.

"Hey!" said Norman, hurrying to keep up with the long-legged twins and his tutor.

Mr. B. let his stride become leisurely but steady, his umbrella tip describing an arabesque with every second step.

"We could be mugged in some far-off neighborhood," said Anna.

"Again, possibly, but also unlikely. Remember, all of this great city's neighborhoods are filled with grandmothers, grandfathers, children, babies, uncles, cousins, aunts, and only a relatively few muggers, who are most likely concerned with other things than us, at this time. Come, do not let these doubts dissuade you. I accept and understand your misgivings and worries. They are a perfectly normal part of every voyage. After all, we journey into the unknown."

"Haven't you ever been there?" said Norman.

"Never," said Mr. B.

"What!" said Emma. "I'm going home. Taxi!"

"Emma!" said Anna.

"However," continued Mr. B., all the while strolling, "I carry with me a wonderful human invention—to wit, a map." Pausing at a red light, he tapped his pocket. "You are all perfectly correct in your implications that we would be safer if we stayed home in our rooms, certainly we would be warmer and ultimately less footsore. But we would also be duller, stupider, and, finally, sadder. If you want to avoid danger, don't get born. Once you are born, make something of it! Ah, the light is green."

They walked on, and the chill, clear air pinked their cheeks.

"But we're just walking," said Anna.

"And trying not to get hit by deranged flower deliverers," said Emma.

They walked.

"Look at that building with the big, *roofy*, hanging thing," said Leonard.

"Yes, the exquisite copper cornice of the Peonie-Browne Apartments," said Mr. Birdsong. "Precisely."

They walked.

Emma said, "Look at that lady in six-inch high heels walking her six-inch-high dog."

"I believe that is one of the Peonie-Brownes now. One of the granddaughters."

"But we're still just walking," said Anna.

"Right," said Balthazar Birdsong. "We are walking and seeing."

They walked.

245

"And we are doing more," he continued. "We are establishing our knowledge of the world in which we live by the most effective means: We walk across it in our booted feet. Henry David Thoreau, one of our great countrymen, insisted on walking each afternoon for four or five hours. He rued the day when our country would be so parceled and boundaried that a stroll through the neighboring hills would become impossible due to individual ownership of the land. Private property! The bane of modern man. Every one of us so determined to secure his or her own piece of petty ground. And what have you got? A piece of petty ground. What have you lost? The world!"

Balthazar Birdsong smiled at the clouds. "But not us. No, we, here in our own city, can go where we please. The streets are still ours, thank our celestial domes, and before the entire country becomes one enormous gated community, we will walk them! Ha-ha!"

"My dad would say you were rabble rousing," said Norman, shooting a glance at his tutor.

"Would he call you rabble?" said Mr. B., cocking his head. "Never mind, I am merely spewing and spouting. I am spewing nonsense and spouting nitpicks. These pastimes being two more reasons to walk. Spewing and spouting come easily to the walker, thus clearing his lungs of stale gas and his mind of cantankerousness. Onward, slowly and steadily. We've already crossed eleven blocks, can you believe it? At this rate, I should say we'll be at the Fifty-ninth Street Bridge in another hour, and then we will look for a place to sit down to drink something warm and eat something sweet. To the bridge!"

"To the sweets!" said the Quadrumvirate.

And so they marched on, sometimes two by three, other times two by two by one, or one by one by three, sometimes on an empty block all five shoulder to shoulder, but this was rare, as it was the day after Thanksgiving, and the sidewalks were especially full of every kind of New Yorker.

Slowly, they crossed the heart of the great city, its high buildings surrounding them and hiding from them the bridge they sought. At last, glimpses of the bridge's suspension towers tantalized them, and then, around a corner, the bridge loomed above.

"The bridge!" said Mr. B. "Like stout Cortés, who, as you may remember, looked upon the Pacific, we look upon the East River with a wild surmise, and we ask ourselves, 'Where is the nearest coffee shop?' Keep your eyes peeled, we need refreshment."

* * *

Half an hour later, warmed and sweetened, the Quadrumvirate found with its leader, after some back-and-forthing among the blocks, the pedestrians' entrance to the immense bridge. Cars whirred past them as they stepped up the ramp.

"We'll take it slowly here. Again, slow and steady. If we have learned anything from Aesop over these years, it is slow and steady." The roadway lifted them, nevertheless, rather

 quickly up over the rooftops of the townhouses and tenements, where they were eye to eye with the middle floors of the new luxury apartment buildings into which the four now eagerly peeped, making up stories of the residents as they marched along.

"Ah, look, we are about to step out over the river," said Balthazar.

They were now at least a dozen stories above the waves of the river, which cast back the low, slanting rays of the sun, warming the cheeks that the dour November wind nipped at.

"Brrrr!" said Emma.

"This is scary," said Anna, but they continued to walk.

The fivesome passed across the central span of the bridge, the wind still whipping and nipping, the Quadrumvirate occasionally whooping, the cars whistling past, oblivious of them and their adventure.

"We have passed exactly eleven pedestrians, our fellow travelers, on this bridge," said Balthazar B.

"How can they be fellow travelers if they're going in the opposite direction?" said Leonard.

"Well, you know what I mean," said Mr. B.

"Besides, some of them were women, not fellows," said Anna.

"Children, children, children," said Balthazar.

When at last the bridge began to lower them gently back down into the neighborhoods on the other side of the river, all five began to skip, the charms of gravity proving to be irresistible, overriding any Greek moralist's admonitions to slowness and steadiness.

At the bridge's far exit, they sank into a twenty-limbed heap on a bench.

Anna said, "I am so exhausted, how much farther to Little India?"

"Oh well," said Mr. B. "Let's see. If this map and my superior mathematical aptitudes are anything to go by, I would say, yes, shortcut there, subtract say ten, around the expressway tunnel there, plus, oh, four, well, ah, let's make it sixty blocks. Sixty blocks."

There was a stunned silence.

"You're right. It's probably more like sixty-five."

* * *

We need not go into the details of each and every one of those, as it happened, sixty-seven blocks that our friends traversed before reaching the patch of neighborhood known as Little India, where they were at last seated comfortably in a red vinyl booth at New Delhi New Deli. Let us say that the first forty or so blocks passed by smoothly enough, as the gentle roll of their various strides worked like the crank of an old organ-grinder, producing stories and jokes and philosophical musings in our four friends, stories, jokes, and musings that they themselves had forgotten or perhaps did not even know they knew. However, in the interest of truth-telling, it must be admitted that the last twenty-seven blocks became tedious, even excruciating, as their destination seemed to stay just out of reach, like a bauble held above a tormented baby's head by its mischievous big brother.

Nevertheless, they made it; it had taken them four and a half hours altogether.

"First of all," said Balthazar Birdsong, "let me congratulate you on this remarkable achievement in city perambulation. Frankly, for a moment or two I was unsure of our success. Still, here we are. Now, second of all, we each of us shall drink a mango lassi, which I assure you will revive your spirits like the best miracle elixir, as you do all seem a bit enervated."

"Oooooo yaa a a a," said Leonard.

"I know that last bit there was a bit trying," said Mr. B.

"Trying?" said Anna, glaring.

"I was just trying not to scream," said Emma.

"Well, yes," said Mr. B., "and yet, somehow, I do believe this trip was quite necessary. Preparation, sound preparation for future challenges. Is it not my sacred task to prepare you for these? And now," he said, looking up and smiling at the approaching waiter with the tray of five tall glasses of mango lassi, "prepare your nerve endings for bliss."

They drank. Inner lights rekindled in four sets of eyes. Not five, as the lights in Mr. B.'s had never dimmed.

"Mmmm," said Anna.

"Yummy," agreed Emma.

"Ah, wow woo wow ow owo wow!" said Leonard.

"I agree," said Norman.

"Now," said Balthazar B., addressing their waiter, "we would like—I am sure we will all like—five paper dosas, please."

The waiter smiled, nodded, and returned to the kitchen.

"That doesn't sound like a firlot of Ring Dings," said Leonard.

"Indeed, no," said Balthazar. "You will find them light yet nourishing, an excellent pedestrian's repast. Anyway, I am proud of you all. I like to think that in only half a day you have been enriched by all of the valuable elements of travel. That is, you have experienced worry, doubt, confusion, and exhaustion of every kind, but also inspiration, illumination, education, and joy. Hmm? For four and a half hours, you have left your daily cares behind," and he raised an eyebrow at Norman. "It is all here before us, and around us. To walk across a city is as good as a flight across the globe. Although I hope you do manage that sometime as well."

"How about just a taxi back to our living rooms?" said Emma.

"No need, no need. I have arranged for Norman's dear

mother to meet us here with her fine automobile and, my goodness, look, here she is, pursuing our waiter to our table."

Norma Normann bustled with fluttering hands behind the steady gait of the waiter, who carried five giant plates covered by five enormous flat breads and bowls of sauce.

As the two neared and Norma began to exclaim her questions and express her relief in seeing them all again, Balthazar B. rose and interjected, "Dear waiter, another dosa, please, and bring this poor woman a mango lassi, instanter."

* * *

That night, feeling no nearer to solving the problem of his father, but still enjoying the enhanced pleasure of sitting in a comfortable chair that only someone who has walked across seven miles of city landscape truly knows, Norman paged open his dictionary to the *T*s and read.

trepang *n* : a large East Indian sea cucumber
trephination *n* : cutting holes into a living skull for medicinal purposes
trepid *adj* : timid, frightened
trepidant *adj* : timorous, trembling
trepidity *n* : fearfulness, dread
trespass *vb* : to enter where it is forbidden to do so
tress *n* : a bunch of hair
trestle *n* : a wooden horse
trews *n* : tights worn beneath a kilt
trey *n* : the three on a domino side
triangle *n* : a three-sided figure

tresses

And he slept.

triangles, trephination, and trepidity

As December began, Norman thought about triangles; more specifically, he thought about people triangles.

First, there was his family; his mother, his father, and he formed a triangle. Sometimes it was long and pointy, with himself at the pointy end, far from his parents; sometimes it was small and cozy, with three equal, short sides around a tight center; and sometimes it was squat and wide, with him at the top, his point falling for a time closer to his father and then to his mother, and then perhaps back to his father, three stars drifting in a triangular constellation: Norman, Norma, and Orman.

Then there were his friends, Anna and Emma and Leonard. They were a kind of triangle, too, tumbling around this way and that. Of course, when he joined them, they were four sided, the Quadrumvirate, a quadrilateral, which, as a shape, had its own interesting possibilities.

But getting back to triangles, there was one more: Mr. B., his father, and himself. This triangle puzzled Norman. It seemed to be spinning all over the place—sometimes his father yanking Norman this way, sometimes Mr. B. coaxing him that way. But Norman wondered: Did he, Norman, ever pull either of the other two his way? Was he able to change where they were going? It did not seem likely. Mr. B. appeared to exist almost in his own world, untouched by anything much. And so far as his father went, all attempts Norman had made to pull him out of his particular warped orbit had thus far either misfired or cratered like a wayward asteroid.

Some days after the Thanksgiving holiday, Orman Normann had announced abruptly, "Gotta split, my cats and kitties. N. T. McSweeney says there's some mice in Katmandu that need my immediate attention." He lowered his voice and hooded his eyes. "So, before whatever is up in Katmandu goes down, I'd better get over there. I'll be right back." He began to push one of his arms into his coat. "Where is Katmandu, by the way, Norman?"

"In the Himalayas, Dad," Norman replied.

"Well, that shouldn't be too far."

* * *

That was the beginning of December. A week later, Norman and his mother received a long e-mail letter from him. Here it is:

> dearest darlings, dearest darlings. darn it!

So it began. It continued:

> i'm now in singapore of all places where it's
> hotter than blazes and they've never even heard
> of the game of football. they play some fool
> thing called cricket!!! saw it with my own
> peepers. imagine a sport named after an insect.
> ha ha! would you believe it? Katmandu was cold
> but the mice weren't biting so now I'm here
> where it's hot—weird. i think i may finally
> have something cooking here, something i've been
> working on all year! tell you all about it later.

don't want to give too much away so's i don't jinx
it—

Norman looked at his mother and frowned.

anyhoozle doozle if i can close this here deal
it would mean a lot to all of us and then if you
really want i spose i could get into the shoe
business with all of my irons in the fire tied up
in a basket. so anyways, that's where i am now.
i'm staying at the pan specific hotel which is
a doozy, biggest doggone insides of a hotel i've
ever seen.

Norma said, "Oh, ah."

i'm meeting someone important this afternoon.
hee hee little does he know that i plan to fill
him full of singapore slings and then make him
sign on the dotted line.

norman—i know you're not much of a football fan—
but will you keep an eye on the giants for me—hey
buddy?

norma darling—take care of your pretty self.
i'll write you again on the innernet as soon as i
can with all the news.

lottsa lottsa lottsa hugs and lottsa lottsa
lottsa kisses—orman

Norma smiled and looked at Norman, who raised a worried eyebrow.

* * *

Toward the middle of December, Norman thought about trephination. He held Alfred the Great, walking him across the table with a swagger.

Alfred the Great was saying, "I'm sorry I'm late for your party, Knut, but I've just come from performing a rather ticklish trephination on a young squire suffering from chronic hiccups."

"A trephination, really?" said Inga, a young damsel. "What's that? It sounds complicated."

"Well, Inga, it isn't really. It just takes a certain knack . . ."

"I didn't know you were a doctor, too, Alfred," said Inga. "You really are great."

"Eeeeeeyoooof," said Alfred. "Can I get you some mead?"

* * *

"Eeeeeeyoooof," said Norman, collapsing onto the living-room sofa after the last of the tremendous gabble of holiday parties: school parties, family's and friends' parties, drama-club parties, and even basketball parties. Norman was completely exhausted from so much fun.

* * *

And when December was nearly at an end, and with the winter break coming, Norman thought less about triangles and trephination, and more about trepidity, his own trepidity. He mentioned this to Mr. B. as they walked along the cold river.

"My upcoming Amalgamated Schools Test scares me," said Norman.

"Why?" said Mr. B.

"I'm trepidant before my trial, I feel like a trespassing trepang before a trephination."

"Dear, dear Norman. Concentrate on the weather, notice how the cumulus clouds are ragged and sailing like loose kites over the land. When your big trial arrives, I know you'll be ready."

They walked three miles along the river, stopping when they reached the pier where an enormous U.S. Navy aircraft carrier pulled almost imperceptibly against its mooring lines. Norman looked up at the name—U.S.S. *Intrepid*—not sure if he should feel encouraged or mocked by the thirty-six-thousand-ton behemoth.

* * *

Intrepid or trepid, it was remarkable that Norman and his mother had managed all their holiday engagements, especially so, since they were without Orman Normann, one of the essential triangle legs, after all, who was still not back from his, perhaps, final bomber mission. This, of course, added to the burdens and worries of Norma Normann, who, on top of the regular festivities, needed to prepare the Normann house for three guests; namely, and much to Norman's delight, Anna, Emma, and Leonard, who were to arrive on Friday evening, after the last day of school before the break. Anna and Emma's parents were on two separate holiday-show tours and Mrs. Piquant was to be away in a southern state overseeing one of her firm's building projects—some convention center or other was Leonard's understanding.

All of this left Norma and Norman both happy and tired, and definitely missing a husband and a father.

Night arrived early on the last day of school, and Norman

sat down at the kitchen table with the dictionary to get the *U*s out of the way before his friends arrived.

uh-huh *interj* : used to express agreement, affirmation, comprehension, or interest; also, yes

umber *n* : a brownish shade

umbrella *n* : a small, portable, usually cloth canopy that is fastened to a frame with hinged ribs radiating from a center pole, having a convex shape when open, with the ability to be opened or closed by means of a sliding catch and providing protection against the weather

umbrous *adj* : shadowed

umi *n* : a Japanese apricot

umiak *n* : an open Eskimo boat

umiri *n* : a fragrant balsam derived from South American trees

umland

umland *n* : the environs of a city, town, or village

umph *interj* : usually used to express skepticism or doubt

"Darn it and umph," said Norman. "I wish Dad would get home already. Didn't he say anything about when he would be back?"

"No, dear," said Norma, who had joined Norman at the table. "He just always says not to worry, everything's just fine, and he hasn't been kidnapped."

"Hasn't been kidnapped?"

"Yes, he says not to worry, everything's just fine, and he hasn't been kidnapped."

Norman closed his dictionary. He said, "Mom, how many e-mails has Dad sent?"

"Oh, just about one every day. They always say pretty much the same thing—'don't worry, I haven't been kidnapped.'"

"Mom, can I take a look at these e-mails?"

"Of course, darling. I'll just get the computer thingy."

Mrs. Normann brought the computer to the table and then leaned on the back of Norman's chair, looking over his shoulder. He hit the power button and waited as the screen slowly flickered to life.

When it lit up, he said, "Crumbs, Mom, don't you ever clean up your desktop? It's a mess. You should really drag some of these things to the trash and empty it from time to time. Look at this, folders lying all over the place, some of them empty, even. How many times do I have to tell you to put your folders away? Really, Mom."

"I'm sorry, dear. I'm just afraid they'll disappear and never come back."

"No, Mom. Okay, let's see. Norma's mail. From Orman Normann—here it is, and this appears to be from today."

"Yes, dear."

"Opening, and here we are. You don't mind if I read it, right?"

"Yes, dear. I mean, no, dear, go right ahead."

```
nurrma, dahlink,
pleaze to not vorry, ahmm jest stayink a coupla
mor daiis to vinish my verk here, ja. jest
verking, thet's ride. no problims. no problims,
no. not.
alzo. ahmm devinitely not bin keednappt.
devinitely no.
bussi bussi, orrm
```

"Are they all like this?" asked Norman in a dry voice.

"Pretty much," said Norma.

"Dad's been kidnapped!" shouted Norman, leaping up, causing the vinyl chair to make a great whooshing sound and nearly throwing Norma over.

"No, dear," said Norma, righting herself. "Didn't you read the letter, it said he was 'devinitely not keednappt.'"

"Mom, can't you tell that's not Dad writing?"

"Oh, it's so hard to tell with e-mail," she said, now kneading her fingers.

"'Jest verking, dahlink'?"

"Your father was never a good speller, dear."

"What's the address on these e-mails, anyway?" said Norman, sitting back down with another whoosh. "Imperialalfurnianspies .org. Imperialalfurnianspies.org! And look at these subject lines."

"Oh, I never read those."

"'Devinitely not keednappt,' 'don't vurry yer priddy liddl hed,' 'ewcritink is vine,' 'no nid to call da polees.'"

Looking up, Norman said quietly, "Oh my goshnik."

"Orman!" said Norma, plopping down next to Norman with the loudest whoosh of all.

In the midst of this, Leonard arrived at the back door, dropped off by a neighbor, as his mother was already on her flight south. Leonard let himself in, dumped his bags with the boots and shovels, and came into the kitchen.

"Ah, woo woo woof!" he said, by way of hello.

"Ah, woo woo woof is exactly right," said Norman. "I think my dad's been kidnapped!"

"Kidnapped? What do you mean, kidnapped?"

"I mean kidnapped! Like, being held captive."

"Wow! Why would anyone want to keep your father? I

mean, not that he isn't a nice guy, but who would want to be, you know, cooped up with him? What makes you think he's been kidnapped? After all, he's been gone on long trips before. Maybe he's just sightseeing. Maybe he's just eating more Wiener schnitzels."

"They don't have Wiener schnitzels in Singapore!"

"Poor Orman!" said Norma.

"Singapore! Why Singapore?" said Leonard, scooting another chair next to Norman's.

"Look at this," said Norman.

Norman began to scroll through his mother's list of letters, opening them at random.

"Let's see what this one says. Listen."

```
nurrma
     don't vorry yur hed which is pritty liddle. am
     not keednappt. hiy tu nurrmin.
```

"'Nurrma'? 'Nurrmin'?" said Leonard.

"Mom, didn't you suspect anything when Dad misspelled your own name?" said Norman.

"Well, he can be an awfully bad typist when he's in a hurry," she said, now pacing.

Norman opened another letter.

```
     am vine. no nid to be konsernt. am about you
     thinkink hallveys.
```

"Really, Mom, 'about you thinkink hallveys'?"

"I guess I've been a little distracted," she said, rubbing her hands.

The letters continued:

```
hilloo—do nat think I am in any trubbel.
bussi bussi.
```

"'Bussi bussi'? Weird," said Leonard.

"'Bussi bussi,' Mom?"

"Oh, Orman!"

The front doorbell bombilatcd.

"The twins!" shouted Norman and Leonard.

Indeed, the twins had walked themselves over with their belongings and now stood in the front hall, bombarded by both Norman and Leonard, who had run in from the kitchen with the enormous news.

quite prepared

"Kidnapped?" said Anna.

"But who would want to kidnap your dad?" said Emma.

"That's what I said," said Leonard.

"Just look at who sent the e-mails," said Norman. "Imperial-alfurnianspies.org! Darn those Alfurnians!"

"All right, girls, Leonard, let's not just stand around here upsetting ourselves," said Mrs. Normann, holding her hands tightly to her chest. "There's nothing we can do about this now," and she moved her hands to her cheeks. "Now, Norman, I wish you would stop making me so upset with your crazy notions, because that's all they are—crazy notions."

She straightened herself, putting a hand now to the back of her hair and looking in the hall mirror. "Listen, I'm going out for the evening, as Norman may have already told you. I have arranged for Mr. Balthazar to arrive here in twenty minutes with the pizza."

"All right, Mrs. Normann!" said Leonard.

"I'll show everyone to their rooms," said Norman.

"Now wait. Before you do that, Norman, I want you to show everyone to their rooms."

"The twins in the spare room, and Leonard in his sleeping bag on the floor in my room."

"Hold on. Wait a second," said Mrs. Normann, brushing her hair. "The twins are in the spare room and Leonard is in his sleeping bag on the floor in your room, Norman."

"Okay, Mom. Love you oodles, Mom. Have a nice evening,"

said Norman, giving his mother a quick squeeze around the middle before grabbing Anna's bag and leading the others up the stairs.

Twenty minutes later, Balthazar Birdsong stepped through the kitchen door, preceded by the wonderful aroma of pizza. Another tutor might have recoiled from the explosion of young voices that rained on him as he entered, but he, having set down the pizza, calmly removed his coat, scarf, mittens, and hat and said, somewhat austerely, "Indeed?"

"My dad's been kidnapped! I know he has!" said Norman, for the seventh time.

"I don't disbelieve you," said Mr. B. "However, before we take this up, let us lay a pleasant table in your charming kitchen, pour ourselves generous glasses of water or wine, and pass around the pizza, so that our discussion may be both unhurried and thorough."

Accordingly, the table was set, under the strict guidelines of Mr. B., who sent Norman and Emma to hunt for cloth napkins and candles, and Leonard and Anna to look for real glasses and china plates.

When they were at last seated, Balthazar Birdsong lifted his glass to his lips, drank, put his glass down, and said, "Now, Norman, what's it all about?"

Norman, through many a mouthful of pizza, proceeded to tell of his father's e-mails and his own earlier premonitions that something was wrong and now his conviction that his father was in real danger. "I knew that my dad wasn't exactly a model citizen, but I wasn't prepared for this!"

he said, taking a rather savage bite of his slice of broccoli with olive.

"There I disagree with you," said Balthazar. "You are quite prepared. Has it not been my task this year to prepare you for your test?"

"But not this test!" said Norman, choking a little.

"Who is to say? Who is to say?"

"Mr. B., no offense and all," said Leonard, "but, seriously, how have you prepared our friend Norman here for this, as you call it, test?"

Balthazar merely smiled and looked over the top of his wineglass.

Anna added, "From what I can tell, all you've taught Norman is how to walk, take care of rats, fly kites, notice people's clothes or celestial domes, look at the sky, and read the dictionary."

"Precisely so," said Mr. B., putting his glass down and folding his hands, "and all in service of two of the pillars of my tutuorial methodology: observation and imagination." He leaned forward and nodded at Norman. "And see, Norman has observed his father and now imagines that he is in trouble. I have no reason to think Norman is wrong."

There was a silence.

"Norman," Mr. B. continued, "can you tell me what your father was wearing when you saw him last?"

"I think so," said Norman. "His brown suit with a light blue shirt and a red tie and his good brown shoes with a black winter raincoat. I'm pretty sure he packed his gray suit, his black shoes, which he always does, and he mentioned the beach, so I imagine three Hawaiian shirts, his swim trunks, and his flip-flops, which are green. And a bunch of other stuff."

"Fine work, Norman. Now do you see?"

Leonard put away another bite of pepperoni and onion with a large gulp and said, "All I see is a man in a brown suit."

"Yes. Well, at least you see that. Really, at this juncture, there remains but one thing more. To the two pillars we add a third— you observe, you imagine, and now you must act."

Norman, who had stopped eating, was gazing out the window into the backyard and wondering where in the world his father was.

The remainder of the Quadrumvirate looked at Norman.

"So, Norman," said Emma, "what are we going to do?"

"Yeah, Norman," said Leonard, "what's the answer?"

Norman looked at the slice of pizza in his hand, then back out the window, and finally at his friends. "Well," he said, "I guess, I guess"—he took a bite and swallowed—"I guess we're going to Singapore."

"Bravo, Norman," said Balthazar. "You pass the test."

* * *

Later in the evening, after much further discussion and argument, Norman and Balthazar Birdsong stood at the bus stop at the end of the street, where the half-moon seemed to drift low over the trees and the lights of the city behind them.

"Maybe you could come with us to Singapore," said Norman.

"Not me, my dear," said Balthazar. "I must remain in the city due to inescapable obligations." He put his hand on Norman's shoulder. "Besides, this is your adventure. Just remember who you are: Norman Normann—conqueror, discoverer, seafarer! I have no doubt you will meet every challenge with a well-chosen karate chop and just the right answer." Balthazar gave the cold air a couple of silent chops, and smiled. "Ah, here's the bus."

The bus door opened, throwing light onto the dark sidewalk. Norman gave his tutor a sudden hug around the middle, and then Balthazar Birdsong hopped on and, turning, said, "Give my regards to your father when you find him, Norman. Farewell!" And the bus door closed.

As the bus hummed and rumbled away, Norman walked, then ran down the dark sidewalk toward the brightly lit windows of his home, observing the faces of his neighbors' houses, imagining a monster or two in their bushes, and acting like the toughest little superhero he could think of.

more prepared

"Where is Singapore, anyway?"

"Beats me," said Leonard.

Leonard and Norman lay in their sleeping bag and bed the following morning, staring at the ceiling.

"Let me check," said Norman, scrambling out of bed and over Leonard to retrieve a globe from his desk, then placing it on the floor. They sat one on either hemisphere.

"I found Copenhagen," said Leonard.

"Here's Tokyo," said Norman.

"Spin the globe once."

Norman spun it.

"Aieeeyeee! We're flying through space!" said Leonard.

"We are flying through space. Keep looking for Singapore. How are we supposed to go to Singapore if we don't even know where it is?"

"All right, all right. Lima, Peru!"

"Johannesburg."

"Mexico City."

"Athens."

"Look, I found where we live," said Leonard, placing his finger on New York City. "Right here where my finger is. Let's see what's on the other side, exactly. I'll keep my finger on the top over here, now you look on the bottom over there."

"Okay," said Norman, bending down to see the bottom half of the globe, "exactly on the other side of the world from New York is . . ."

"Is?"

". . . is blue. Ocean."

"Which ocean?"

"I don't know which ocean. Let's see. The Indian Ocean."

"Well, what's around there?"

Norman swiveled the globe left and right. "Australia. So that's where Australia is."

"What else?"

"Sumatra and Java."

"Isn't Java coffee?"

"I'll ask Mr. B. Oh, and one more thing," said Norman, with his right index finger on a spot just above the equator. "Here's Singapore."

*   *   *

The boys peeked into the spare bedroom. The girls were awake and reading.

"We found Singapore!" said Leonard.

"I didn't know it was missing," said Anna. "In fact, I would put it at two degrees north latitude, one hundred and five degrees east longitude, at the southern tip of the Malay Peninsula."

Norman and Leonard deflated.

"We looked it up online," said Emma.

"All right, now how do we get there?" said Leonard.

Norman and Leonard sat down at the foot of Anna's bed, and the Quadrumvirate scratched its four heads.

Norman said, "I don't know about how we get there, but this is all starting to make sense to me. I was thinking about it some more last night. Mr. B. says your brain works on things even when you sleep."

"No wonder I'm so tired in the morning," said Leonard. "So, when does your brain sleep?"

"Well, in your case," said Emma, "I'd say from about nine to five."

"Ha. Ha," said Leonard.

"Let me finish," said Norman. "We thought the Alfurnians were chasing us, when all along, really, they were chasing my dad. Every time we saw them was on a family outing. Remember the Halloween parade? Dad always goes, he loves Halloween. They obviously thought he was with us!"

"But why would they want your dad, that's what I still don't get," said Emma.

"Who would really want to spend a lot of time with your dad?" said Anna.

"Besides you and your mom, of course," said Emma.

"I know it sounds pretty unlikely. But I'm sure it's them. And I'm sure he's in trouble," said Norman. "My guess is it has something to do with the deal he's been trying to close with the Alfurnians all year. Maybe the Alfurnians lured my dad to some secluded spot to grab him so's they could find out all he knows about the Katong Luangans or the Blinesians or the Jakartians or something. Maybe they want him for their grand vizier or something. I don't know! He's a shady used-bomber salesman! Anything's possible! Darn it. Why isn't my dad a shoe salesman?"

"Everybody needs shoes," said Leonard. "Who needs bombs, anyway?"

"The Alfurnians," said Anna.

"Getting back to what are we going to do . . ." said Emma, beginning to brush and braid her sister's hair.

"Here's what I propose," said Norman. "Anna and Emma, you go online again and find out how we get to Singapore, all five of us. I think we'll have to bring my mom along, although maybe we won't tell her what exactly is going on. I think if we all just smile and act like we know what we're doing, she won't be any trouble."

Anna began to brush and braid Emma's hair.

"Leonard, you go back down to the kitchen, my mom's computer should still be down there. Print out all the e-mails from the Alfurnians or from my dad in the last month. Then see if you can discover some kind of code or hidden coincidences, or something to help us figure out where exactly my dad is right now." Norman stood up from the bed. "And in the meantime, I'll get my mom to go out and get us doughnuts for breakfast so she's safely out of the house, and then I'll go to my dad's study and see what I can find there. Let's meet back here in seventy minutes."

"Why seventy minutes, exactly?" said Anna.

"I don't know, it just sounds cool," said Norman.

* * *

An hour and ten minutes later, they sat again on the spare beds and ate the doughnuts Mrs. Normann had dutifully gone out for, saying merely, as she handed them around, "Try not to drop any crumbs."

"So what have we got?" said Norman, his mouth full of half a marble-frosted.

"Not a whole lot," said Leonard. "All the e-mails were pretty much the same, full of dahlinks and nurrmas, N-U-R-R-M-A, and nurrmins, N-U-R-R-M-I-N. And they were full of things like, I am devinitely not in eny dencher and sur hevenot bin keed-nappt. I mean, how dim do they think your mom is, anyway?"

"Oh, I'd guess about fifteen watts," said Anna.

"Fluorescent or incandescent?" said Emma.

"Incandescent."

"Oooh, that is dim."

"Hey!" said Norman. "Well, I guess they know her pretty well."

"After all," said Emma, "it worked until now, and would have kept working if you hadn't gotten suspicious."

"Wasn't there anything else?" said Anna.

"Well, in what looks like the last genuine e-mail from your dad, sent on December sixteenth—"

"Beethoven's birthday," said Emma.

"Sh!" said Anna.

Leonard continued, "He mentions a meeting with the Alfurnians in the Tall Bar of the Snaffles Hotel."

"All right!" said Norman. "That's where we've got to pick up the trail. That fits with what I found in my dad's office. Listen, there were a bunch of different copies of various contracts lying all over. Two things I know about my dad. One, except for the occasional catalogue in code, he rarely puts anything away. And two, he eats a lot of fast food. Keeping this in mind, I made careful observations of the papers on his desk. By a close visual analysis of the relative hardness of the mayonnaise, ketchup, and french-fry stains, I concluded that the most recent bomber contract in my dad's office was one for the Alfurnians. But it was unsigned. That means he really was going to try one last time to close an Alfurnian bomber deal, if they would meet with him again. And that would confirm what Leonard found in the last e-mail."

"Brilliant!" said Anna.

"But disgusting!" said Emma.

"Brilliant and disgusting," said Leonard.

"Okay, so that puts my dad in the Tall Bar at the Snaffles Hotel in Singapore in the third week of December. Now we've got to get there ourselves. We've done everything we can here."

"That's where we come in," said Anna.

"Look," said Emma, turning her computer around for Leonard and Norman to see. "We've booked five seats on Singapore Airlines."

"Two windows, three aisles, all together, so we can trade around during the flight, which by the way is going to be kinda long."

"And kinda expensive."

"How kinda long and expensive?" said Leonard.

"Don't worry about the expense," said Norman. "I can handle my mom. I call it giving her the moisturizer. I raise this eyebrow this way, this eyebrow this way. I let the corners of my mouth twitch thusly, and the hands and fingers work like this." Norman twisted his hands together and contorted his face. "Or if Mom's hands are available, I work them like this." Norman twisted his hands over Emma's, who tried to yank them away. "It's never taken me longer than forty-five seconds to get the American Express extracted and into action."

Norman let Emma's hands go. "All right, we're ready to get this operation under way."

"By the way," said Leonard, "what's the name of this operation going to be?"

"How about Operation Hooner Po?" said Norman.

"Didn't we use that already?" said Leonard.

"How about Operation Bad Dad?" said Norman.

"He's not my dad," said Anna.

"Operation Bomber Bummer," said Emma.

"Winter Summer Bomber Bummer!" said Leonard.

"Winter Summer Bomber Bummer!" chanted the four, and so it was decided.

"There's just one thing," said Anna.

"Yeah," said Emma. "Because we're getting these tickets kind of last minute, we could only get them for Wednesday night."

"Uh-huh," said Norman.

"But?" said Leonard.

"So, the flight takes eighteen hours."

"But—" said Leonard.

"And according to the flight times, we leave on Wednesday night and we don't arrive until Friday morning."

"Uh-huh."

"But—"

"Wednesday night is Christmas Eve," said Anna.

"So?" said Norman.

At last Leonard burst in, "But that means we'll completely miss Christmas! Christmas Day will come and go, and the whole time we will never have one toe on the ground!"

"Exactly," said Emma.

"I think that's maybe against Santa's rules!" said Leonard.

"Look, he can still deliver your presents," said Emma.

"But not on an airplane! Santa doesn't work for NASA, you know. He can't do a midflight delivery. Where's the chimney on a 747?"

"Anyhoozle," said Norman, "we've got to rescue my dad, right? This is going to count big-time for the nice list. What could be nicer than rescuing a grown man from Alfurnian spies?"

"Rescuing a puppy from Alfurnian spies?" said Anna.

"There's no puppy. Forget about the puppy. Come on, Leonard, are you in on Operation Winter Summer Bomber Bummer or out?"

"I'm in," said Leonard with a sigh.

The Quadrumvirate placed its hands together in typical pre-game pep-talk fashion. Norman slowly looked into two sets of identical brown eyes and one of hazel green.

"Winter Summer—"

"Bomber Bummer!" answered the three.

* * *

On the eve of Christmas Eve, in the midst of books and socks, packs of cards, his monocular, T-shirts lying all about him, Norman held his Alfred the Great figurine in his left hand, then tossed it to his right, weighing it there. Norman's eyes were fixed out of the window at a gibbous moon.

"Alfred," he said, "Alfred the Super-Great, I mean. I'm going to put you back in your plastic egg. I think I'm going to go it alone on this one. I'm going to need all of my senses, including my inner ones, focused on finding my dad."

Norman held Alfred the Great up to his face. "Don't look at me like that. You'll be fine. Of course I'll miss you. Besides, lately all you've been thinking about is that damsel, Inga. Now let me finish packing, I've got to concentrate." Norman gazed about him. "Umph, I can't forget my umbrella."

Sometime later, his packing at last complete, and with Leonard already snoring very softly, Norman threw himself onto his bed and closed his eyes. A moment later, he opened them again; he jumped off his bed, unzipped his suitcase, dug until he found his Ingmeister's Compact International Dictionary, and leaped back into bed. He snuggled his shoulders into his pillows, switched on his bedside lamp, and opened to the *V*s. He read:

Vandyke red *n* **: a grayish red that is bluer and deeper than Pompeian red**

vane *n* : a movable device attached to
a spire for showing the direction
of the wind

vanguard *n* : the leaders of thought,
taste, or opinion in a movement

vanillism *n* : "grocer's itch," a skin
irritation caused by handling
vanilla pods infested with mites

vanish *vb* : to disappear entirely

vanity *n* : something that is empty, vain, or valueless

vanman *n* : a van driver

vanquish *vb* : to conquer

vane

operation w.s.b.b.

Norman blinked open his heavy eyelids. Squinting at the diffuse light around him, a rumbly hum in his ears, he wondered where he was or if he was even awake. A soft grunt and lip smack emanated from what appeared to be a sack of some kind next to his right arm. As Norman studied this grumbling sack, it slowly resolved itself into Leonard, happily asleep beneath a blue Singapore Airlines blanket. With this dawning recognition, a tingle of excitement, or possibly apprehension, ran up and then down and then back up Norman's spine. He remembered he was on Flight 94 to Singapore; all fuzziness fell away like a piece of tissue paper torn from a Christmas box. Norman's senses of sight and hearing were back to normal, and even his sense of smell kicked in as he breathed in the odd smell of airplane, the aroma of beige.

Norman looked around. Beside him in seat 38B, as we have seen, was Leonard, curled like a pill bug; across the aisle, Norman could see his mother in 38C, also sound asleep. Norman leaned forward and peered between the seats, where he saw two heads of braided hair mingled together in 37A and 37B: the twins enfolded like kittens.

The soft clinking and clanking of the few passengers who were awake was subsumed by the profound purr of the enormous airplane. A flight attendant wearing a yellow, flower-printed dress, her hair pulled back and piled to make an enormous, black, glossy pincushion, ghosted down the aisle, checking on her sleeping brood, removing an empty glass here, tucking up a pillow there. She smiled a perfect smile at Norman as she passed, so smoothly as to seem to have ten feet where presumably there were only two. But as her dress reached all the way to the floor, it was impossible to check.

Norman sat back in his seat and let his mind wander over the flurry of the day just passed. It had been a long one, full of last-minute scrambles for one missing item or another. There had been a quick trip to the bookstore for guidebooks. Then there had been a trip to the grocery store for snacks. "They'll have food in Singapore, Mom," Norman had said. "But what if it isn't properly sanitary?" had said Norma. And at two o'clock in the afternoon, Emma announced that she had lost her passport somewhere in the Normann house. It had taken forty-five minutes and all their combined efforts to find it, Leonard ultimately guessing that she had probably been staring at her passport photo, looking for blemishes or a bad-hair moment, before going to sleep. Indeed, Leonard imagined well, for the passport turned up within the tangled sheets and blankets of her bed.

You might think it unlikely that the various parents had agreed to this scheme. Actually, Anna and Emma's parents were thrilled that the twins would get such fine entertainment over the holidays. It was only Mrs. Piquant who had to be persuaded. Though she trusted her friend Norma to do her best, she knew that she was not much of a match for the combined wills of Norman and Leonard. Still, she also knew Leonard would not allow not being allowed to go along.

"Eeeeeeeyaaa!" had of course been Leonard's comment.

Norman smiled in his seat 38A.

The Quadrumvirate plus one mom were already pretty exhausted by the time they gathered at the gate, waiting to board their flight, late on Christmas Eve. Before the blue runway lights had much receded below them, they were all helplessly asleep.

Norman raised his window shade and peered out. What time was it anyway, he wondered. He had no idea. The sky was a brilliant black, a living black of infinite depth. The numberless stars looked close and far at the same time; it was more stars than Norman had ever seen before. He pushed his face close to the glass of the inner window to see farther. He could not find the moon, but he imagined it somewhere, and then looking down he saw its proof, as the great, wide earth was glazed in moon glow, whitely shimmering, sparkling but gauzy. With a start he knew it was the North Pole. Norman remembered now that the captain had said they would fly directly over it. It was beautiful, so immense. It was vanilla frosting.

Wait a second, Norman thought. It's Christmas Eve. It's the middle of the night. And we're directly over the North Pole. Do you suppose . . .

And Norman pressed his face to the glass again, feeling the cold against his cheek and eyebrow.

For a moment Norman thought he saw a red, blinking light flying through the night sky, but then he could not bring himself to believe it, not enough to wake his sleeping friend, at any rate. He turned his gaze back to the stars above the frosted earth. What were they telling him? He had read that, because they were so far away, whatever they were telling him was already ancient history, billions of years old. Still, they seemed to be winking directly at him, as if knowing all those years ago that he would peek at them this night.

Norman checked for Santa one more time—had he heard reindeer bells?—pulled his blanket close around him, and fell back to sleep.

"Norman! Wake up, it's Christmas!" Leonard had emerged from beneath his blue blanket and was shaking Norman by the shoulder.

Norman raised a heavy lid.

"Merry Christmas," said Leonard. "Look out the window! Sunshine."

Norman raised another heavy lid to cast gummy eyes at the shafts of yellow light glancing off the snowy world so far below them.

"Merry Christmas," said Anna and Emma, their heads now popped above the seats.

"Good morning, dears. Merry Christmas," said Norma, stretching in her seat across the aisle.

Norman heaved himself up.

"I saw the North Pole last night," he said through a yawn.

"Did you see any sign of Santa?" said Leonard. "I only ask in the interest of science."

"Maybe."

"You did not!" said Anna.

"I think I saw something blinking," said Norman.

"An airplane," said Emma.

"It was red—"

"A Sputnik," said Anna.

"What's a Sputnik?" said Leonard.

"I thought I heard tinkling—" said Norman.

"In the bathroom!" said Emma.

"No, seriously," said Leonard, "did you see or hear something?"

"Well, it's a little hard to remember," said Norman. "But speaking of tinkling, I have to get up."

"Oh yeah, sure," said Leonard. "I'll go with you."

Norman and Leonard rose from their seats and walked down the long aisle, picking their way past their fellow passengers, who read or slept or watched films or manipulated the screens on the seatbacks. Norman glanced at each face he passed; any one of them could be his neighbor at home, and yet all together they created a new world for him, a place he had never been, foreign, frightening, exciting. Where were they all going?

After Norman and Leonard used the lavatories, they decided to explore farther aft. They discovered a small side room where they could stand and look out the windows.

"Eeeeeyooof!" said Leonard. "Where on earth are we? Look at all that snow."

Norman pressed his face against another window and again felt the cold on his cheek, this time with the glare of sunshine in his eyes.

"I don't know, but it sure is snowy."

"We are above Siberia now," said a soft voice above them.

Norman looked up and recognized the flight attendant he had seen the night before.

He smiled hesitantly as Leonard turned from the window as well.

"Merry Christmas," she said, also smiling.

"Merry Christmas," said Leonard and Norman.

"Excuse me, miss," said Leonard.

"Yes?"

"I was just wondering, since this is my first trip to Singapore, I was just wondering, um . . . do you even have Christmas in Singapore?"

"Oh, why yes indeed. We have Christmas, Hanukkah,

Ramadan, Vesak Day, and the Festival of the Nine Emperor Gods. We have nearly every holiday there is."

"Have you ever heard about Santa Claus?"

"But of course. Singapore is a country full of many, many different people with many different faiths and traditions. There are Buddhists and Taoists from China, Muslims from Malaysia, Hindus and Buddhists from India, Christians and Jews from Europe. We all live together. Temple next to mosque next to synagogue next to church, and you are welcome everywhere. Just read the signs before you go inside, to see if you should take something off, like shoes and socks, or put something on, like shawls or kipas. Oh, you will have a wonderful time in my city. Come, let us have a toast to the day."

She began to glide away, then turned and held out her hand.

"By the way, my name is Ronita Kim," she said.

"Norman Normann," said Norman, taking her hand.

"Leonard Piquant," said Leonard.

"Wonderful to meet you both."

Ronita Kim led them a few steps farther aft to the galley, where she stooped to open a silver cabinet. She stood up, holding a green bottle in her hand.

"A bit of the bubbly."

"Champagne?" said Leonard.

"Even better," said Ronita Kim. "Spark-ling cider." And she popped the cork and poured out three plastic cupfuls.

"Chin-chin," she said.

"Chin-chin," said Leonard and Norman.

"So you do have Christmas," said Leonard. "Do you have snow?"

"Good heavens, no. Singapore lies almost

on the equator. The temperature is always warm, usually hot. At present, on this airplane, we are just a couple of hours past the North Pole. We still have to travel approximately one quarter of the way around the globe to get to Singapore."

"A quarter of the way around the globe?" said Leonard.

"Another quarter. Eight hours or so."

"Eeeeeeyaaaaaa," said Norman.

"All right, boys, back to your seats. I've got to finish up the breakfast service, yours are possibly already on your trays right now. Wait, here's a little something to pass the time," she said, diving for another drawer and then handing the boys a small package each.

"Could we possibly have two more for our friends?" said Norman.

With two more packages in their hands, Leonard and Norman hurried back up the aisle, Ronita Kim's musical "Bye-bye-la" echoing in their ears.

"Merry Christmas! Ho ho ho," said Leonard.

"Merry Christmas yourselves, we got you breakfast," said Anna.

"Merry Christmas, Anna," said Norman, sitting down and passing forward her package. "Merry Christmas, Emma," said Leonard, doing the same. The packages proved to be compact travel games and puzzles, which were traded back and forth as everyone drank their orange juice and ate their yoghurt and munched their breakfast rolls with much holiday merriment.

At last, quiet and thoughtful again, all four gazed out their windows.

"Which way are we looking, anyway?" said Anna.

"East," said Norman.

"We just finished breakfast and it's already getting dark again," said Anna.

"Wow," said Leonard. "Time sure flies when you're having fun."

"I'd say the reverse is true," said Emma. "Time sure has fun when you're flying."

* * *

Norman clutched the armrest of the taxi van, which propelled them over a smooth roadway bordered in palms and flowering bushes, the blue of the sea now and again beckoning between the foliage in the twilit morning.

"I think that was the cleanest airport I have ever seen in my life," said Leonard.

"That was the cleanest building, period," said Anna.

"I wonder what their hospitals look like," said Emma.

Their taxi driver leaned back, smiling, and said, "Yes, we have very well-organized public services here, yes, we do-la. Did you have any trouble in customs?"

"No. Thank you. Everyone was very helpful, really, very helpful," said Norma Normann.

"Very good," said the vanman, "so long as you don't bring chewing gum with you, ha-ha!"

"Why no gum?" said Anna.

"It is a one-thousand-dollar fine if you spit it out. Also, one-thousand-dollar fine for jaywalking or bicycling on the sidewalk. That is why we say, Singapore, a fine city. Ha! Ha!"

"Oh brother," said Emma.

The flowering bushes and the palms began to give way to the first high-rise towers. Red and green and blue lights made the pavement, still wet from a recent rain, sparkle and flash around them. The taxi driver sped them quickly and smoothly through the mostly empty five a.m. streets.

"Soon you will see the beautiful fountain we are building to welcome all visitors to our city."

"Will it spray a fine mist?" said Emma.

"Good one, ha-ha, bravo. Here it comes, you see it there on your right? When it is finished, it will be the biggest fountain in the world."

"Oh my," said Norma. "What will it be called?"

"It will be called the Biggest Fountain in the World. Yes, we are all very proud of it-la."

Leonard said softly to Norman, "These people are nuts-la."

"Shh!" said Norman.

"Now look here on your left, our new giant Ferris wheel, the Singapore Flyer."

"Why isn't it called the Biggest Ferris Wheel in the World?" said Leonard.

"Because it isn't. Ha! Ha! The ones in China and Kuala Lumpur are bigger."

"You didn't want to name it the Third Biggest Ferris Wheel in the World?" said Emma.

"Ha-ha-ha! Very good! Here we are, your hotel, the Pan Specific Hotel. My friends, just between us, the atrium is the fifteenth-tallest in the world."

"You're joking," said Emma dubiously.

"Yes, I am. Ha! Ha! Come let me help you inside. Enjoy your stay here in my city, and remember, tipping is not necessary," he said, bowing to Norma, who had a fistful of crisp Singapore dollar bills, "not even to me. Bye-bye-la!"

As the great revolving door slowly waltzed them into the hotel lobby, Leonard said, "That has got to be the Nicest Taxi Man in the World."

"Clean airports, friendly taxi drivers who refuse tips, the

sun rising when it should be setting. My world has been turned upside down!" said Emma.

Five minutes later, having been speedily checked into two adjoining rooms on the twenty-seventh floor, our five slightly disoriented globe-trotters stood frankly slack jawed in the elevator, staring out its glass sides at the triangular, balconied atrium of their hotel, which gave the impression of plunging infinitely down and soaring infinitely up.

At last, Anna said, "This is like otherworldly-la."

the tall bar in singapore

There was a tap at Norman and Leonard's door.

"It's me and Emma. Let us in," said a quiet voice.

Leonard eased open the thick wooden door a crack, peered out, then closed it quickly, removed the safety chain, and opened the door wide.

"Your mom's asleep," said Emma.

"Good," said Norman. "Operation Winter Summer Bomber Bummer can commence. Let's synchronize our watches."

"Mine says three," said Anna.

"Mine says eleven," said Emma.

"Mine says six, but I think it might not be running right," said Leonard.

"You're all wrong, and I'll tell you how I know," said Norman. "I never changed my watch."

"But then you're still on Eastern Standard Time in America," said Anna.

"Wrong-o. We went one hundred and eighty degrees around the world, and for every fifteen degrees you go east, you lose one hour, so we are exactly twelve hours ahead."

"How do you know this stuff?" said Leonard. "And I still don't get it."

"Don't you see? You don't have to change your watch settings, you just have to change your mind settings."

"All right, all right," said Emma, "time's having fun again. What time is it, then, here, exactly, so I can set my watch and my mind?"

"Nine a.m.," said Norman.

"And how long were we on the plane?" said Anna.

"Eighteen hours," said Norman.

"And how long did we sleep?" said Emma.

"I dunno, exactly. Probably ten hours."

"And what day is it again, here?" said Leonard.

"The day after Christmas."

"Well, if it's nine a.m. on the day after Christmas, no wonder I'm famished," said Anna. "Let's go look for some breakfast."

"What about Mrs. Normann?" said Emma.

"She'll sleep at least until the afternoon," said Norman. "Let's go."

Norman and Leonard gathered up their maps and guidebooks and knapsacks and left behind all their excess layers of clothing.

The Quadrumvirate descended swiftly in the marvelous elevator and passed through the now busy lobby, back onto the wide, curved sidewalk in front of the hotel. The heat rolled up and around them like a long-lost aunt's damp hug. Rainwater dripped from the wide-leaved bushes and palms as five black birds—like Crick, only with yellow heads—hopped and argued among themselves on the curbside.

"Hot, hot, hot," said Emma.

Norman pulled his map out and bent his head to it, then straightened and pointed an emphatic thumb to the right, in which direction they then proceeded, down one long block skirting the Sun Sun shopping mall. They crossed the spacious boulevard before them by pedestrian bridge, from which Anna spotted a breakfast place. Diners sat in twos and threes at tables on the sidewalk. Toward this oasis they now hurried.

The menu was displayed above the counter in large photos

of each combination of some familiar and some unknown items. After a hushed consultation, Anna approached the counter and ordered: "Four toast sets, please, with hot chocolate."

The old woman behind the counter smiled up at Anna, who was considerably taller than herself, counted out the change from the money Anna had offered, then gathered several small plates of things and arranged these on four trays. After which, by means of some eyebrow-waggling and further smiling and head-nodding, the members of the Quadrumvirate at last understood that they were to take the trays away and find a place to sit down.

They found a table on the sidewalk outside.

"Oh boy, what did we get?" said Emma.

"Toast sets," said Anna.

"I know what we ordered, what I want to know is what did we get?"

"Well, looks like a dish of two undercooked, runny, slimy eggs," said Anna.

"Mmm, strangely delicious," said Norman, wiping his eggy mouth with a napkin.

"And a stack of fat, perfectly square, toasty breads with green stuff oozing out between the slabs," said Leonard.

"Mmmm," said Emma. "Crispy, sweet, and buttery."

"Coconut?" said Norman. "Yes, coconut."

"And a surprisingly normal-looking cup of hot chocolate," said Leonard.

They all slurped, crunched, and sipped contemplatively, shyly taking in the bustling scene around them.

"I wish Mr. B. were here to try the coffee," said Norman.

"I wish Mr. B. were here to find your dad," said Anna.

"Urp," said Leonard, "we can do it ourselves."

"Look, our nice lady is making the coffee, I think," said Norman.

Turning in their seats, they watched her through the glass as she repeatedly and rapidly poured coffee from one long-spouted pitcher into another, the coffee flying through the air.

"How'd you like to do that every morning, all morning?" said Anna.

"No Sanka," said Emma.

They turned back in their seats and contemplated their maps and guidebooks.

"Eureka!" said Norman.

"No, Sanka," said Leonard.

"No, I've found the Tall Bar and the Snaffles Hotel, which"— Norman scrutinized his map—"doesn't look that far from here."

Revived after their long flight and thoroughly satisfied, for the toast really was delicious, with its creamy butter and coconut jam—nothing could have been better—they rose, bused their table, and followed Norman.

* * *

Norman led the way with determination until they reached another broad boulevard of many lanes of traffic, which appeared to offer no way across.

"Look, I think we have to go in here," said Anna, pointing at the entrance to a sleek building. They wove themselves into the flow of people and were quickly swept onto a descending escalator that carried them to a glittering subterranean shopping center.

"Follow the signs to Snaffles City," shouted Norman. A number of passersby paused and pointed in which direction they should go, which they duly did, following a long arcing hall of shops and restaurants.

They threaded their way through the throngs of people,

often bumping awkwardly into them, until Norman called the Quadrumvirate to a halt.

"I just remembered something," said Norman. "Did you observe that the taxi driver drove on the left this morning?"

"Everything's backwards here," said Emma.

"I imagine they walk on the left, too," said Norman.

Now proceeding on the left—that is, the correct side of the hallway—they moved at a quicker tempo.

Rising up again to street level, they found themselves at the edge of a small park, with a war memorial at its center.

"War means bombers, which means we must be getting close," said Leonard.

"You're right," said Norman, checking his map again. "On the other side of this park is the Bras Basah Road. All we need to do is go one block along it and we should bump right into the Snaffles Hotel."

Leonard said to Emma, "Did he just say 'bras'?"

"Yup," said Emma.

Norman was quite right, and in five minutes they stood before the hotel.

The Snaffles Hotel occupies an entire square block of the old center of the city. Within its countless pink-columned verandahs, since the days when Queen Victoria ruled the

British Empire, business propositions have been floated and sunk, fortunes have been won and lost on the turn of a card, writers' pencils have been sharpened and dulled, and spies have always lurked and been lurked upon.

"If ever my dad was going to get into some shady dealings, this looks as likely a spot as any," said Norman.

"Maybe we should go to the Singapore police. They're probably the finest in the world," said Anna.

"What if we get a one-thousand-dollar fine for burping, or parting our hair on the wrong side, or something?" said Emma.

"Or for being out without our mothers?" said Leonard.

"Or for being sarcastic without a permit?" added Emma.

"Don't be sarcastic," said Anna.

"Without a permit," said Leonard.

"No, let's see what we can find out ourselves, first," said Norman. "Come on, let's look for the Tall Bar."

The Tall Bar, as any tourist could tell them, and did, is on the second floor at the northeast corner of the hotel. They climbed the outside stairs to the verandah and pushed open the door.

The polished wooden bar stretched before them. The few customers at that hour were seated in deep leather chairs or lounged on bentwood chaises, lifting slender glasses of pinkish drinks. Above them, an ingenious, many-bladed, slow-flapping fan, looking as though it had sprung from the pen of Dr. Seuss, kept the humid air gently moving.

Norman eased himself up onto a tall barstool, motioning the others to follow him, and prayed that the bartender was not going to ask them how old they were.

He, the bartender, glided along the bar, wiping it with a rag as he came, and stopped before the Quadrumvirate. Placing a companionable elbow on the bar, he said, "What'll it be, mates?"

Norman cleared his throat squeakily and said, "Is the lemonade fresh?"

"The freshest," said the bartender.

"Made on the premises?"

"Can you doubt it?" said the bartender, examining his eponychiums.

"We'll take four."

"Pink or yellow?"

Norman threw a questioning glance along the bar to his friends.

"Pink," said Anna and Leonard.

"Yellow," said Emma and Norman.

"Two pink, two yellow, with ice, I do presume?"

"Yes, please," said Norman.

Norman took a deep breath and smiled as the bartender slid away.

"What do we do now?" said Anna.

"We gently steer the conversation around to his customers, find out if he's seen anything out of the ordinary, you know, but casually like, so he doesn't get suspicious."

"Right," said Emma.

They swiveled quietly on their barstools.

"He's coming back," said Anna.

"Four lemonades. Two pink, two yellow, all with ice," said the bartender.

The Quadrumvirate sipped.

The bartender drifted down the bar to attend to an elderly gentleman.

When he returned, Norman yawned and said, "Nice weather today."

"Nifty," said the bartender.

"I did, however, notice some cumulonimbus to the east," said Norman.

"Say, you're pretty sharpish. Most likely, we'll have another bit of a rainstorm this afternoon."

There was a pause.

The bartender smiled at them.

"I see Singapore will play Australia in a cricket match on New Year's Day," said Anna nonchalantly.

"Right again. We have no chance."

In the following silence the bartender sailed up to the other end of the bar to freshen a young woman's pink drink.

The Quadrumvirate sipped again as he returned.

Leonard said, "Have you ever seen a couple of guys come in here in tall furry hats and blue coats, with big black mustaches and boots?"

Looks of mingled shock and horror registered across the three brows of his three friends.

"Oh, you mean Nigel and Reg, the Alfurnian spies?" said the bartender. "Sure, they come in all the time. Usually around four-thirty. Ish."

"Great. Well, uh, thanks a lot," said Leonard, slipping off his stool. "The lemonade was very refreshing," and he ankled to the door.

"Oh yeah, thanks very much," said Norman, pulling Singapore dollars out of his pocket.

"My pleasure. That'll be twenty dollars. No tips required."

Norman paid and, with the bartender's "Toodle-oo" in his ears, caught up with the others.

Leonard said, "What? We got the information we wanted, didn't we?"

* * *

That afternoon, dozing on the covered terrace beside the pool, the Quadrumvirate watched the tropical rain come hissing straight down, as if poured from an immense, widemouthed pickle jar directly onto the hotel pool, making a tremendous noise.

"Maybe I'll find out what to do next in here," said Norman, drowsily opening the dictionary to the *W*s.

Leonard dozed in the next lounger.

Remembering something, Norman turned first to *Wi*. "Here it is," he said.

Winchester bushel *n* **: the volume measure equal to a cylinder 18½ inches wide and 8 inches deep**

"So that's what a Winchester bushel is."
He went back to *Wa*.

wahoo *n* **: an American tree and shrub**
waif *n* **: something ownerless, usually found by chance**
wailful *adj* **: sorrowful, mournful**
waist *n* **: the narrowed part of the body between the thorax and the hips**
wait *vb* **: to stay in place, usually in hopes of some event**
waiting game *n* **: a strategy in which the participant does nothing, hoping for a future occasion for better action**

waif

Norman looked up and said, "Of course!"
"What?" said Leonard, waking.
"We wait."

"We wait?" said Leonard. "What?"

"We play the waiting game."

"Like a spider?" said Leonard, yawning.

"Like four spiders." Norman flopped back into his deck chair and let his eyelids slide slowly closed until he could just peek through them slitwise. "We will be the four katipos. Katipo, noun, a small, deadly spider of New Zealand."

The rain hissed like a thousand Russell's vipers and Norman slept.

act! act!

And they waited. And they watched. And they checked in at the Tall Bar at four-thirty. Ish. But their furry-hatted prey eluded them.

The bartender just raised a friendly eyebrow when he saw them at the door and shrugged his shoulders to let them know that Nigel and Reg had still not been in.

The first days in Singapore went like this: sightseeing in the morning with Norma along; lunch; then a much-needed nap for the maternal Normann. Having her unconscious for a bit served not only her need for recuperation but the Quadrumvirate's need to hunt and reconnoiter, ending up, as has been mentioned, at the Tall Bar at four-thirty. Ish.

In sum, the first three days had netted them nothing.

The next day Anna said, "Let's go to Little India here, for lunch. It'll give us a taste of home."

"How do we get there?" said Mrs. Normann.

"We walk," said the Quadrumvirate.

"Oh dear."

This time their walk brought them out of the city's center into neighborhoods of shop-houses, the first floors of which were packed completely, from wall to wall and from floor to ceiling, with whatever wares were being sold, all the business seeming to take place on the sidewalks. The five walked stickily past mechanics squatting next to disassembled motor scooters, and ducked as plumbers pulled copper pipes out of nearly exploding shelves, and shuffled sideways around upholsterers stuffing their sofas.

In the Kampong Glam, golden-domed mosques towered above them as they peered through the twisted wrought-iron fence of a forsaken cemetery. The streets were no longer quite so clean; here and there the Quadrumvirate lifted its feet over broken bottles and discarded food wrappers.

"This place should be fined," said Emma.

"And dandied," said Leonard.

At last, they came to the Serangoon Road, with spice markets, textile stores, and shops filled with bangles. One large store sold every religious figurine imaginable, from twice double-armed Ganesh, with his noble elephant's head, to Mary and Jesus, four arms and two heads between them.

"God-a-rama," said Anna.

Outside the Sri Srinivasa Perumal Temple, everyone took off their shoes and socks, except for Leonard, who was sockless already, then entered the high entrance tower adorned with tiers of painted statues. Within the temple they happily did what they saw other families doing: They simply sat down on the floor and watched the drama, in painted stone and living flesh, unfolding around them.

"Look, a blue man with a monkey's head," said Anna.

"I observe and I imagine," said Leonard. "This is a tale of an old man who evolved backwards."

Shoes and socks back on, as the noon bells rang around them, they stopped at a curry shop and squeezed themselves into a tiny booth to feast on dosas with lentil curry and coconut chutney, washed down with mango lassis.

"Ah," said Leonard, stretching back, "a taste of home."

"Mr. B. should be here," said Anna.

"Mr. B. most definitely should be here," said Leonard.

"Mr. Should B. most definitely here be," said Emma.

"I wonder what he would say, if he were," said Norman.

"Find the answers in your friends, oh faithless ignoramuses," said Emma.

"Well, friends," said Norman, "what do we do, now that the waiting game is washed up?"

The Quadrumvirate sipped.

Norma Normann, fanning herself, said, "Maybe we should go back to the hotel and have a nice lie-down in the AC."

"Wait, Mom," said Norman. "We need a plan. What else would Mr. B. say?"

"Welcome to Singapore, now read the dictionary," said Leonard.

"Okeydokey," said Norman.

As they sipped their lassis, Norman paged through his travel dictionary. "Maybe something in the *X*s will give us a clue about what we should do next."

He read aloud.

xanthene dye *n* : a yellow dye
xanthic *adj* : tending toward yellow

"Norman," said Emma, "maybe you'd better lay off the sunscreen a little, you're looking a little xanthic."

"I feel thic," said Leonard.

xenophobe

xebec *n* : a three-masted sailing ship
    of the Mediterranean
xenophobe *n* : someone who is afraid
    of anything that is foreign or strange
Xmas *n* : short for Christmas

"Emma," said Leonard, "stop eating the table. I swear you're getting more xylophagous every day."

"Come on, Norman," said Emma. "Let's, like, make for the X-it."

* * *

Before returning to the hotel, they spent half an hour in one of the many Internet cafés, composing a summary of their trip for Mr. B., which they sent in hopes of receiving some kind of direction from him. The waiting game had gotten them nowhere.

And time was running out; the next day was Tuesday, their fifth day in Singapore, one day before New Year's Eve, when they were scheduled to depart for home.

At the Tall Bar that afternoon, there was still no sign of Nigel and Reg.

* * *

Over their toast sets the next morning, Norman convened the morning powwow.

"Well, we're starting to look like four very hungry katipos. Nothing has wandered into our web. By the way, we got an e-mail from Mr. B.—I checked on one of the computers in the lobby."

"And," said Emma, "did he send us any bright ideas?"

"He just said, 'Point your noses to the sky and carry on, carry on.'"

"Big help," said Anna.

"He also said he knows we're all well prepared."

"Terrific," said Emma.

"He also said, 'Observe! Imagine! Act!'"

"'Observe, imagine, act, observe, imagine, act.' What does he mean?" said Leonard.

Anna and Emma looked at each other.

Anna said, "Are you thinking what I'm thinking?"

Emma said, "We didn't go to Camp Ess-Ay-Tee for nothing. Give us a piece of paper."

The twins, muttering and elbowing each other, began writing strings of letters on the hotel stationery until, looking up, they shouted together, "We've got it!"

"What is it?" said Norman and Leonard.

"It's a code!" said Emma, passing the paper back to Norman. "He sent us a code. Read it."

"'Beaver sin toe magic,'" said Norman. "'Beaver sin toe magic'? That's the code?"

"Yes!" said Anna. "That's 'observe, imagine, act' un-scrambled."

There was a silence.

"Okay, so maybe it's not a code," said Emma. "Give me the map. Where haven't we been?"

They bent their heads to the map.

"Chinatown!" said Leonard. "We haven't even been to Chinatown. I feel like we'll find something in Chinatown."

"You can always find something in Chinatown," said Anna.

"Leonard's hunches are sometimes right," said Norman. "Here's my plan. First, we take my mom to Orchard Road and all the fancy shopping centers. She likes shopping. Second, we all shop."

"Till she drops?" said Emma.

"Till, as you so aptly put it, she drops. She drops, and then we drop her back at the hotel. Then we head for Chinatown."

"Question," said Leonard.

"Yes?"

"What if we drop, too?"

As it happened, Norma Normann was the only one to drop, just as they had planned. Accordingly, the Quadrumvirate left her tucked in and happily asnooze in the girls' cool room.

The four took a taxi to Chinatown and had lunch: rice and noodles and dumplings, finishing with ice kachang.

Bellies full, possibly even overfull, they wandered heavily through the Chinatown streets, down Temple Street, up Pagoda Street, then down Mosque Street, the little bud of sweat where their shirts met their stomachs slowly blooming.

Norman observed what he imagined was a familiar face. He looked again and knew it.

"Ronita Kim! Miss Kim!" he shouted, and ran ahead of the others.

Ronita Kim, for Norman was not mistaken, turned from a vendor's stall, with the scarlet cloths she was examining still in her hands.

"Norman?" she said, "Norman Normann?"

"Yup," he said, as the others arrived. "You remember Leonard? And this is Anna and Emma."

Ronita Kim smiled. "Hello, Leonard, of course. Pleased to meet you, Anna and Emma."

Everyone shook hands.

"Did you enjoy your little games?" said Ronita Kim.

"Very much," said Emma.

"Have you found everything that your hearts desire here in Singapore?"

"Well, almost. Not quite," said Norman.

"Not quite, you say. Well then, I know exactly what you are missing. Follow me, please," said Ronita Kim, and laying the cloths back down on the shop table, she plunged into a side lane and from this into an old building with a large, open first story full of food booths with tables piled impossibly high with fruits and vegetables, spices, and sometimes meats and fishes of frightening aspects.

"Ah, here we are. Here we are," said Ronita Kim, stopping at a table that bent beneath a pyramid of heavy-looking, green-spiked fruits just about the size and shape of footballs. Choosing one she liked, she had the seller cut it in half lengthwise.

She displayed one of the halves in her outstretched hands. "This," she said, "is durian, the king of fruits. Your hearts have not yet known that they desire durian, but they do."

Now she plucked out, one by one, giant seeds the size of small plums, each covered in a thick whitish goo, and handed them round to the Quadrumvirate, keeping one for herself.

"We eat it like this," she said, daintily pulling off a largish gob of goo with her teeth. She consumed it with a blissful, closed-eyed smile upon her face. She said, "Just one thing. Remember, tastes like heaven, smells like hell."

As she said this, an aroma that can rightly be described as the essence of rotting rodent reached the four young noses, and everyone but Ronita Kim quickly held the offending objects at arm's length.

"Come on. You're almost there. Don't give up now."

Slowly, whimperingly, with eyes held tightly shut, Emma and Norman brought the wet blobs to their faces.

Norman shouted, "Eeeeeeyaaaaa!" and bit.

Emma followed him.

They chewed, and slowly their foreheads unwrinkled, their eyes opened, and smiles spread across their faces.

"Delicious!" said Norman.

"Hooeee," said Emma. "Out of this world!"

Anna and Leonard smiled false smiles and placed their own gobs back into the halved fruit and began to wipe their hands on their shirts.

"Your hearts don't know what they're missing-la," said Ronita Kim.

"Oh well," said Anna, still wiping her hand, "ignorance is bliss."

"Well, two out of four is about the same proportion of durian lovers to haters here in Singapore as well. The four of you show a healthy balance."

"We may be balanced, but we're still looking for one particular item," said Leonard.

"Then may I recommend our newest attraction, the Singapore Flyer? It offers the best views of the city. From there you are guaranteed to spot whatever you seek."

* * *

The four, not having any better idea, allowed Ronita Kim to find them a cab and point them in the right direction.

"Now be careful and maybe we'll meet again somewhere. Here, there, or above the clouds. Bye!" she called, waving after them.

The taxi sped away from the shops with paper kites and bamboo brooms and into Singapore's twenty-first-century financial district, built straight into the sky, where the only merchandise for sale was billions of bits of encoded information.

Pushing their way through the canyons of metal-and-glass buildings, the driver alternately laughed and grumbled at the antics of his fellow drivers, until they crossed the Singapore River.

"I see it!" called Leonard from the back.

An enormous structure with the delicacy of a bicycle wheel flickered between the hotel towers as they approached. A cylinder as big as a train car, where the passengers rode, hung at the end of each spoke. Soon the cab man dropped them off near the end of the queue, and the four stood, heads back, staring nearly straight up at this fabulous, grown-up toy.

"It sure looks like it should be the biggest in the world," said Norman.

The four seekers purchased tickets and joined the others waiting to climb into the next car. When their turn came, they quickly found their way to the good spots by the windows. The great wheel turned, passing through thirty degrees of an arc, and they rose, moving outward and up, coming to a gentle stop after a minute. The car behind them slowly filled with passengers. As they began to drink in the wide views of the city spreading below, Emma shrieked.

"*Eek!*" she said. "Look!"

In the line of passengers waiting to get into the next car, two tall, furry hats projected, unmistakably, above the crowd.

"It's Nigel and Reg, at last!" said Leonard.

"Ohmygoshohmygoshohmygosh, staycalmstaycalmstaycalm," said Norman in a twitter. "I guess I never really imagined we'd find them. Oh, darn it. I wasn't prepared for this!"

"Yes, you are," said Leonard. "Balthazar B. said so himself. Now make an educated guess at what we should do next."

"Okay. You're right," said Norman. "I've just got to calm down." He took a breath. "All right, if our guesses are correct, the Alfurnians aren't after us, and probably have no idea we're even here. So I think we should be able to follow them without their even knowing it, so long as we don't get too close."

"Look! They're getting on," said Anna.

They all looked as two furry hats bowed, passing through the doorway.

Leonard said, "We are now actually riding in the third-largest Ferris wheel in the world, with two international spies."

"This is kind of like eating that weird fruit Ronita Kim gave us," said Emma, "delicious and horrible at the same time."

"Winter Summer," said Norman quietly.

"Bomber Bummer," said the others.

The Flyer began to turn once more. The radius of the wheel was so large, and its movement so smooth and slow, that the experience felt neither roller coaster–like nor airplanelike, but cosmic and moonlike: not thrilling, but awesome.

"Awesome," murmured Leonard.

For the moment, the Quadrumvirate forgot its nearby prey and filled its eyes with the sights farther away: the indigo-blue sea, dotted with scores of oceangoing ships; the aquamarine mountains overtopped by the ever-threatening cumulonimbus clouds; and the towers of the great city-state of Singapore itself.

"I can see our temple," said Anna, "the Sri, um, Sri, um, um, Sri temple."

"Look at the islands," said Emma. "I didn't know there were islands!"

On their second orbit, they watched the car behind them, occasionally glimpsing the tops of two furry hats.

"Are we even sure it's them?" said Leonard.

"I'm sure it's them," said Norman. "Who else would wear furry hats in this weather?"

When the ride at last came to an end, the four debarked from the wheel in their turn as casually as possible.

"Sunglasses," said Norman.

The four put on their sunglasses.

"And hats," said Norman.

And hats.

They sauntered over to the snack stand and lingered, pretending to peruse the menu.

The passengers in the next car began to file out, including their quarry, Nigel and Reg, who passed the snack stand, heedless of their hunters.

"It's the waiting game no more," whispered Norman, and the Quadrumvirate followed thirty paces behind them.

"The deadly spiders have spun their web, and now they gather up the flies," said Leonard.

The Alfurnians crossed Snaffles Avenue, then descended below the street on an escalator.

"Now it's a game of cat and mouse," said Anna.

"Looks like they're taking the subway," said Norman.

The Alfurnians lined up to buy tickets at a window; the four hunters bought theirs more quickly at an automated ticket machine and waited at the entrance to the trains.

"Act casual," said Norman.

"How?" said Anna.

"I don't know. Pretend to tie your shoelace," said Norman.

"I'm wearing sandals!"

"Shh!" said Emma. "Here they come."

The Alfurnians passed them, walked onto the platform, and two minutes later boarded a train headed for Boon Lay. The Quadrumvirate quickly boarded the car behind them.

At Outram Park the Alfurnians and their pursuers changed for a train to the harbor.

Arrived there, the Alfurnians crossed the wide, palm-lined boulevard opposite the station and proceeded to a long, arcing esplanade bordering a narrow sand beach. At the end of this, they passed along a walkway beneath spreading, umbrous trees, which led to a number of piers pushed out into the sea. At the base of the second of these, the Alfurnians passed through a gate.

The four, with Emma in the lead, dashed forward, arriving just as the heavy gate fell shut with a profound clang; the green sign at nose height on the still-vibrating door restated the obvious: MEMBERS ONLY.

All four pressed their foreheads to the white wrought iron, peering between the bars. Nigel and Reg, apparently without a care in the world, sauntered to the end of the pier, jumped into a sleek, open motorboat moored there, undid her lines, and shoved off.

"What does a deadly New Zealand spider do when the fly strolls through its web and leaves in a motorboat?" said Leonard.

flying horse

Norman gazed dreamily at the kites floating above the water, illuminated like bright lanterns by the afternoon sun. These were not ordinary kites, however, because they were passing back and forth over the shimmering sea at high speeds.

Norman ran through the trees to the beach and then down to the edge of the water.

The others caught him up and Anna shouted, "Is this really the time to indulge your yen for kites?"

"Definitely. Because those aren't just kites, those are kiteboards," said Norman. "Come on!"

"What?" said Anna.

"What!" said Emma.

"Eeeeeeeyaaaaaa!" shouted Leonard.

Norman raced along the sand. Coming nearer to the speeding kiteboards, he smiled, though he was breathing hard, for he spotted what he wanted: a rental shack.

He ran up to it and said, panting, "One kiteboard, please."

The teenaged attendant leaned across his counter and looked skeptically over the top of his sunglasses. "You know your way around kites?" he inquired.

"Oh, most definitely!" said Norman.

"And boards?"

"Absolutely," said Norman, less truthfully.

"Okay, you can have a rig and board till sundown. That's about two hours. I'll get the gear. In the meantime, you sign here, here, here, and here, here and here, and here twice, plus the date."

Norman took the stack of papers and quickly signed them as the others arrived.

"Norman," said Anna, "what do you think you're doing?"

"It's the only way," said Norman. "I'll follow Nigel and Reg on the board. They're probably just headed to that island over there. You can take the ferry, there must be one, and I'll meet you in an hour at the marina on the island—there has to be one over there someplace. The crucial thing is that we don't completely lose sight of the Alfurnians. Can you still see their boat?"

"Yeah," said Leonard. "They stopped at the last pier. Maybe they're getting gas or something."

The kiteboard man returned. "Everything signed? Cool. Here's your harness. The kite and board are ready to go, down at the water."

The Quadrumvirate ran off down the slope of the beach as the teenager shouted, "Hey! Are you going in those clothes?"

Norman paid him no mind. Instead, he slipped off his backpack and bent over the kite and board, focusing on the complicated set of lines and fabric arrayed before him.

"All right. This must be the control bar." He lifted it, a shoulder-width bar attached at each end to a number of lines stretching out to the enormous, elliptical kite, lying flat in the sand.

"Hook this in here, I suppose," he said, and he hooked the harness onto the bar with a kind of leash.

"Here's your life vest," said Emma. Norman slipped this over his head and cinched it tight.

In the meantime, Leonard and Anna walked over to the kite and then lifted it when they saw Norman give them a thumbs-up.

The kite filled with air, becoming a wide, blunt wing with the power to drag all four of the Quadrumvirate as far out to sea as it chose. Instinctively, Norman leaned back and directed the kite with the bar, sending it straight up, dumping some of its tremendous power. Now it flew like a champing racehorse directly above them.

"Whoa," said Norman.

"You going to be all right?" said Emma.

"I'm going to use every trick Mr. B. ever taught me," said Norman. "Remember, I'll meet you at the marina in an hour. Can you still see their boat?"

"It's over there!" said Leonard, pointing to a red flash on the water. "It looks like they're headed to the island, all right."

"Okay. Next stop, Treasure Island. Here goes."

Norman carefully bent his knees, keeping both eyes glued to his gently bucking kite, and grabbed the board and tucked it under his arm. Wishing he had taken a closer look at it beforehand, he eased himself into the water. With quick glances he could see that the board had two shallow fins at each end. Also, it was hot pink, with two padded spots where straps were secured, under which his toes would slide to keep him on it, he presumed.

Norman kicked off his sandals.

"I'll bring them and your backpack with us," said Anna. "Oh, Norman, be careful!"

"Oh yes."

Stepping deeper into the water, Norman dropped the board. For a moment he could not imagine what to do next. He looked around nervously; he spotted another kiteboarder lying face upward in the water, knees up and sliding his feet into the foot straps as the kite flew above him.

"Ah ha!" said Norman.

Norman slowly lay back into the water, the kite supporting him on the surface now. After slipping his feet into the straps, he took a deep breath. And then one more. He glanced at his friends and looked up at his kite. "Let's go!" he shouted.

"Hooner Po!"

He pulled down on the bar a smidgeon. Immediately, his transcendent flying horse sprang away in a gallop, lifting Norman fully out of the water and nearly into the air. The front of the board was waving wildly back and forth as the tail alternately dragged and skipped in the water. The kite bucked at this and plunged to the right and downward. Norman summoned his kite skills and pulled the kite out of its dive.

"Easy, big fella," he said.

Now Norman kept a watchful eye on his kite, holding it well under control, but still the board seemed to have a life of its own as Norman tried to direct the kite's power through his own legs into the board.

"How do I do this?" he yelled to no one in particular.

Just then a foot-high wave hit him on the right. Norman thought his grand experiment was over, and he was thinking of his life, but the little wave had good intentions; it lifted Norman up and forward just enough to trim the board so that, with a truly thoroughbred acceleration, Norman was sent skimming, no, blasting, no, flying across the water.

"Eeeeeeeeeeeeeeeeeeeeyaaaaaaaaaaaaaa!"

Norman barely heard a faint "Eeeeeeyaaaa" answer from the beach as the spray flew from the bow of the board, which chattered and bounced across the choppy water.

Norman tried to take a breath and relax into the thundering speed, but it was impossible. Instead, he narrowed his eyes and let every last bit of instinct and knowledge help him stay in control of his watery Pegasus. He looked at his feet for a moment and cautiously began to carve gentle turns in the water rushing beneath him by pushing on his toes or heels. He sliced a slightly larger arc and sent up a magnificent spray.

"Yaaaaaaheeee!" he shouted.

Feeling confident now, he looked ahead and around him. There were a number of boats cruising and playing in the strait between the mainland and the island. It was difficult to focus on anything other than his whistling kite and the board, clattering against the waves like a castanet. But he was just able to spot the Alfurnians in their motorboat, thanks to their hats, which stood out like two short smokestacks.

"I bet they're bald under those hairy things," Norman said aloud.

Norman heard a roar and snapped his eyes around to see the large wake of a passing powerboat rolling at him, but in an instant he was sent fully airborne. Naturally, he clutched the bar for dear life, which only sent him soaring higher, higher than a house, higher than two houses, higher than two houses and a pup tent, and then down slowly, then faster, until with a huge *wham* he splashed into the waves.

The sudden jolt spilled most of the air from the kite, which began to crumple and fall. Norman heaved back on his bar. The kite seemed to shake itself sober, then to re-form itself into its

312

proper wing shape, at last standing, as if expectant, on edge on the water.

Norman took an internal roll call. "Foot bone still connected to the ankle bone, ankle bone still connected to the leg bone, leg bone still . . ."

He leaned back again, the kite rose into the air, and with a splash he was back up on his horse.

"Giddy-yap!" he shouted, skimming after the Alfurnians like a cowboy of the sea.

Five more life-altering minutes later, during which Norman kept a watchful eye on his kite and any unusual waves, he was approaching the island. He could see Nigel and Reg slow their boat and then idle it into the marina. Norman aimed his kite for the white sand beach next to this.

"Attaboy, big fella, time to head for the corral."

* * *

Landing the kite proved to be the most challenging part of the whole affair; this flying horse just did not want to return to the barn.

Getting onto the beach had not been a problem. Norman managed to slow down and stop by letting wind out of the kite, thereby reducing its tremendous lift. He then let himself lie back in the shallow water, slid his feet out of the straps, and, grabbing hold of his board, carefully walked out onto the beach, mindful to keep the kite directly above him, catching only enough wind to keep it up. But how was he to bring the kite down without being dragged through the possibly thorny boscage? The answer appeared in the shape of two friendly locals—kiteboarders, too—who, just as in any good Western, took the reins of the bucking bronco and let the gunslinger, in this case Norman, dismount. They grabbed the lines and expertly brought the kite down to the beach, where it lay folded and limp, its energy gone.

"Dude!" said the first local. "You were righteously rippin'! Rippin' righteously-la!"

"How long ya been kiteboarding?" said the second.

"Feels like a lifetime," said Norman truthfully, with a grin.

"Yoo-hoo-la-la. I hear you," said the first.

"Killer-diller," said the second.

"Um, could I just leave the kite here on the beach for a bit?" said Norman.

"Sure, dude, we'll watch it for you," said local number one.

"No worries!" said local number two. "Lim Robinson, the shop owner, is one of our best mates."

"Thanks! I mean, righteous!" said Norman.

As he passed his sleeping steed, he gave it a quick pat. "Righteous thanks to you, Pegasus," he murmured, then nipped up the beach.

now or nothing
for the karma

Norman looked around to see if he could spot the two Alfurnians. Once again, their infundibular helmets bobbed like harbor buoys, leading Norman along. They were just leaving the marina and entering what appeared to be a sprawling resort, dominated by a large hotel.

Norman hurried forward, hoping his soaking-wet clothes would draw no attention. He walked in among the various outbuildings unquestioned.

Hanging back a little, he waited to see where the spies would lead him. They were headed for a patio bar. Aha, thought Norman. Maybe while we've been looking for them at the Tall Bar, all this time they've been at this bar. Maybe it's the Short Bar. Or the Medium High Bar, or the . . .

Norman followed them, crossing an open courtyard cautiously and as inconspicuously as possible.

He slipped behind the spidery boughs of a frangipani tree and peered past its scented petals. Trying to keep his teeth from chattering, Norman watched as Nigel and Reg climbed onto high bamboo barstools. After setting their furry hats down on the bar (not bald after all!), they leaned forward and called for service.

The scrape of a gate and a voice—its timbre one Norman had tried to forget—sounded behind him.

"Zounds! Narmin Narminn! Ye doog! Wot be ye a-dooin'
here?"

All the fine hairs on the back of Norman's scarlet neck stood
straight up, only to be flattened by the boisterous slap of an
epollicate hand.

"Narmin Narminn, ye wee rapscallion. Ah'm nae sure if ye
mayn't be oop tae nae gud, but naerteliss Ah'm pleased tae see
ye, dinnae wurry yersilf aboot tat. An' soo will yer fadder be,
when he sees ye. Coom alang noo, he's nae far."

Norman could only gasp for breath, no words were available,
as No Thumbs McSweeney's thumbless hand, still upon his
prickly neck, guided him along a pebbled path. No words were
available, but questions chased one another pell-mell through
his mind. Was No Thumbs one of the kidnappers? Or was he
kidnapped, too? Where were the guards? Did they have guns?
Why was No Thumbs so happy? Would he be tortured? Where
was the Quadrumvirate? Had he just peed in his pants?

Norman could answer that one. Yes, he had peed in his
pants, but only a little, and since his pants were soaking wet
already, he trusted that no one could tell. This calmed him.
Then a thought so horrible that his neck hairs tried to stand
up again, even against No Thumbs's gnarly hand: What if they
cut off his, Norman's, thumbs, too? He would be epollicate. For
the rest of his life. Never able to
give the thumbs-up sign again.
Not that, not that, not that,
thought Norman. Not that.

"We'll just coot off"—Norman peed into his pants a wee bit
more—"the carner here," said No Thumbs. "The pool's aroond
tis tree."

What would Mr. B. advise? Reading the dictionary was out.

Balance. Norman's mind raced again. That's it. Find the balance between imagination and observation. Norman's imagination was in hyperdrive—he realized that. Got to slow down the imagination. Now observe, observe!

The pebbles crunched beneath Norman's feet. Palm trees stretched up and out, toward the sea behind him. From beyond a hedge of white bougainvillea came a splash.

No Thumbs guided Norman past the hedge and onto wide flagstones beside an oval swimming pool. They stopped, and Norman looked up at No Thumbs expectantly. Birds whistled and a woman laughed somewhere, and then from across the water a voice shouted, "Norman! Norman!"

Again it was a familiar voice. Norman stiffened, turned his head slowly, and then stood there, his mouth falling agape. On the opposite side of the turquoise pool, beneath gently waving palms, stretched out on a white chaise longue, in a fuschia-and-puce Hawaiian shirt, cargo shorts, flip-flops, and pith helmet, lay his father, a tall, pink drink in his large pink hand.

"Norman! Well, I'll be jiminy-jiggered!" he cried. "Come here, son! This must be some kind of Santa surprise!" He struggled to sit up without spilling his drink, chortling and purpling in his cheeks.

"Dad!" shouted Norman, pulling himself from No Thumbs's grasp. "Dad!" Norman ran helter-skelter across the flagstones and around the end of the pool, finally throwing his arms around his father, who now sat with his legs astraddle the chaise longue.

"Daddy!" Norman said gleefully.

"Whoa, whoa, my drink, son, my Singapore sling, ha-ha!"

"Dad, are you all right?" Norman held his father's face in his hands. "You look all right. Are you okay? How about psychologically? You haven't been brainwashed, have you? You still remember your name and everything? Let me see your thumbs." Norman felt for his father's hands. "Tell me, who is the president of the United States? How are your palms? Moist? Dry? What?"

"Haven't been brainwashed? Remember my name? What in Katmandu, Oklahoma, are you talking about, son?" Orman Normann put his drink down and swung his legs over to one side.

"The Alfurnians! Your kidnappers! Them!" said Norman, suddenly cringing as the Alfurnian spies themselves sauntered toward them, tall glasses in hand.

"Avtahnun, Meestir O. Avtahnun, Meestir Meckess," they said as they passed.

"Afternoon, fellas," said Orman Normann.

No Thumbs clapped one of the Alfurnians on the back, saying, "Wot ye drinkin', boyos? I could use sommat mesilf," and he followed them off toward the hotel.

"Them, Dad, them!" whispered Norman.

"Nigel and Reg? Kidnappers? Ha! Ha! That's richer than Houston, Ohio!"

"Then who kidnapped you?" Norman sat down next to his father and looked into his eyes.

"But I haven't been kidnapped!"

"Dad, what are you saying? Your e-mails, we read the e-mails, they weren't from you at all!"

"But didn't the e-mails say I wasn't kidnapped?"

"Yeah, but . . ."

"I specifically told Nigel and Reg to tell you and Mom that I wasn't kidnapped." Orman Normann puckered his lips to the straw, slurped, and burped. "How is Mom, by the way?"

"But why didn't you write?!"

"Son, it's a long story." Orman Normann put down his glass and, leaning toward Norman, spoke softly: "Son, I'm onto something big here."

"You mean, you haven't been kidnapped?"

"Norm, that's what I keep trying to tell you! Now listen." Again his voice grew quiet. "I'm onto something truly colossal. Bigger than big. This could put the goo back in good and the doll back in dollar. I've got the Alfurnian foreign minister, Mr. Pajakbaru, in a bidding war with the Katong Luangan foreign minister, Mr. Bg Kabong, and when this deal finally goes through, hoooooeeeeeeeee, it's gonna be the biggest bomber bamboozle I've ever brought in." In spite of his wish to keep quiet, he whistled and slapped his knee. "See, first Mr. Bg Kabong nibbled, and then Mr. Pajakbaru bit, and then the thing started to get a little sticky, with all the special meetings and so forth, and that's why I couldn't write to you, see? They both started to get nervous about me cutting a deal with the other one on the side, so they wouldn't let me use my e-mail, which is why I had Nigel and Reg send you those letters for me. I made sure they sent one every day just so you wouldn't worry. Really, a couple of nicer guys you couldn't meet—"

"Dad . . ." said Norman, who had himself been slowly pinking as his father talked and was now a pretty light purple color.

"A couple of nicer guys you could never meet, and Mr. Pajakbaru—"

"Dad."

"And Mr. Kabong—"

"Dad!"

"What is it, Norman?"

"Dad, listen to me very carefully." A steely note had entered Norman's voice. "Put that stupid drink down. Thank you. Have you got a good grip on your flip-flops? Good. Because we are now going to stand up and walk quietly and calmly away from the pool and then out of this hotel, and then as quickly and carefully as we can, we will return to the Pan Specific Hotel, where your wife, my mother—remember her?—awaits us."

Norman stood, satisfied with his speech, feeling his father's karma safely within his grasp.

"But, son, haven't you been listening to a word I said? I'm maybe an hour away from the biggest bomber deal of my life. We can't leave now!"

Norman felt his father's karma slipping.

"Dad, have you got any idea—"

"Or maybe two hours."

". . . any idea at all—"

"Or maybe half a day, or maybe two at the most, honest."

". . . how worried we were about you? I nearly broke my neck three times to get here!"

"Well now, I see that, but that couldn't be helped, and I knew you'd understand once you realized how much this could mean for all of us."

Norman looked down at his father. It was now all or nothing for the karma.

"Dad, I understand one thing. You can either have the biggest bomber deal of your life, or you can have me and Mom. You can't have both."

"But, son, really."

"Dad," said Norman, beginning to turn away.

He looked back at his father. "What's it going to be, Dad. Me and Mom, or your bombers?"

There was a small commotion under the palm trees, and then a larger one, as Leonard, Anna, and Emma came running, vaulting, and, of course, "Eeeeeeeyaaaa!"ing over chairs and towels.

"We watched you the whole way, from the ferry," shouted Leonard. "It was überawesome! Hey, Mr. Normann. Long time no see."

Norman said, "Mr. Normann here was just making up his mind whether he'd like to see you or Anna or Emma or Mom or me ever again in his quickly shortening life. Because if he doesn't get up out of this deck chair and come with us right now, I will never let him in our door again!"

Norman glared as the others stared large-eyed at Norman's large father.

"Oh, all right, all right, all right! I'm coming, I'm coming, I'm coming!" Orman Normann swung himself around on his chaise and clapped his hands on his knees. "Cheese, I'm sunburned! I'll just go get my things from my room."

"No time, Dad!" Norman couldn't take any more karmic chances. "The hotel can send you your things. We're going before Nigel and Reg come back. Anna, toss me my sandals, quick."

Just then, wearing nothing but furry bathing trunks, Nigel and Reg came back.

"Nigel, Reg," said Orman Normann, "meet my son and his friends."

"How do zyou do?" said Nigel.

"Ve've heard zo much about zyou," said Reg.

"Pleased to vinally meet zyou," said Norman.

"How come you aren't wearing your hats?" said Leonard.

"Oh, ve don't alvays vear dem, zyou know," said Nigel with a smile that made his mustache wiggle.

"Say, Nigel," said Leonard, "you remember last summer in Vienna?"

"Gosh, Leonard, I wish we could stay and chat, but my dad was just saying he'd love to show us around the hotel, weren't you, Dad?"

"No, son—I mean, why yes, son, I was," he said. "Reg, Nigel, see you later."

"Allighator!" said Nigel.

The Quadrumvirate plus one father walked slowly around the pool, then around the corner of the changing cabana, and then a little more quickly toward the marina.

"You know, Nigel and Reg aren't going to like it when they notice that we're gone," said Mr. Normann. "They might start to wonder what I'm up to. And No Thumbs would truly not be pleased if he thought I was cutting him off. He's awful sensitive about cutting off anything."

"I know, I know," said Norman. "That's why we've got to get out of here as quickly as possible."

At the marina they checked the schedule for the next ferry back to the city.

"Six-thirty," read Anna.

"That's an hour from now," said Emma.

"Isn't there any other way?" said Norman.

"Well, we could take the cable car," said Mr. Normann, looking up.

Four heads tilted back. Sure enough, off to their left, beyond the roofline of the hotel, a tramway of red and blue cable cars could be seen rising gracefully out over the island and, by means of many tall pylons, reaching all the way to the mainland.

"Come on," said Norman.

Hurrying away, they passed over a broad promenade

beneath more palms. They mingled with the people there, hoping to blend in with other tourists and Singaporeans out for a bike ride or a holiday stroll. After half a mile, they came to the tramway station and quickly bought tickets.

Mr. Normann said to no one in particular, in the voice of a mourner, "Money isn't everything, right, heh, heh?"

"Give it up, Mr. Normann," said Emma.

"Maybe, if I just went back for a minute, I could give them an ultimatum."

"Get in the cable car, Mr. Normann," said Leonard.

The cable car was otherwise empty, and for the first time in four hours Norman was able to take an unhurried, deep breath of air.

"Whoo!" he said.

The five were quiet for a moment, staring out the window as the cable car rose smoothly from the station.

"The kiteboarders are still out," said Emma.

"The motorboats are, too," said Anna.

"Say," said Leonard, "is that—"

"Eeeeeeyaaa! It is!" said Norman. He yanked his monocular from his backpack and scanned the water through it. The Alfurnians, along with No Thumbs McSweeney, were in their motorboat, pointing and, by the look of it, shouting. In the back of the boat were two very small men in midnight-blue suits wearing dark wraparound sunglasses. Norman passed the monocular to Anna.

"Who are those guys?" said Anna.

"Is that Ronny and Rinny?" said Leonard.

"It is!" said Norman.

"Who in this upside-down world are Renny and Runny?" said Emma.

"Ronny and Rinny," said Norman. "They're my dad's Katong Luangan friends."

"Hoo boy, darn it, now I am in trouble!" said Orman Normann.

The cable car slowly swung into its city station, just as the pursuing motorboat pulled into the marina. Norman, Anna, Emma, Leonard, and even Orman Normann dashed across the boulevard into the subway station, down the steps to the ticket machines. Norman fumbled madly with Singapore dollars, at first cramming them into the wrong slot, then into the right slot but entering the wrong amount, then correcting it as Anna and Emma screamed instructions and Leonard paced and Orman Normann simply said, "Why don't we just go back and talk things over." The machine, however, at last dispensed the tickets, which Norman grabbed and quickly distributed. The five bumped and jostled through the turnstiles just as a city-bound train was arriving.

"On, on!" cried Norman, not daring to look behind them.

As the train doors opened, they fell into the car, then waited, with fingers crossed, until the doors closed again. The train eased out of the station with a whirring crescendo, and Norman, peeking out the window at the receding station, saw Nigel, Reg, Rinny, Ronny, and No Thumbs run onto the platform, plainly cursing in Alfurnian, Katong Luang, and above all in Scottish.

"Hooeee, son, we did it!" said Mr. Normann.

"Not quite, Dad," said Norman. "We still have to get on our plane tomorrow morning without them finding us first. What are we going to do?"

The five sat down in a row, glancing shyly at the Singaporeans around them, perhaps hoping to find the solution somewhere in their faces.

Leonard, staring at the placards above the riders' heads, said, "Look! There's a night safari at the zoo. See the poster?"

"Leonard, is this really the time to be thinking about zoos?" said Norman.

"No, Leonard's right," said Anna. "We could hide out most of the night at the zoo, they'll never think of tracking us there."

"That's it!" said Norman. "Sorry, Leonard." Norman checked his map as the train eased quietly into the next station. "Quick, if we're going to the zoo, we've got to change trains here and head the other way."

The five jumped out and just managed to catch a train for Jurong East. As this train was pulling away, the train behind them pulled in, containing, to the mingled horror and delight of the Quadrumvirate, two Alfurnians, a couple of Katong Luangs, and an epollicate Scotsman in the midst of a heated, presumably polyglot argument. The evasive maneuver went undetected! Changing trains again three stops later, they sped on to Choa Chu Kang.

"That should do it," said Emma. "By now our international friends of the underworld are probably whacking each other on the head with their flip-flops."

"Okay," said Norman. "Now I've got to make two phone calls. Dad, phone, please."

Norman punched in a number on his father's cell phone, waited, then spoke: "Mom? It's me! We've got Dad! Yes! We had to kidnap him ourselves. Yes! We'll give you complete details later. But first I need you to do something. Okay, listen carefully. Check out of the hotel. Have a porter help you with our bags. Then take a taxi to the Snaffles Hotel and check us all in there under some fake name. What name? I don't know what name . . . How about Longhouse? That's it, Mr. and Mrs. Woody Longhouse and their four charming children. Okay. Get a couple of rooms just for tonight. If you see any short men in blue suits or tall men wearing furry shorts, or one red-haired man with eight fingers, duck. We'll meet you in the Tall Bar at midnight. Got that? Midnight at the Tall Bar. Okay, here's Dad. Give him a lecture about what is and what's not truly meaningful in this life. Bye, Mom. I am positively, absolutely sure we're all right. Love you, Mom."

Norman held out the phone to his father. "Here, Dad, it's your honey-bunchums."

We need not go into detail regarding the phone conversation between Mr. and Mrs. Normann, which is after all private and potentially nauseating to some. Let us just say that Norma Normann has a tender heart of gold, which is a precious metal and flexible enough to forgive.

Norman's second phone call was to Lim Robinson. But before Norman could even begin to explain he was buffeted by a loud "Dude!" and an "awesome hang time" and numerous "no worries." As it happened, locals one and two had continued in their roles as helpful cowboys, corralling Norman's Pegasus and returning him to the barn. With many well wishes on both sides, Lim Robinson rang off.

"Righteous," said Norman.

* * *

With the nearly full moon coating the hot skyscrapers with a sticky sheen, and the shop-houses glowing in their own red-paper-lantern light, at eleven-fifty-five exactly, our five adventurers, now quite exhausted, unbent out of a cab at the foot of the stairs to the Tall Bar. Norman led their stumbling way up the wide steps, then cautiously pushed open the bar door.

Beneath the languid fan blades sat Norma Normann, dozing with a magazine in her lap. She awoke with the first "Eeeeyaaa!" and the ensuing group hug might have gone on all night if not for the polite cough of the barman, standing to one side with a tray.

He said, "Four lemonades, two pink and two yellow, and two Singapore slings. I'll leave them on the table."

It was already the morning of New Year's Eve when, in the boys' room, Leonard, Norman, and Orman Normann pulled the crisp sheets up to their weary noses.

Norman was simply too tired to even think of looking at the *Y*s, but if he had, he might have read these, some of which might even have pleased him.

yerk *vb* : to pull tight in making a shoe
yes *adv* : an expression of agreement in answer
    to a question, command, or request
yesterdayness *n* : the feeling of yesterday
yetzer *n* : the human impulse, according
    to Jewish traditional belief
yeuky *adj* : itchy

yeuky

a bit more of the bubbly

The plump Singapore Airlines jetliner flew smoothly and steadily on an east-northeasterly heading, high enough so that even the few cumulonimbus clouds were far below it. Within, about halfway between the wing and the tail on the starboard side, now sat six where before there had been only five. In rows 36, 37, and 38, seats J and K, the Normanns, Mr. and Mrs., were holding hands and chatting quietly; Anna and Emma sampled bits of the many movies on the screen menus; and Leonard laughed, karate-chopped, and eeeeeyaaaaed over the classic arcade games.

"These games are so cool! They're medieval! Look at how they made the asteroids!"

Norman, his forehead to the window, watched the green-and-yellow islands drift by, far below them in the South China Sea.

We can be all the more thankful for this peaceful scene, as it followed a bit of a to-do at the airport. Our travelers had not quite made it to the security line when their way was blocked by Mr. Pajakbaru, Mr. Bg Kabong, and N. T. McSweeney, standing shoulder to shoulder with arms crossed, along with Nigel and Reg, and Rinny and Ronny, lurking sternly behind them. For a long moment, no one spoke. The bomber dealers had glared and the Quadrumvirate had glared back. Only Orman Normann had squirmed. Like a worm surprised by the hook he was stuck on, he wondered what the future held.

But where Norman had been the karmic victor the day before, on this morning it was his mother, Norma, whose eyes, normally so mild, had flashed enough fire to make the assembled members of the used-bomber market suddenly shift uneasily, look at their shoes, and mutter something about working things out. If N. T. McSweeney had had any thumbs, he might even have twiddled them nervously.

She had let them all have it properly with a frank discussion of her feelings that brought a little embarrassed color even into the stubbly cheeks of Nigel and Reg.

"P'raps she be right," N.T. had said. "P'raps it be best if ye dae leave the bomber bissnez—ye've been nowt but trooble tae me, all tese years, arfter all." And to show that there were no hard feelings, N.T. had extended an epollicate hand.

Norman's forehead at the window grew cold. Gliding high above the Sea of Japan, the airplane entered a quick dusk, then night.

"Leonard," said Norman.

"Eeeeeeyawp! Die! Die slowly! Now die fast!" said Leonard.

"Leonard."

"Ah! They killed me! What?"

"You know what day it is, don't you?"

"I'd say, if we're somewhere between Singapore and home, it must be either Monturday or Thursnesday. Or is it Suesday?"

"It's New Year's Eve! And look. It's dark over the ocean already. Pretty soon it'll be midnight. Let's go to the back again and see if we can get a bit of the bubbly."

"Anna, Emma!" said Leonard. "Say good-bye to your movie-star boyfriends, come with us to get a bit of the bubbly."

The four made their way to the same small roomlet in the back of the airplane. They stood at one of the high, bistro-style tables, waiting shyly to catch the eye of a steward.

From behind them came a voice: "Norman! Leonard! Anna and Emma!"

Of course it was Ronita Kim.

"Happy New Year!" she said.

"Happy New Year!" said the Quadrumvirate.

"Wait here one second. I have to bring some coffee to the gentleman in 32A and a diet cola to the lady in 29C."

She passed through the roomlet to the galley, then glided back up the aisle on the other side.

"I wonder if Ronita Kim ages faster or slower, flying around the world like this all the time," said Norman.

"Maybe she only looks young, maybe she's really a hundred and four," said Leonard.

"Or maybe she's only fourteen, and one trip doubled her age," said Anna.

"Yeah, maybe they grab kids like us, age them, and then make them work forever on the planes, constantly circling the globe," said Emma.

"I think Ronita Kim may be trying to lure us to our doom, hee, hee!" said Anna.

"She is not!" said Norman.

"Who is not?" said Ronita Kim, returning with the empty tray.

"Oh, nobody. Nobody is not," said Norman, blushing.

"Oh, 'nobody' is not," said Ronita. "Well, this somebody wants to celebrate. It's New Year's Eve! How about a bit of the bubbly?" She proceeded to the galley and began rummaging in one of the small refrigerators.

Norman looked out one of the windows. He could not see the full moon rising in the east, but he could see the silvery glimmer it cast on the icy waves miles below them.

"A bit of the bubbly," said Ronita, pouring out glasses of cider. "To the coming New Year."

"To the coming New Year," said the Quadrumvirate, raising four glasses.

They clinked as well as they could with their plastic champagne flutes and quaffed.

"Well, friends, the Tiger of Singapore will miss you," said Ronita.

"You mean, the one we didn't see when we were at the zoo?" said Leonard. "You know, the poster did promise a tiger."

"I'm sorry about that, dear Leonard, but no, I mean the symbolic tiger, the symbol of Singapore. Did you find your hearts' desire, by the way?"

"Definitely!" said Norman.

"I think you'll find more of what your hearts desire when you get home. Now go back to your seats. Turn off your movies and arcade games and get some sleep. When I bring you breakfast, I'll have a surprise for you."

"First, I miss Christmas, and now it's the shortest New Year's Eve party of my life," said Leonard.

Nevertheless, the friends returned to their seats, tucked the senior Normanns in—they were already snoring in a gentle duet—and then themselves.

Norman gave one more glance at the moon, which, from his window, he could now see sailing along in the south, and then he slept.

* * *

And what felt like only a moment later, he woke to Ronita Kim's friendly "Good morning, boys."

Norman smiled through stinging eyes, then peered out the window at the rays of sunshine, which lit the high mountain peaks emerging from the clouds below.

Ronita Kim passed out hot chocolate and croissants.

Leonard yawned and, stretching, said, "Happy New Year!"

"Nope, not yet," said Ronita.

"What do you mean, 'Nope, not yet'?" said Leonard.

"That's my surprise. While you slept, we crossed the International Date Line. You get to see the sun rise twice on the same day. It's New Year's Eve day again."

"So, if we want, we can have another party in New York," said Norman.

"Yes, indeed."

"Eeeeyaaaa!" said Leonard.

"Hey, keep it down back there, I'm trying to sleep," said Emma.

The rest of their second New Year's Eve day passed slowly or quickly, depending on how you looked at it. On the one hand, it was many more hours in the airplane; on the other hand, it was a very short day.

The remarkable airplane, surely getting tired at last, had passed over the Bering Sea, to the right of Mount Denali in Alaska, over the Rockies in Canada, then across the plains of the middle of the continent and hundreds and hundreds of frozen lakes like shards of smooth tinfoil, until, with only an eastern state or two to cross, it began to descend toward its destination, New York City.

Ronita Kim came by once more with seltzer water and slices of lemon and wished them another Happy New Year.

"Have a bit more of the bubbly when you get home," she said.

"But you won't be home yourself," said Norman.

"I'm at home anywhere in the world," she said with a warm smile. She waved, and then, following her captain's orders, she prepared the cabin for landing.

zowie

At the curbside of the chaotic airport, taxis careening past pell-mell, Mr. Normann looked for some little while before finding one that could carry six.

Norma Normann said, "I called all your parents this morning to let them know when we'd be arriving. It was funny, though, they seemed to think it was yesterday."

"Mom, it *was* yesterday to them."

"What time is it now, anyway?" said Emma, scrunched between Anna and Mrs. Normann. "My watch says eleven-thirty."

"Mine says three-thirty," said Mrs. Normann.

"Wrong again," said Norman. "It's five-thirty. See, the sun's gone down again."

"Sometimes I wish either the world or my head would stop spinning," said Leonard.

The taxi van swam out into the river of other cabs and cars on the wide dirty expressway, where, at this hour, the traffic moved at anything but express speed. Horns blared. Drivers cursed one another. Everyone looked tired and cantankerous.

"Ah," said Emma, "it's nice to be home. Dirty streets, rude cabbies, and obnoxious traffic—my world is right side up again."

One hour and fifty-five long minutes later, the taxi van turned down the Normanns' street in Buddingdale Heights.

"I think we'll all just go to our house first and then I'll call your parents," said Mrs. Normann.

As the vanman helped to unload the bags from the back,

and Mr. Normann counted out the fare and tip, Norman ran up to the front door. Digging for his house key in his backpack, he jumped when the door opened by itself. There, in the warm light of the hall, stood Mrs. Piquant, Anna and Emma's parents, and behind them, wearing a kitchen apron and with an espresso pot in his hand, Balthazar Birdsong.

"Welcome home!" they shouted.

Norman stepped back, dumbfounded, but not Leonard, Anna, and Emma, who whooped and ran past him, launching themselves into an appropriate parent's outstretched arms.

Mrs. Normann, shuffling with the weight of four bags, which she was lugging up the walkway, wet and slippery with half-melted snow, just managed to say, "What a wonderful surprise!"

Balthazar Birdsong leaped from the threshold. "Dear Mrs. Normann, do let me help you."

Mr. Normann called from the street as the taxi van drove away. "Kids! Come back here and help me with these bags! Darn it, it's cold here! I think I forgot that it could be anything but hot in this world!"

Soon bags and suitcases were thumping against steps and walls, and then were left in heaps in the hallway.

"Oh dear," said Mrs. Normann. "Well, we'll sort through all of this later."

"Everyone!" shouted Mrs. Piquant. "Listen a moment. We took the liberty of preparing a little party—it was Balthazar's idea, really—and so a modest holiday feast awaits you. After you children have washed some of the intercontinental dirt off your hands and faces, we'll meet you in the dining room with all the goodies."

In the midst of the tumult of their loud return from the bathrooms, one could hear Norman say, "I could murder a firlot of Ring Dings," and Leonard say, "I'll eat anything except a fruit that smells like three-week-old roadkill," and then silence, for all voices were stilled when the four turned the corner into the dining room and saw before them, lit only by candles, a table filled with delicacies. Among these were cheeses, olives, salamis, fish, breads, jams, butter, fruit, cookies, and chocolates. On closer inspection, they saw that the table was spread with Muenster, Gouda, Jarlsberg, and Morbier cheeses; almond-stuffed, garlic-stuffed, pimento-stuffed, Greek, Niçoise, and herb-cured olives; mortadella, prosciutto, and Genoa salami; creamed and

pickled herring, whitefish salad, Scotch salmon, and lox; flat breads, black breads, sourdough, ciabattas, peasant loaves, and bagels; strawberry, raspberry, peach, and blueberry jams; sweet and salted  butter; apples, oranges, red and green grapes, and clementines; and too many chocolates and cookies to mention.

Leonard summed the whole thing up with a simple "Eeeeeyum!" and grabbed a plate.

After an initial half hour or so of jubilant feasting, the Quadrumvirate, with parents and Mr. Birdsong, plates and glasses refilled, found cozy spots in which to settle in the living room. There, a warming fire—the first in the house since the Normanns moved in, and made specially by Mr. B.—crackled discreetly in the fireplace.

At last, Balthazar B. said, "The last time I saw you, Norman, Leonard, Anna, and Emma, we had a lively discussion, which led us, then, to the conclusion that it was time for you to act.

Well, you have acted. And I see, what's more, you have acted well. Now I wish—I'm sure we all wish—to hear what you've done and seen. Give us a proper account."

Well, as you can imagine, all four of the Quadrumvirate began to speak at once.

"A moment!" said Mr. B., raising an admonishing palm. "I would like to propose Anna for spokesperson. I believe she is the oldest."

"Phooeey!" said Leonard.

"Go ahead, Anna," said the twins' mother, who sat on the carpet with her long legs folded beneath her. "Tell us what we missed."

Anna sat forward on the sofa and began to tell the tale, which, having just experienced it ourselves, we need not repeat in detail here. This is not a Wagnerian opera, after all. Wagnerian operas, though sometimes soul stirring, are a bit repetitious. The twins' father, who stood next to Balthazar's chair, handsome and smiling, with a glass in his hand, would be happy to discuss this.

Anna's audience was an appreciative one, and Leonard's occasional annotations, such as "It was the most awesome atrium in all of hoteldom," were not unwanted. Emma insisted on telling the story of the durian herself, as only she and Norman had eaten it, producing a satisfying groan from the squeamish parents.

As the story unfolded, sometimes questions arose along the lines of Mrs. Piquant's "But, Norma, you were with them, weren't you?" to which all the children quickly responded, saying that yes, she nearly always, very nearly always, was.

To Norman's great satisfaction, Anna described his kiteboarding episode with flair, making Norma Normann give herself away with loud gasps, weakening considerably the idea that she might have been there.

Norma finally cried, "Norman, how could you?"

Mr. Normann filled in some of the aspects of the case from his point of view. "Really, I had no idea anyone was the least bit worried!" he said, amid the furrowing brows of the other parents.

In the meantime, Mr. B. filled and refilled everyone's glass, and now said, "Still, but for Mr. Normann's lack of maturity and consideration, all four of these delightful children would have missed this marvelous trip to the Far East and been much the poorer for it. Cheers!" And he raised his bit of the bubbly, as did everyone else, even Orman Normann, the forgiven villain of the tale.

Balthazar Birdsong also took it upon himself to keep the fire blazing in a friendly manner, and its soporific warmth soon cast its spell. Mr. Normann was sound asleep in his recliner by nine-thirty; Mrs. Normann followed in hers at nine-forty-five; and at ten-thirty, Anna and Emma's parents took their daughters home to the comfort of their own beds.

As Mrs. Piquant shut the front door, she said to Leonard, "I've made up the beds in the guest room for us, so we can stay up as long as you like." But even Leonard's eyes would not stay open once the clock struck eleven, and so Mrs. Piquant led him off to bed.

"Happy New Year, Leonard!" called Norman after him.

"Eee yaa a wn . . ." said Leonard.

Norman and Balthazar sat with their chairs turned so they might watch the fire dance brightly and hear it whisper and snap.

"You would like the coffee in Singapore," said Norman.

"They call it kopi." And Norman described how he had seen it being made.

"Oh, ah," said Mr. B.

"And the clouds were fantastic!" said Norman.

"Yes. A tropical cumulonimbus is truly one of the earth's most wondrous things. I never did give you a proper lecture on them, did I? Must remedy that in the new year."

"And the way it rains there! Straight down. It's like you're two inches tall and standing straight under a tap."

"Ah, wonderful."

"We went into a church where you had to wear long pants and sleeves, and you took your hat off. We went into a synagogue where you put your hat on. We went into a golden mosque where you took your shoes off and walked around in your socks. We went into a Hindu temple with hundreds of statues where you took your shoes and socks off and walked around barefoot. And we went into an ancient Buddhist temple where it didn't seem to matter what you did."

"Ah, our feet and heads, the connectors to the earth and sky," said Mr. B. "Oh, look, the clock!"

Norman turned his head and saw that it was seven minutes after twelve.

"Happy New Year, Norman."

At last, Norman was properly exhausted. As he went off to brush his teeth, Balthazar Birdsong gathered plates and glasses, bringing them to the kitchen; he covered the food and generally prepared the house for the next day. Then he covered both of the Normann parents in blankets and left them to sleep in their chairs.

Norman went to his room and climbed into warm pajamas. Beneath his covers, he lay gazing toward the weak moonlight outside his window.

Balthazar looked in on him to say good night and found Norman's eyebrows wrinkling together.

"What is it, Norman?"

Norman said, "Now that I'm home and it's January, I've got to get ready for the big test. It's coming at the end of the month."

"Dear Norman Normann," said Balthazar Birdsong. "Do you still not understand? You have passed all the tests you need to pass already. And magnificently, with flying colors!"

"But what if I don't do well? I don't want to disappoint my parents."

"After all you've done for them, your parents are not likely to be disappointed in you anytime soon—unless they're more forgetful than your average aquarium fish, which let's hope they're not."

"I guess so."

"Have you read the dictionary?"

"Everything but the Zs."

"All right. You read yourself to sleep with the *Z*s." He lifted the dictionary from the desk and placed it on the bed. "And then you'll awake fully prepared to meet the new year."

Balthazar Birdsong smiled.

"Good night, Norman."

"Good night, Mr. B.," said Norman as Balthazar Birdsong quietly pulled the door closed behind him.

Norman opened the dictionary. Alfred the Great sprawled by the bedside lamp, already snoring in the midst of his tangled velvet robes, his gray beard smeared with chocolate, or possibly lipstick, empty bottles of honey mead by his boots.

"Looks like you've had a swell party," said Norman.

Norman riffled to the back of the dictionary, but he soon slept in the midst of dreamt kiteboards and clouds as his nose quietly sounded the letter on the open page: *ZZZ*.

zonelet *n* : a little zone

Zonta *n* : a club for executive businesswomen

zonule of Zinn *n* : a ligament holding the lens of the eye

zoo *n* : a collection of living animals

zounds *interj* : used as a mild curse

zowie *interj* : used to express amazement, admiration, or delight

begin

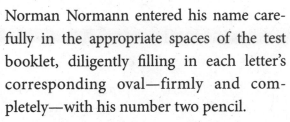

Norman Normann entered his name carefully in the appropriate spaces of the test booklet, diligently filling in each letter's corresponding oval—firmly and completely—with his number two pencil.

Norman Normann—not a bad name, he thought.

But it was the same name, filling in the same spaces in the same test (new year) in the same room (or one just like it) in the same school in the same city on almost the same day in January as the year before.

He examined the tip of his pencil to check that it was sharp and put it down.

"When you have completed . . ." said the same test monitor.

And Norman had the same bad feeling in his stomach.

"The first portion of the test will consist of . . ."

Norman guessed that nothing ever really changes in life.

And for the first time in many months, Norman's guess was wrong. For was it not true that Norman now knew what a cumulus cloud was? And no one could deny that Leonard had mastered the German for "chicken butt." What is more, it could be argued that all four friends understood their city better for having walked across it and their world better for having flown around it. These were all changes for the good.

And finally, how could Norman ignore, most important of all, his own father, Orman Normann, who no longer sold bombers? Where bomber catalogues, weapons inventories, and the telephone numbers of the underworld once lay, now shoe catalogues, leather samples, rubber soles, and laces covered the broad expanse of his desk.

"Norman," his father had said to him just the day before, "call me a heel, but I'm going to get to the bottom of the shoe business and polish it off."

No, a great deal had changed. The karmic health of the entire Normann family had never been better and was looking up.

"You may turn," said the test monitor, "to the first page of section one . . ."

A little shiver passed from Norman's toes to the top of his head as he prepared himself for action. He settled in his chair, shrugged, and turned to the first page.

We will leave Norman here, for we do not wish to disturb him. He must have unbroken quiet and no distractions if he is to make the very best educated guesses in the next few hours.

It only needs mentioning that the test monitor said, "You may begin the test . . ."

Norman Normann picked his pencil up.

"Now."